THE BYGONE

LIBRARY

ANGANDEEP KR. CHATTERJEE

Published by Angandeep Kr Chatterjee in 2018
Copyright © 2018 Angandeep Kr Chatterjee
All rights reserved.
ISBN: 978-93-5346-113-3

Angandeep Kr Chatterjee asserts the moral right to be identified as the author of this book.

THE BYGONE LIBRARY

Cover Design by

Sudipta Chanda Burman

(Picture courtesy : Google images)

THE BYGONE LIBRARY

www.authorangandeep.com

To my mom, Mrs Sarbani Chatterjee

ACKNOWLEDGEMENT

As always with any author, there are a lot of people behind the creation of any novel. For me there are so many people behind the creation of the following novel, that it would be impossible to take each person's name and details in a single book. Still, I am trying my best to acknowledge everyone involved in successfully completing this work of fiction.

Firstly, I would like to thank my Mom- Mrs. Sarbani Chatterjee, whose relentless persuasion regarding the completion of my novel actually helped me in the long run. If it wasn't for her, it would have been very difficult for me to complete this novel. A single mother, raising two children on her own, without any financial or mental health from anyone, it was almost impossible for her to support me on my venture to write the Bygone Library, but she did it anyways. Instead of pushing me to work hard for my day job, she always supported me, pushed me to complete this novel. So, a simple thank you will not be enough to recognize her contribution to the completion of my novel.

Secondly, it's the most important person in my life, my wife- Mrs. Sudipta Chanda Burman who inspired me in writing the novel itself. If it wasn't for her, I would still be juggling between ideas, no way near to put them down on paper and creating a novel. It was she, who supported me, inspired me, helped me in my research, along with designing the cover picture and the back cover of my book. Countless days and nights went by in order to make the things right. In addition to the above, she is also my best critique regarding my ideas and the words being put in the paper. I am always grateful and proud to be a loving husband of her.

Thirdly, my sister deserves the thank you for supporting me on my venture. Though she is not that much into the archeological fiction, but her support and love are something that kept me going.

Lastly, I would like to thank Amazon for its great support to self-publish this book and bring my dream into reality. Without Amazon, it might have been very difficult to publish this book.

Yours truly,

Angandeep Kr Chatterjee

Author's Note

There are many historical events that are used to write this book. All of them are researched and noted down to the best of my knowledge. For some of the events, I have used my imagination to connect the dots between different eras, different occurrences and historical evidence. If something is found inappropriate to any person – living or dead, or any historical event found tampered with in this book, I truly apologize for the same as that was not my intention.

This is purely a work of fiction, and some of the historical details are changed to match the context of the novel in order to provide entertainment for the readers.

The fact that Julius Caesar went to Alexandria following Pompey during the Roman Civil war is a fact, as is the fire burning the Library and his ships. However, the other part of him searching for something specific is a work of imagination as are the details regarding the death of Pompey and Cleopatra being involved.

The fact that Hans Schleif had committed suicide after killing his children and wife is true. The reason for his death is still unknown, and whatever described in the book is a work of imagination. Alexander being a descendant of Hans is also a work of fiction, purely for the entertainment of the readers. If any similarity is found regarding the descendants of Hans, it is purely co-incidental.

The Library of Alexandria was a real Library in Alexandria, Egypt, along with the Callimachus scrolls which were burnt during the siege if Julius Caesar, later again by Caliph Omar. However, as to what are the contents of that scrolls, we are not aware. Whatever mentioned in the novel, is purely for the entertainment of the readers, and doesn't bear any resemblance to anyone or anything historical or modern.

The Indo-China-Nepal border is nearly inaccessible for the normal people and needs extensive permissions from the respective governments. It is inadvisable to try to go there on your own without the appropriate permissions.

As for the translation of Callimachus texts and the details regarding the *power* mentioned in the book, they are not included in this first installment of the series. The readers have to read on through the series as it comes up to know more about the power and the translation of the Callimachus scrolls.

The *Kastellet* is a real building in Denmark, though it is a museum currently. So, Alexander living there currently is a work of fiction, as is Sam studying in Cambridge for PHD in archeology and his professor getting killed in broad daylight.

The characters and events are all created from my imagination, nothing to do with anyone living or dead.

Lastly, I would say that I have tried my best to put my knowledge, research and imagination into the Sam and Mark series and would appreciate the support from my readers. Thank you.

Dear reader, read on...............

If you do not hope, you will not find what is beyond your hopes.

--- Clement of Alexandria

PROLOGUE

ALEXANDRIA 48 B.C.

The Key to unrivaled power is out there.

Julius Caesar looked towards the port of Alexandria. His red robe hung from his neck like a forgotten cape, occasionally fluttering in the winds coming from the Enipius River. It has been a year since the Roman Civil War had started. On 10th of January last year, it was him who crossed the Rubicon river, the boundary between the Cisalpine Gaul province to the north and Italy proper to the south, a legally prescribed action forbidden to any army-leading general. That was when it all began. And now, after more than a year, he was still struggling to stop this war.

But it's not about that anymore.

At first, Julius thought that he would be the hero of the Romans and began his triumphal progress. But the problem occurred when the Roman Senate started supporting Pompey or Gnaeus Pompeius Magnus, as he was known in Rome.

That fool.

Caesar still can't believe Pompey had escaped to Capua and created his own military regime. Being the son in law of the Great General Julius Caesar, he was supposed to be smarter than that. They had an alliance for ten years, and in a single foolhardy decision, Pompey had started the Civil war.

Not a single decision, Caesar thought.

It had started a long time back when Pompey sided himself with the optimates, the conservative faction of the Roman Senate. And those scoundrels were still supporting Pompey, until a few days ago. But Domitius, on the other hand, had been smart. After being isolated and trapped near Corfinium, he had surrendered, and most of his troops have promptly joined Caesar's army now.

However, looking at the port of Alexandria, Caesar had understood what made Pompey to take refuge in Egypt.

He could still remember that day from a couple of years ago and his conversation with Pompey.

'My Liege.' Pompey said. 'It seems to be in Alexandria.'

'In Egypt?' Caesar said in disgust. 'Ptolemy XIII doesn't have the balls to decide what to do with it.'

'Yes. But if we don't work on it now, all might be lost.'

'You speak the truth, Pompey.' Caesar replied while thinking, looking straight at his son in law in the eye. 'We must go to Egypt to find it. Do you know where it is?'

'It's in a Library, my Lord.'

Caesar was not able to go to Alexandria in search of the Library though, mainly because there were so many other things to take care of. Now, looking at the building looming in front of him on the port of Alexandria, he realized why Pompey had taken refuge here.

He wanted it for himself.

But that was not in his fate. After defeating him in the Battle of Dyrrhachium, Pompey fled again, though Caesar still can't fathom why he fled after being the triumphant, and after a series of mis happenings, had reached here and taken refuge.

But, Caesar received word a week ago, that Pompey was murdered, by an officer of Ptolemy XIII. Though he had no idea of the reason, he was glad. Still, there was one part of him, which mourned for this. After all, Pompey was his son-in-law and a close person for nearly a decade.

All was looking good for him, when suddenly two days earlier, he reached Alexandria, and now was involved in the Alexandriñe Civil War. A war between a brother and a sister. He was yet to take a side, but as far as he has heard, Pharaoh Cleopatra VII probably was the most beautiful woman in the world and thus inclining himself to side with her.

But that was yet to be decided. Now, being besieged on all sides with the Alexandrian army, he has done the only thing he could think of. He had asked his army to set fire on one of the ships, thus spreading the light to the enemy ships as well. But as most of the times in his life, things backfired.

Some more of his ships were on fire right now due to the fluttering winds from the side of Enipius River, along with the enemy ships. The troops have jumped into the water to save themselves. However, that did not deter him from reaching the shore of Alexandria and marching towards the library, the same one which Pompey had told him about.

****

The big bronze door fell off its hinges with a loud *Bang*. Julius Caesar and his band of soldiers marched forward.........

............and stopped dead in their tracks.

'What the hell?' Caesar shouted with his mouth fell open.

The northern part of the building was on fire, which was not supposed to be, considering the fact that the ships were burning on the port side at the south of the building, from where there was no chance of the fires to reach the building, especially on the northern side. And that's not all; the fire was spreading in all parts, slowly but surely.

But the most astonishing fact was that the whole Library seemed deserted. Not a single soul could be seen there.

Realizing something was amiss, Caesar ran forward.

After a few minutes, he sat on the reading room with his hands supporting his head.

Everything was lost. The whole Library of Alexandria was empty. All the scrolls were gone.

BERLIN, GERMANY
APRIL 27,1945

Hans Philipp Oswald Schleif looked in the mirror to find a haunted ghost looking back at him. His hairs have gone thin over the years, and the specs shrouded his blank hollow eyes.

Been in the Nazi party for last eight years, had taken its toll. At the age of 43, he was the *Standartenführer* of the Ahnenerbe, the Archeological project of the Nazi Party. For these last few years, he had dedicated himself to research the Archeological and cultural history of the Aryan race. Of course, the führer was the one who had always been interested in the history of the Aryans, believing the Nazis were the real successors of the Aryan race. But Hans had his own agenda too.

He looked at the bed beside him in this vast bedroom. It hosted the dead bodies of his twin sons - Alexander and Konstantin, both of whom were just 18 months old. His wife Lora lay just near the bed, with a bloody hole in her head.

The semi-automatic Luger was still smoking, which he held in his right hand.

At least their death was quick. And I have sent the details away from here.

The *Reichsführer*, Heinrich Himmler has voiced his suspicions about Hans today to the führer, and as per the latest report, the Protection Squadron was coming for him. If they had caught his wife and children, the torture would have been gruesome. Hans had seen the torturing process of the Nazi Third Reich for the last two years, and his family was not ready for that.

The secret he had learned, somehow Himmler got a hint of it. But it was too massive a secret for the Nazi party to get a hold on.

Hans put the Luger in his temple and pulled the trigger without thinking anymore.

Blam.

Darkness.

THE FIRST ORDEAL

THE WAY TO THE TRUTH

CHAPTER ONE

CAMBRIDGE, LONDON

November 10,

Friday, Present Day

7.30 A.M

'Hey, C'mon.' Rita looked at her husband as he hugged his son the second time. The boy was pleading to take him with them. But both his parents knew it was not safe for him to go with them.

'We will be back within a fortnight. Until then Granny will take care of you.' Hemanth let go of his son, who was just above eight years in age. The little boy obviously was despondent to stay at the home while his parents were going on an expedition out of his homeland.

'Your exams are at the doorstep.' sighed Rita. 'Or else we would have taken you with us, dear.'

'Why should you have to go now?' The boy was about to cry. 'Can't it wait till my exams are over?'

'Dr. Berthold has called us immediately, said it is urgent. So, we have to go in a hurry my son. But I promise to take you on our next tour, just after your exams.' Said Rita, smiling. 'Promise me you will study for the exams & won't fight with Granny.'

The boy never seemed to like the idea of it. But, he had no choice. 'I promise Mom.'

'But be quick, you must come before my exams start. I need you to help me with the history. I don't like the subject at all.'

Rita smiled. 'You will like it, my dear. I will be back before the exam starts.'

Both Rita & Hemanth stared at him for a moment. Then both of them kissed the cheeks of their son.

'Goodbye Mom, bye Daddy.'

'Goodbye, dear.'

Tic tic……tic tic….tic tic.

There was a sound somewhere. He can't make out what it was. It was as if he had been swimming for a long time and his senses have gone inert. The sound was getting louder.

Sam woke up with a jolt. The alarm had been ringing for quite a bit now. He slid his right arm from under the sheets and stopped the alarm from ringing further.

The dream always kept coming back. It was eighteen years ago that his parents had left for *Leipzig*, a populous city in the federal state of Saxony, Germany. It's located some 160 Kilometers from Berlin, the capital of Germany. Dr. Berthold Weber, a fellow archeologist from German Archeological Institute or DAI as it's known among the archeological world, had called Rita and Hemanth Rawath, the husband-wife duo, for their expertise on World War II history to unearth some artifacts from somewhere within the city.

It was then that the duo started for Germany. That was the last time Sam saw them.

It was after a week that a telegram reached their home. Granny had received it, and a minute later Sam has heard the shriek and came running down. The telegram contained the news of the untimely death of his parents in an accident, and their bodies were yet to be found. They have presumably drowned somehow when searching for something in *Markkleeberger See*, a lake near Leipzig.

Sam went to the restroom. Half an hour later he was supposed to meet Professor Richard Hedley. The Cambridge archeology Department has made it clear that without the submission of a live and realistic project, students pursuing the Ph.D. on Archeology will not be able to get their research papers out this year.

The date of submission was nearing every day. Just three months remaining.

He had no idea on what he could submit as a project. A month earlier he had tried to write up a blog regarding the truth behind the myth of the Hanging Gardens of Babylon, but it was denied by the Board saying – 'A waste of time and talent.'

He had then spoken to Professor Hedley about a project he was working on. No one in the campus knew surely about what he was working on, but the Professor had been traveling between weeks. The Prof. had said no…. until yesterday evening.

'Sam,'…. the Prof had said over the phone. 'We need to meet.'
'Is….is it regarding the Project submission?' Sam had asked tentatively.
'It's about much more Sam.' He replied cryptically. 'I think you would want to know about it.'

19

'Sure Professor. Where should we meet?' Sam replied, apparently surprised.

'The Stickybeaks Café.' He said. *'8 AM.'*

Click. The Prof hung up.

****

Professor Richard Hedley, the Head of the Department of Archeology in Cambridge, was sitting alone, nursing a cup of Coffee and scribbling something very carefully on a tissue paper, on the northern side of the café, when he saw his student Sameer Rawath coming in a cab.

It's not easy to tell him.

The cab took a turn to the left and started heading towards the café.

It's been already a long time that I have kept things secret from Sam. But what I have discovered now……

Suddenly the Professor felt a sharp sting on his neck. It felt like a syringe sunk deep in his neck and the next moment it was gone. He checked his surroundings but saw nothing unusual. A couple was having a romantic morning on his left side table with coffees and salad in front of them, a man behind him in black suit moving towards the exit, the waitress flirting with a young man, people walking on the pavement.

Sam just reached the café, exited the cab and saw his mentor waving his hand and replied in kind.

But to his horror, the Prof suddenly slipped off his chair and fell, his watery eyes looking directly at him.

He ran towards Hedley.

<u>CHAPTER TWO</u>

8:01 AM

The man in the black Cassini Suit left the Café quietly through the Northern Exit. He smiled picturing the scene he just left behind.

It had been few minutes that he was watching his prey from his vantage point, the table just beside Hedley, for an opportune moment. The old man was waiting for somebody, just as the man in the black suit was told. As soon as the Indian boy made his appearance, the Professor's expression changed, suggesting that this was the guy whom he wanted to meet.

So, this is Sam. Can't wait anymore.

So, the black suit did what he was ordered to do.

'Make sure the Professor doesn't speak to the boy. We don't need that guy's intervention.' His employer had said.

The Nerf N-Strike Maverick he was carrying was a special of its category. Weighing just a little more than a quarter of a pound, it was equipped with a 22g gauge, which contained 5 grams of botulinum, one of the deadliest poisons known to the humankind. Experts agree that botulinum—several orders of magnitude deadlier than sarin—is the gold standard among the known toxins. The nervous system fails in a matter of seconds, and the person dies with severe pain.

So, the dark-suited man had used this little gun for accomplishing the purpose. After the poison mixes into the blood, it would be untraceable once the man dies. As a result, the exact cause of the death will be a mystery. No sound took place when he fired the gun. And he made sure that the syringe can also be not found by pulling it out of the old man's neck in between shooting it from his table and moving towards the exit.

A simple trick of the hand, when no one is noticing.

The man smiled once more. He had timed his kill perfectly. On the morning of a busy Friday, there were not many people to watch the old man dying. More importantly, the old man was not able to speak to the young Indian. If it were a bit earlier, then there would have been unwanted chaos before the boy reaches, and if it were late, then the opportunity to do the next thing would have been gone up in smokes.

Now the boy would be busy with the Professor's body leaving him to execute the next phase.

Just as his employer had commanded.

He put the dart gun back in his pocket, along with the syringe with a drop of blood on the needle, recovered from the neck of the old man and took out the wire-rimmed black sunglass.

Time to go.

CHAPTER THREE

8:02 AM

'Oh...god...no!' Sam hurried through the door towards Hedley. There were not many people sitting in the restaurant at this early morning. A lady started screaming, and Sam thought he heard someone calling 112, the UK emergency number, equivalent to 911 in America.

But Sam could only look at one person at that time while moving forward.

The professor's eyes were bulging out and had gone red in a matter of seconds. The intense pain he was feeling in his chest caused his face to twist. Sam immediately understood what was happening.

The Professor is dying.

He reached the older man just as he fell off his chair. The Coffee mug landed on the floor of the café with a loud *clang* and broke into a thousand pieces just as Sam reached near the Professor.

'You're going to be ok.' Sam took Hedley's head on his lap and tried to console him as much possible, himself sitting on the floor. First, he thought the Professor couldn't recognize him, the eyes quickly becoming red and blurry due to blood condensation. But then he saw a hint of recognition in his eyes.

'S…SAM'. It was merely a whisper. 'The…. the not…. the note…,' was all Hedley could say.

Sam couldn't even think in his wildest dreams what the Professor was trying to say to him in his last moments. But whatever Hedley wanted to say must be very important, or else he wouldn't have said these in his dying moments.

'Yes, Professor.' Sam said, nodding his head quickly.

Or maybe it's gibberish…a garbled thought at the end of the man's life, Sam thought. Whatever it was, it seemed best for Sam to soothe the dying man with his words.

'Someone, please call the Ambulance,' he cried, looking desperately on all sides.

'It's on its way.'…... Sam heard someone say among the crowd that gathered around him and the Professor.

'Fin…find it.' The Prof. was losing his power to speak. 'You must find the path to….'

'Path to what?'

But Hedley was not able to speak anymore. His nervous system started to break down. First, his eyes were blurred, then his body went limp. His face muscles tensed, and suddenly…….

Nothing.

There was simply nothing. The Professor's head lolled soundlessly to the side and his eyes closed. Sam just felt a sudden weightlessness in his lap.

Someone behind drew a large breadth, probably letting a single breath out after holding it for some time now.

'Professor!!!' The Indian's eyes became moist, and a single tear dropped on the forehead of the Professor lying below.

Flashes of the older man came in rapid succession in his mind………

The Professor coming first time in their house in Delhi, taking him and his Granny out to see the museum, consoling him about Rita and Hemanth's death, arguments with Granny upstairs at night. The Professor left the house the next day early morning.

'Be a very good boy,' he had said just before leaving… 'you have to make your parents proud.'

Again, Hedley coming back to the same house during Granny's funeral, taking Sam with him to study in London, the Professor visiting his hostel room for the freshman year, countless nights spent speaking on the history of the World, on Ancient and recent Wonders of the World, on historical anomalies, on unnatural events and so on.

He had always wanted Sam to study under him in Cambridge.

Sam closed his eyes, half expecting the flashes to vanish. Tears started dripping now constantly, soaking his idol's shirt.

'Somebody call the ambulance.'

Even though the words came out of his mouth in a whisper, Sam knew quite well that no one could do anything about the person lying on his lap anymore.

The cops and the ambulance were coming. Sam could hear the sirens of the CPD, the infamous Cambridge Police Department, approaching. But he could barely contain his emotions. The man now dead in his hands had been his mentor for so many years.

Hedley had been the only person after the death of Granny to be a part of his life. Sam had considered him not as a teacher, but as a friend, philosopher, and guide.

Now the Professor was dead. Sam felt an emotion which he has not felt for quite a long time. It was the same that he felt after hearing the dreadful news of the death of his parents. The feeling was a mixture of loss and grief.

It was then that he saw it, a piece of tissue paper and a pen, lying beside Professor's limp body....... most probably fell from his trousers' pocket when he fell from his chair.

Sam took the paper and saw something written on it. It would have to wait. Before anyone knew he hid it in his own jeans.

He would have to check it later. Maybe it was important, or perhaps it was just a piece of paper, like so many on the Professor's desk he had seen always.

Sirens were now just outside. The cops were here.

CHAPTER FOUR

8:32 A.M

The Silver Daewoo Nexia Hatchback 3dr was passing the Fitzwilliam Museum. Inside the well-furnished car, on the driver's seat was the man in the black suit. It would take some time to reach his destination.

He reached for the dashboard and took out his phone. With only three fingers on the left hand, he always felt uncomfortable to get hold of a cell phone. But his employer had made it clear that before starting the second phase of his day's work, the black suit must call him.

He parked the car just outside the Museum and dialed a number and waited for the phone to ring.

'I was waiting for your call.' A metallic voice said on the other side of the line, electronic masking enabled.

'The first phase completed.'

'Then you must proceed to the next phase.' The voice said without any emotion.

'What about the payment?'

'Your one Million Dollars will be transferred to your Swiss account in the next hour as usual.'

'In that case,' he paused, 'consider your work done.'

'Good. I expect your call within the next hour. Your transport will be ready.'

'You will get it.'

'I'd better.'

The person hung up.

Black suit stared at the phone for a few moments. Then, stashing it in the passenger seat, he started the engine.

He must complete the second phase before his employer's patience wears off.

CHAPTER FIVE

WASHINGTON D.C., USA
3:10 AM

'I got the call just a minute ago,' the voice from the other end said. Mark was still tired, being woken up early in the morning. The preceding day had been very tough for him. Being the Special Operations Officer in the MRR Division of MARSOC takes a toll. The Marine Raider Regiment, better known as MRR always see the direct action in the field. And being the SOO of United States Marine Corps Forces Special Operations Command or called merely USMC MARSOC, Mark was always in the front seat of any battles. Not that it matters much, mainly because he was used to the battlefield for more than one and a half decades courtesy of being in USMC FAST earlier.

After that, he was offered the position in MRR as a CSO, short for Critical Skills Officer. They had to go through a more thorough training on each type of combats known to man. As a person previously working in FAST, it was easy for Mark to grasp the exercise much more quickly than his comrades, and then a few years to climb the ladder for the position of SOO there.

FAST is the Fleet Anti-Terrorism Security Team which deals with the terrorism in the United States soil. They also help the allies of US when necessary to deal with International Terrorism or foreign threats. Most people think FBI, CIA or NSA handles such situations, courtesy to the countless Hollywood movies. But the truth is the men with black suits there identify the threats and men like Mark march into the battlefield experiencing and witnessing such threats, eliminating them.

Being the SOO, he should lead the squads of Special operations forces explicitly. Post-Nine-Eleven, such ventures have started more. As a result of these, there were very few places on earth where Mark have not been to.

He had thought that after this he would become the Special Operations Commander and retire early after a few years. But all that changed a month ago when he had received the call on a rainy night. Mark still remembered every detail of the call that night.

It was an off-season rain. After a tough day on the field, Mark just wanted to sleep. His apartment at Capitol Hill provided all the comfort necessary after an unusually long day that Mark was craving for. He had a good dinner with Laura, and all he wanted was his cozy bed to sleep on.

It was 1 AM at night when the call came. Mark woke suddenly at the sound of his phone vibrating on the bedside table. He looked towards the watch, checked the time and grunted in disdain.

'Holy shit…goddamit,' was all he could say.

He took the phone in his hand to check who the hell was calling at this hour. To his surprise, there was no number shown. It only showed 'Private Number' in the Caller Id. He knew about this process of masking the IP of the internet call.

His curiosity piqued, Mark answered the call.

'Good Evening Mark.' The voice on the other side sounded full of authority, someone who is accustomed to being listened to and obeyed.

Mark's eyes grew wide. He immediately recognized the voice on the opposite side of his phone.

It can't be- was his first thought. Why would he…….

His chain of thoughts was broken by the words coming from the other side.

'I understand its late. Probably you were savoring your victory today', the voice continued ….'I have kept tabs on you for a long time now.'

'Y..yes, sir.'

'You seem surprised to hear my voice Mark. As I understand you already knew that I have been keeping tabs on you'.

By now Mark has got a grip on himself. If he was calling at this hour, then it must be important. This was the first time the person has called him, though Mark had his doubts that he may be spied upon. He had seen this person on many occasions but never had he thought that he would actually be able to speak to him, let alone now…especially after this person has become…….

He shook his head. He needs to answer correctly; he must show confidence.

'I know very well sir about your people watching my every move for some time now.' Mark continued, 'But I would like to know why.'

'That is the reason you are coming to meet me tomorrow at the House.'

'I'm sorry……. Did you say the House, sir?'

'I did, yes. It takes a great deal of courage and intelligence for someone to know that he was being spied upon by me, especially now. And the fact that you could find it out and confront one of my men a few days ago proves that you are worth much more than credited for, and your intelligence is proved by the way you were able to investigate and find out that I was the one who was spying on you.'

'I am honored sir, but I am not sure why you want to meet me, or as a matter of fact why you were spying upon me.'

'If you want to know what I want Mark, you will have to meet me tomorrow after lunch.' Said the voice, 'We have a great deal to talk about. I have a job for you'.

The phone hung up.

Mark had met the man the next day. It was there that he learned about the nature of his job. It seemed the person kept Mark in his highest regards. And so he agreed to the job.

He was told it might take some time. But it seems his employer was wrong.

'The Professor died today in a restaurant in Cambridge.' The voice said.

'Was it a murder? Or was it something else?' Mark asked.

'From what I heard, it might be a heart attack. Nobody has seen anything unusual, just suddenly he fell from his chair and died. But I don't want anything to be missed. And he was meeting the boy when he was murdered. He told me last week that he will tell the boy everything now. Considering everything, it seems that it was related to that.'

Of course, Mark thought. The Professor if not dead, would have been able to tell Sam about everything.

'Someone is after it, Sir.'

'Exactly my point. This is when you come into the picture. You need to go now. The jet will be ready when you reach'.

'Yes, sir. I am moving now'.

Mark kept the phone as the caller hung up. He needs to get ready now. The danger was luring, and he needed to be there soon, or else…….

Everything might be lost.

CHAPTER SIX

CAMBRIDGE, LONDON
2:30 PM

What was he talking about?

'S.....SAM, the not....the note…find it….you must find the path to….'

The Professor's words still played in his mind. There were thousands of questions running in his mind – How Hedley died? What path was he speaking?

It had taken the whole morning and some part of the afternoon to sort things out with the cops. The entire University was still shocked upon hearing the news of the Professor Hedley's death.

The cops have taken statements from all the other Professors in the University and the people in the restaurant. Sam and some other people in the restaurant were the eyewitnesses, but that didn't help much. According to the eyewitness accounts, the Professor was having coffee and suddenly fell from his chair.

'It may be a heart attack.' Officer Harvey Jones said. 'We need to send him to the lab for the postmortem.'

Sam heard from the restaurant that Officer Jones was the In-charge of this murder investigation. The man looked more like a TV star than a cop. The salt and pepper beard, the luxuriant hairstyle and a handsome face contributed to the thought. The only anomaly was the tummy, the size of a car tire that belied this thought.

At five feet nine, Sam himself had a lean cut physique, courtesy of many years' habit of hitting the gym after hours. The close-cropped hair, well build body and brown complexion represented his Indian heritage. Because of his features, many people in the past have thought of Sam as an athlete. Partially that's true, courtesy of the fact that he liked to play basketball.

After the formalities were done, statements taken, Sam came back to his room. This was the first time after the day's events that he was alone. He tried to gather his thoughts. The questions filled most of his thoughts.

Suddenly he stood up. Something clicked in his mind.

What if………

He knew then what he must do.

<u>CHAPTER SEVEN</u>

2:50 PM

Mark came out of the Private Jet massaging a kink in his back. Being in the employment of someone as powerful as his employer, there were certain advantages. The Jet has taken a little more than 6 hours to reach Cambridge.

He was grateful to come out of the Jet. The elegant environment and two beautiful Airhostesses did little to make his journey comfortable. It's not that he didn't like the atmosphere inside consisting of great leather seats, a private room and some of the most expensive liquors he ever had the pleasure of tasting… but the problem for him was to sit in the same place for more than 6 hours.

He has never been known among his friends to be the most patient one, and in a way, that's true. During missions, he could wait outside an enemy line for days, but when it comes to the office jobs or travels, it has always been difficult for him to stay in the same place for long.

'I am a man of action,' he always told when confronted with this question about his patience.

'I like to be on the run rather than sitting on my butt,' was his usual answer.

So, it's easy to conceive that the journey was not that much comfortable, though that didn't discourage Mark to consume a bottle of *Dom Perignon 2003 Rosé*, known to be one of the most expensive Champagnes in the world and a lavish lunch.

After clearing the customs, he made his way to the waiting Mercedes. His employer has made sure that the car would be waiting for him when he arrives. Collecting the keys from the dashboard, he threw the bag pack in the passenger seat and sunk into the driver's seat.

His employer made the arrangement to have a private car to himself. The main reason was to protect the anonymity of Mark as much as possible. The fewer people know about Mark's destination and work, the better.

Mark inserted the keys into the ignition and started the engine.

He needed to reach quickly, if not already late.

CHAPTER EIGHT

AIRSPACE ABOVE BRUSSELS

4:00 PM

The Boeing 757 soared through the air. The city of Brussels could be seen below. Inside the flight, the lights were dimmed for providing comfort to the passengers while taking a nap.

Sabir was reviewing the notes in his hand with the overhead lamp projecting directly towards them. He had changed into a more casual look with a Denim Trousers and a V-neck in contrast to the dark suit, to look the part of a tourist on his way back. He had taken whatever he could in a hurry from the Professor's office and home. It was easy to break into the house and get copies of all the notes and notebooks of the Professor. But his employer wanted him to get the notes from the dead man's office as well.

It had been a risk for Sabir, but he had managed it in an exemplary manner. A blow to the head took care of one of the security guards who went into the ground floor washroom to relieve himself.

Then a change of clothes and posing as a security in the University was just a matter of minutes. From there making his way to Hedley's office and then gathering everything and leaving was not that much difficult.

He had a fair idea of what his employer was searching for. But checking most of the notes for the last hour in the flight had not yielded anything useful. If his employer was correct regarding the fact that the historian was working on something important, then the dead man was very secretive about his work.

It was just last week that Hedley got the courier. Sabir had been looking out for any unusual activities since the Professor's visit from Frankfurt. And this parcel stood out to be a significant event for the old man, precisely because it was one of the events his employer had suspected.

The listening device inside the Professor's desk in his study room provided the required details just a week ago.

'I have received the package,' Hedley said in the phone. 'Seems like the claim was legitimate. I could have helped them, saved them'. His voice resembled sobbing.

After a few seconds, hearing the answer from the person on the other line the Professor had said – 'I will tell Sam everything, I need to.' After a few more words, Professor kept the phone.

That was when the wheels were set into motion. The package needed to be secured and the Professor to be stopped from speaking to the boy. There was the matter about the person with whom the Professor has spoken, but that didn't matter much. The Professor was dead, and all his notes were with Sabir now.

It must be somewhere within these worthless bunch, and he must find it, before the plane lands.

<u>CHAPTER NINE</u>

CAMBRIDGE

4:00 PM

urznagu ebbz. qryuw, onfrzrag ylpxvre friar

- - - - - mlechh

The writing seemed random, not making any sense at all. The letters were English no doubt, but it didn't result in anything.

That doesn't make it less bizarre than it appears.

He had gone to the Professor's office at Cambridge to try and find out a clue that could give an answer to the mystery. But it seemed like someone has cleaned the room recently. Indeed, there was not a single sheet which could be seen, much less something resembling a letter or a note, which was very unlike the old man. Sam had visited this same room for more than a few years now, and it always looked the same. The messy look, the scattered books, notes, and sheets – that's how it's always have been. It was like a signature of the Professor.

But it sure as hell didn't look like that anymore. Sam had enquired to the staffs in the University if anyone had seen someone entering or exiting Hedley's office but always got the answer in negative.

Nobody had seen anyone coming in or out of the office, and none of the staffs cleared the room.

That left only one conclusion. Some outsider was in this office. But whoever he was, he was brilliant to keep himself invisible. A guard was found unconscious inside a stall in the ground floor washroom, and he couldn't remember anything other than the fact that someone had hit him hard on the back of the head. The reddish black bump on the lower right side of his head supported his narrative.

But why would someone come to Hedley's office? There was nothing of importance there at all. But Sam's gut told him that there was something wrong with the Professor's death. And maybe whatever was the reason for his death was either in the office or his home. This was no coincidence that the day the Professor wanted to tell him something, he died; and moreover, on the same day someone entered in his office, and all the notes and sheets were gone, except the old man's books in his shelf. All these seem somehow connected. The Professor's urgent call last night to meet him, his death and now this. But Sam was still not able to figure out why.

It was then that he remembered the piece of tissue paper that he had kept from the restaurant. As soon as he remembered, Sam came rushing back to his room and searched for the paper.

Damn…where had he kept it? After the day's events, it's difficult to….

There it was.

Sam saw the paper on the floor, probably fell when he took out his phone earlier while changing.

Is this the note he was referring to?

Maybe, maybe not. But it was something to go on with. Whatever it was, he had to solve it.

All the mysteries might be connected to this gibberish. Sam decided to follow this lead, without anyone else knowing.

CHAPTER TEN

FRANKFURT, GERMANY

4:45 PM

'Motherfucker.'

The plane was coming down to the Frankfurt Airport for its final stop.

Sabir couldn't contain his anger anymore. He had been going through every note, every sheet of paper the Professor had in his house or the office. Still, there was no sign on anything remotely related to the parcel.

Oddly, there was no reference to his travels in the last month as well. That could mean only one thing.

The fucker was paranoid, which would also mean that he may have stumbled upon the very thing Sabir and his employer were after for nearly two decades. It was only an assumption, but a good one nonetheless.

Or else, the guy wouldn't have been so paranoid to get rid of anything related to his recent travels, his interactions, and the parcel. His employer would not be pleased about it.

He has been waiting for more than a decade to get hold of it.

If only that crooked couple had helped. It would have been so much easier.

But Sabir knew that nothing good could come quickly. The path to something so awesome, so powerful could only be found through many hardships. And he was someone who had seen difficulties in life.

<u>CHAPTER ELEVEN</u>

<u>CAMBRIDGE</u>

4:30 PM

The house seemed lonely to Sam from outside. It was as if the Professor was the heart of this house.

In a way, that was true. All his life's work, all his days were mostly spent in this house other than his lecture times at Cambridge. Sam felt a pang of loneliness, picturing the lifeless body of the Prof in the café this morning.

After getting the note from the tissue paper, it felt like coming in the house was the correct course of action. It seemed like there was some mystery related to the Hedley's death, something that he couldn't put his finger on. Something seemed to be alluring him here. The Professor's sudden call last night, today his death, his note in the tissue paper of the café and too much tidiness in his office; all seemed off to Sam.

The first time he ever entered this house when he was in high school. After the death of Granny, the Prof came to his home in Delhi and took him to London. He has taken care of Sam ever since like a father would. Hedley himself was childless and took Sam as his own son. Sam has always been a brilliant student in his school life, and that helped him get admission into Regent High School, one of the most prestigious schools in London. After completing, he went to college to study history and archeological studies. All the time the Professor guiding and helping him with his studies and providing a much-needed father figure.

The house was a single-story building with two bedrooms, a lounge, a kitchen, and a study room. Most of the nights the Professor would be asleep in his couch in the study, with a book open in front of him. A lawn could be seen in the front of the house.

****

The door opened, and Sam entered inside.

The note was what seemed like the biggest mystery. Sam took the tissue paper out of his pocket and checked again.

urznagu ebbz, qryuu, onfrzrag ybp.xre friar

- - - - - mlechh

It was the Prof's handwriting all right. But the only problem was, there was no telling if it was an old man's dying note or just a simple gibberish, a way to pass the time in café waiting for Sam.

Maybe I will get some clue inside his house.

The lounge was a neatly kept room. Hedley spent very little time here, except when there was an occasional visitor. So, it was expected to be clean and neat. But Sam was struck with the familiar gut feeling of something being wrong as soon as he entered the study room. It too was neat and clean.

Too much clean.

He has seen this room numerous times in last few years and never in his countless visits he had seen this room so well ordered and organized. Granted, that the shelves were filled with the books kept in an orderly fashion, but the whole study room was very different always. There were his notes and sheets sitting everywhere in the room; some in the recliner, some in the study table and few on the floor as well sometimes. Adding to that, there was always few notebooks sitting in a completely random order in his study table and a minimum of five books always going with them.

But today it seemed that the room was thoroughly cleaned by the Prof. The study table was immaculately arranged. There were no sheets or notebooks present there. Only a few books arranged in a neat order one above the other.

That was totally inappropriate for the Prof.

Sam came to the study table and opened the first drawer slowly……
…….and he froze.

CHAPTER TWELVE

4:32 PM

Mark looked towards the house where just a minute ago, Sam got inside the Prof's house.

He has been sitting in his car just a hundred meters away from Hedley's house for an hour to check if he can find anyone curious enough to come to check for something. Nobody had come till now, except the Indian boy.

He remembered what was told to him on the day he went to meet his new employer.

'Sameer Rawath is a special boy.' The man sitting opposite Mark said.

Mark nodded his understanding, all the while checking the photos of Sam. These photos were taken during various times of Sam's life ranging from his school life in Delhi to his Ph.D. classes in Cambridge.

'He seems to be very close with Richard Hedley.' Mark noted seeing a photo of Sam with the Professor. Hedley holding the young twelve-year-old boy's hands and showing him a fort in Delhi.

'Indeed, they are.' The man said. 'And that's where you are up.'

Mark was still a bit in shock. He still can't believe that he is sitting inside one of the most famous rooms in the world. Not to say anything about the man he is meeting now.

'What do I have to do?'

'May not be anything.' The man said sighing. 'But if what I believe is correct, then you will be encountering Sam very soon. Maybe in the next few months.'

He was dead right.

But Mark had never thought that he would encounter Sam so quick. It seemed Sam was also not believing in the story of the Professor dying due to a heart attack. And if that's true, then Mark needed to do what he has been sent to do and put an end to this.

He exited the car and marched towards the Prof's house. A smile crept on his face.

Time to meet the boy.

CHAPTER THIRTEEN

00:00:10

The stopwatch started the countdown.

Beep.

00:00:09

Sam was frozen for a moment. His mind took an extra nanosecond to process what he was seeing. The timer countdown was all too familiar to him, courtesy of the Hollywood movies he has seen all numerous times.

It's a C4 explosive. Need to run. NOW.

His mind screamed.

He had seen documentaries on the bombs a few days ago in Nat Geo. The host was showing a lot of different kind of bombs. And among them was a C4 plastic explosive bomb. He can still remember the composition of the C4 explosives from the show. It contains 91% of RDX(Research Department Explosive), 5.3% of dioctyl sebacate (DOS) or dioctyl adipate (DOA) as the plasticizer (to increase the plasticity of the explosive), 2.1% polyisobutylene (PIB, a synthetic rubber) as the binder, and 1.6% of a mineral oil often called "process oil".

There seemed to be 4-5 blocks of C4 attached together and covered in black plastic cover and around them the timer was set.

00:00:08

'Shit.'

Sam cursed himself. The documentary never showed how to diffuse a bomb. And he was not a bomb expert. The only way to save himself was to run.

00:00:07

Sam ran towards the kitchen. It was the nearest exit from the study room.

00:00:06

Somebody must have rigged the explosive in such a way that if anybody came to investigate the house and opened the drawer, the timer for 10 seconds countdown would start, and the bomb should blow up the whole house.

00:00:05

Sam reached the exit door from the kitchen and stopped.

'Oh no.'

The exit was locked, and Sam only had the key to the main entrance that the Prof used to keep under the mat. There was no time to search for another key.

00:00:04

Sam ran through the kitchen and reached the study room. The study room window was closed too.

No way to escape through there.

00:00:03

He reached the bedroom and crossed the bed in a single jump.

00:00:02

He reached the lounge and……

…….and saw a man entering the house through the main door. He seemed like an American to Sam.

No time to think.

'C4 BOMB.' Sam shouted on top of his voice.

00:00:01

The American seemed to understand the word quite clearly and made an about turn to exit the building. Sam jumped through the door after the man, and both tumbled together on the lawn just as they felt a searing heat.

The sound followed a moment later.

BOOM....

CHAPTER FOURTEEN

FRANKFURT, GERMANY

5:33 PM

Peep...peep.

The transmitter sounded the alarm.

Sabir was nearing his safe house when the transmitter sounded. He looked at his phone and a crooked smile formed on his face.

Must be someone curious to find out more about the Professor.

Someone must have gone to the Professor's house to do their own investigation. Sabir had made sure before coming back from Cambridge that nobody else could investigate anything in the old man's home. The jerry-rigged C4 plastic explosive was set with a motion sensor, custom created by Sabir himself.

He savored the moment. It has been a long time that he had used this kind of expertise in the field. It was last during the fight in Afghanistan that he had used a similar type of bomb to eradicate some American tourists and the Delta forces that have come there to save the hostages. That's the price of war.

After being discharged from the Syrian Army for insubordination, Sabir had taken up mercenary jobs all over the world, providing covert under the radar jobs to his clients.

Whoever pays money.

He had worked for various dictators and leaders of the world to help them with many out of books cover works and had been paid handsomely. He even worked in Basra for some time, for Saddam Hussain himself. So, violence was never off the books for him.

His current employer would be considerate of the progress so far. Though he had not found what he was looking for, so does nobody else in the world as of now.

And the Professor was dead.

CHAPTER FIFTEEN

COPENHAGEN, DENMARK

5:40 PM

Alexander Penbrose looked out from the window of his private lounge. The view itself was a breathtaking one. From his estate, it's just 500 meters where the beach starts. And from the window, there's a direct view of the *Little Mermaid*, one of the best-preserved sculptures in Europe.

Alexander was probably the Sixth wealthiest person in the world, thanks to his numerous businesses starting from footwear, healthcare, and furniture. He himself had never bothered to calculate the net worth of his fortune.

The media does that for me.

From what he has gathered recently, it seemed his net worth right was 96.8 billion Danish Krone, which had landed him into the sixth position of the world's wealthiest list. The renovation and preservation of the most of Denmark's history were done using his generous donations to the Danish Government every year.

Those who see him for the first time could never guess that the person opposite to them was a 62-year-old. With all his hairs a blood red color, a powerful physique comparable with Arnold Schwarzenegger himself, and a height of six feet four inches, he looked more like a Rockstar than an accomplished businessman. Indeed, he was a well-known person among the world's businessmen.

He was wearing a white Dunhill suit with a stylized shirt and a blue tie. In twenty minutes there was a meeting with Bill Gates regarding some off-shore business he was investing in.

'Sir, they are on the way.' Rhony Freds, his Public Relations Manager, prompted from behind.

Alexander nodded absentmindedly. It seemed Bill Gates is on his way to *Botanisk Have*, the botanical garden of Copenhagen to meet him.

Triing…… Triing.

Finally, the phone rang.

He had been waiting for this call for an hour now.

'Yes.' He said picking up the call.

'It's all done.' The voice from the other side said.

'Good.' Alexander's response was crisp. 'How about the item?'

There was a pause on the other end which gave him the required answer.

'This is unexpected.'

'I…. I understand sir.' The other person's voice became very low. 'I have checked all his notes, notebooks, sheets and books. But there no mention….'

'That doesn't mean the item is not real.' Alexander said in a crisp voice, clenching his cell tightly making his knuckles white. 'I need it. Find it anyhow; I don't care what you have to do for that.'

With that, he hung up the phone and moved out of the room.

The helicopter was waiting at the terrace to take him to the Garden.

Only one thought crossed his mind when the aircraft took off.

The professor has been very secretive about his work and travels. He surely knew about the item.

CHAPTER SIXTEEN

CAMBRIDGE
4:30 PM

'Ohh…... ouch'.

Sam cried out while trying to sit. The pain was terrible but still bearable.

Addenbrooke's hospital was one of the best in Cambridge, sitting on the Hills road from 1976. Owing to the strong affiliations to the University of Cambridge and being an internationally renowned teaching hospital, the doctors were always on their toes to help the patients. Dr. Howard completed bandaging Sam's shoulder and left hand.

'Take rest, Sam.'

Sam looked at the person saying this. It's the same person who was at the Prof's house.

Now he got the time to see this guy fully. At first, glance just while the bomb was exploding, he didn't have time to ponder on the presence of an outsider, least of all an American. But here he was in the hospital, beside Sam's bed, advising him.

Now that he got a good look at the American, he was amazed. He seemed a tall guy, much more than Sam himself…. at least six feet three inches. The way he handled himself when Sam had told about the bomb was nothing ordinary. Sam himself was frozen for a moment after seeing the time bomb in Professor's home, but this guy just turned in a second and jumped out of the room without a second thought or any hint of fear in his eyes. The way he carried himself made Sam think of Keanu Reeves in *The Matrix*. Indeed, the handsome and an almost elongated and clean shaved face, buzz cut blonde hair made him think of the military people he had seen in different movies over the years. The stranger had a tattoo on his neck, but from this angle, Sam couldn't make out what it was. It could be a scorpion, or it could be a butterfly as well, as far as the Indian can tell. The guy was wearing jeans and a white shirt, but still, from what Sam could see, the muscles were bulging out of the shirt.

'What happened?' Was the first thing that Sam could ask.

'You saved me from the bomb in Professor Richard Hedley's house, that's what happened.' Said the man with a casual shrug, as if the blowing of a bomb was an everyday thing. 'And in the process, you hurt yourself, and for some time you lost consciousness.'

'I was unconscious?' Sam asked incredulously while putting his shirt on.

'Or maybe you slept after getting hurdled with shrapnel, hmm?' The stranger said with an irritating smile.

'Thanks for being sarcastic.' Sam said with a humorless smile. 'Then I presume you are the one who saved me now by bringing me to the hospital?'

'Yes Sam.' The man said while lifting himself up from the chair.

'Looks like we are even on playing the savior game.'

Sam noticed a little surprised that this person knew his name.

That's odd. How would an American know my name? Unless he knows something else too. Maybe he is somehow related to the death of the Prof? And the bombing in the Prof's house?

No. He didn't seem like that kind of person to Sam. If he had planted the bomb, then at the last moment there was no need for him to enter the house when the bomb was about to explode. He would have gotten killed if not moved quickly.

Then who was he?

'Then let me ask you something.' He said to this seemingly stranger.

'It seems you know my name, but I don't know yours. Who are you? And why are you here?'

The American came in front of Sam and extended his right hand for a handshake.

'My name is Mark Brent.' He said dramatically. 'And I am here to help you.'

What he said next confused Sam more than he already was.

'We need to leave. NOW.'

CHAPTER SEVENTEEN

MARYLAND, USA
12:30 PM

Cryptanalyst Eva Brown was working on the top floor of the building no. 2B in Fort Meade when the call came.

Not everybody knows, but the current Headquarter of the National Security Agency or NSA, as its commonly known, is at Fort Meade, consisting of four buildings together called as the "Big Four." NSA's mission, as outlined in Executive Order 12333 in 1981, is to collect information that constitutes "foreign intelligence or counterintelligence" while not "acquiring information concerning the domestic activities of United States persons."

However, apart from providing valuable intelligence on the foreign works, another important work of NSA is to work on the field of Cryptography. They usually work on breaking the numerous codes that are encountered in everyday intelligence gatherings.

Eva was one of the three hundred cryptographers taken in NSA as part of extending their cryptographic division in Fort Meade in 2012, to divide the works of cryptography in hopes of quickly achieving the result of breaking available codes every day.

'Oh god.' She said, seeing the name of the incoming number in her cell. 'Not again.'

She still remembered the day they met.

It was almost six years ago. The imminent threat of an attack on the now ex-president's life had put everyone on edge in NSA and CIA. The latter had particularly promising information regarding the same, an encrypted message with a sixty-four-character key that they were not able to break. MARSOC was with the presidential detail at that time when the President was traveling from Moscow to Washington.

The NSA had received a copy of the message. Eva, as one of the brilliant cryptanalysts of NSA, was looking into the message when suddenly she found a solution to break the encryption by writing a three-liner code and unlock it.

Fifteen minutes later, she was talking to Mark on a secured line and provided the useful message to him, which saved the life of the then most powerful man in the world.

It was later that night in the basement of the White House that they both met. The medals they received were a reminder of the common threat they dealt with, though they can't show it to anyone.

Eva and Mark have been in contact ever since. It was not dating or anything romantic, but they have become excellent friends over time. She has asked for his help or passed necessary information many times in the last six years. They both have seen each other rise through the ranks over the years.

The only problem was Mark's sense of humor. Sometimes it felt like too much over the edge.

She came out of her workstation to the lobby outside to take the call.

'Hello, Mark.'

'Hey, darling.' Mark's voice came from the other side. 'How's the day going?'

'As usual. What's up with you?' She said with a smile. 'Where are you today?'

'At Cambridge. In London. In a problem. Need your help.' The words came through the other side of the phone in four installments.

'Oh! Is it? And here I thought you were missing me.'

'Hard time. I need…'

'And what are you doing in Cambridge?' She said with mock humor. 'Thinking of starting the studies again?'

'Hardly. But now that I think of it, it would have been better to start the studies.'

'Well…… Better late than never.'

'Listen Eva.' Mark's voice turned serious. 'We need your help. I have sent a picture of a message to you. I need it to be decrypted.'

Ping……

She heard the incoming message tone in her phone, indicating the picture had arrived.

'Oh! …. So that's why you need the Cryptographer.' She said feigning anger. 'Don't worry; it will be done by the evening.'

'Nope Eva. We don't have time. This needs to be decrypted ASAP. And it has to be under the radar.'

She thought for a second. If it's under the radar, that means no computers, no resources from NSA. That could be tracked easily. And she was better off asking any details on it.

'Who are we?'

'Later dear. Right now, gotta go.'

The phone clicked off.

CHAPTER EIGHTEEN

FRANKFURT, GERMANY
6:30 PM

'He what?'

Sabir had just freshened up in his suite in the hotel he had checked in. It was used as a safe house for the whole year, being booked in an alias. It was good that he has kept his second in command, Ashir Ahmed in Cambridge to check for any proceedings there, in case anything new happened.

And he just received news that in one hand was a bad one, and in another side might be just the thing he needed right now.

After the discussion with his employer, Alexander Penbrose, he was struggling to find a way to retrieve the item that the Old man had received last week. The news he just got from Ahmed, might give him a chance he needed.

It appeared that the Indian boy Sam was unharmed by the blast and had fled with an American.

'Do you know where he is?' He barked on the phone.

'Yes, sir. It seems the boy and the American are going towards the airport.'

'Good. Follow them. I need to know every detail of their movement.'

'Yes, sir.'

'Losing them out of sight is unacceptable Ahmed. We need to know every step they make.'

After getting the positive response from Ahmed, he clicked off the phone. In between everything a new concern rose in his mind.

Who is the American?

CHAPTER NINETEEN

CAMBRIDGE
5:34 PM

'Who was that?'

Sam and Mark left the hospital half an hour ago, and on Mark's suggestion going towards the airport in his Mercedes. After a brief discussion in the hospital, they both were now sure about one fact; someone did kill Professor Richard Hedley or wanted to kill him along with whatever he was working on. Or else, there was no reason to keep a booby-trapped bomb in his study room.

Why would anyone want to kill the Prof?

The main problem was that there was nothing to prove or to go on. The explosion at his house can well be indicated as a gas leak, and the Prof's death was already being told as a heart attack.

There were other things that he needed an answer too.

Who is this guy? Whom was he calling now? Why is he here? And what he has to do with it all?

Mark looked at him from the driver's seat.

'That's a friend of mine. A Cryptographer.'

So that's why Mark had taken a picture of the tissue paper with that note.

'Dude.' Sam said, exasperated. 'Stop the car. I need to know what's going on.'

'It's ok Sam. I will tell you on the way.'

'On the way to where?'

'On the way to Washington.'

'Washington?' Sam said, surprised. 'Why the hell should I go to Washington?'

'You will understand once I tell you everything.'

'STOP.' Sam said in the top of his voice, losing his cool.

Such was his voice that Mark was forced to stop the car.

'I need to know what is going on.'

****

'I am here to help you, Sam.'

'The hell you are.' Sam said, angry. 'You may very well be the killer of the Professor. You might have been the one who put the bomb in his house.'

'Oh great.' Mark said, throwing his arms on both sides. 'And then I have gone back there to commit suicide, is it?'

The sarcastic tone in his voice was not lost to Sam. *He is right.*

'Then tell me what's all this about?'

'Ok. What do you want to know?'

'How about starting from who you are?'

Mark paced the road, deciding how much to tell. After a second, he came to a conclusion.

Honesty is the best policy.

'My name is Mark Brent, which I have already told you in hospital. I work in the United States Marine Corps Forces Special Operations Command.'

MARSOC, Sam thought. He had heard of them before. It's one of the most elite army panels of the world.

'What has a MARSOC personnel has to do with the Professor?' Sam asked, his curiosity piqued.

'You know that the Professor went to Berlin last month?'

'Yes.' Sam remembered the Prof leaving for Germany last month.

I am going on some personal work, he had said.

'He went to Germany in search of some clues related to the Nazi rise in Germany. I don't know the details, but from his dossier what I can gather is that he was searching something specific about the Nazi's rise in power in Germany.'

'Yeah, I know about his obsession with the Nazi history.' Said Sam sadly, remembering something.

'Ok. Now, from what I know, he met someone there who had offered him a lot of money for some item related to the Nazis.' Said, Mark. 'I would have taken that amount of money to build a good life, but Hedley thought otherwise.'

Again, that humor, Sam thought.

'However, the person he denied, doesn't like to hear no. Still, when Professor came back, calls were coming to him from that person.'

Mark continued - 'But in between the Professor received something from somewhere I am not sure about, and then left for three days during the last weekend.'

Yes. He was out on Monday as well this week.

'So, after that, we believe the Professor came to know something, something nasty enough to piss off one of the most powerful persons on the planet.' Said Mark with a smile. 'And it's our assumption that same person might have the Professor killed.'

Sam listened carefully. Some of the things were correct like – the Prof going to Germany, and mysteriously disappearing for three days after coming back. And what Mark said matches with what he himself suspected regarding the death of the old man.

But something he heard, made him question.

'Who are we? Who are you working with?'

'Well Sam, there are some things I can't tell you right now.' Mark said seriously. 'All I can tell right now is that if you come with me to Washington, you can get a safe haven there as well as maybe some of the answers on what happened today.'

Sam stayed silent, satisfied for the moment. *Will need to know what's happening exactly. And I alone cannot do that.*

The American also seemed to relax a bit and yanked open the door to the driver's seat in the car.

'Wait a minute.' Sam said, suddenly remembering something which Mark had said. 'Who is the person who wanted to pay the Prof and whom you suspect for his murder?'

Mark's facial expression became grim on hearing the question. He looked Sam directly in the eyes and replied with only two words.

'Alexander Penbrose.'

CHAPTER TWENTY

MARYLAND, USA
1:00 PM

Due to the work pressure, she was not able to check the message for the last half an hour. The three-fifty-six-digit encryption key took the whole morning for her team to break. At last the signal was decrypted and sent to the Interpol.

Eva guessed the guys in Brazil would be looking for the warlord's assets there now that the code was broken.

And as she felt hungry seeing the burger and the Donut in front of her, Eva suddenly remembered the picture Mark sent.

Now, what was it he said?

We don't have time. This needs to be decrypted ASAP. And it has to be under the radar.

That means no NSA computers could be used. And she couldn't use the home computer too, courtesy to the fact that NSA would track every decryption she does in her personal system as well. She exhaled.

That's the price to be paid to work in NSA. No Privacy.

But who was Mark working with? And why under the radar?

As far as she knew, Mark only needed some decryption when he was working for MARSOC.

If he was not working for MARSOC.......

She opened her iPhone and went to the gallery to check the picture Mark sent in her inbox. She stopped short seeing the image of the tissue paper.

Well, that's interesting.

The handwriting seemed to be that of an Englishman, aged between fifty-five to seventy. Being trained on Graphology on joining NSA, it was an easy analysis for her. The person probably was in stress judging by the way everything was written in the note.

But the most interesting was the one-word note below the line.

Mlechh.

She had heard of it.

But if it's that.........

The person who was writing it was interrupted while writing.

She quickly opened a notebook and started copying the words from the picture of the tissue paper. And then she started breaking it.

After a few minutes, she stared down at her handiwork and felt her pulse quicken.

This was more than just an email or phone call decryption. Someone had been writing this when he was interrupted, but he left a clue in the note itself on how to decrypt it.

Need to call Mark. ASAP.

THE SECOND ORDEAL

LEARNING THE TRUTH

CHAPTER TWENTY-ONE

DELHI, INDIA
November 11,
Saturday
9:30 PM

Sam and Mark were waiting for the last half an hour outside the airport. After the call from his friend in Maryland, Mark and Sam decided to reach Delhi via the Safdarjung Airport near Delhi and drive the rest to reach the Delhi Airport to lose any trail they may be having.

Sam was not approving of this idea, but after Mark's discussion with the American lady, his friend from NSA from what Sam now have heard, Mark had decided to take this route. There was no telling if someone knows about them or if they were being followed.

But Mark's gut was telling him that there was someone following them always. Someone knew about their whereabouts.

****

To Sam, coming back to India felt like a Déjà vu. It had been eleven years that he had left with Professor Richard Hedley. Now coming back made him feel nostalgic.

The roads have changed, the airport looked very different, there was much more population than he could remember. The flyovers were new; the freeways were new. Now Delhi was divided into three sectors- New Delhi, Gurugram, and Noida. But sometimes, while driving here, he was able to see the different forts which reminded him of his childhood.

His parents used to take him to the forts on weekends and show him the rich history of the Delhi Sultanate, the Mughals and the British. It was those memories that made him study history and archeology. It made him feel somehow connected to them and their interests.

But right now, there was only one thing on his mind.

Why are we here in Delhi? And who this guy really is?

To Sam, the person standing next to him was still a stranger. True, the guy had a Gulfstream G650ER Private Jet at his disposal, but what was making Sam suspicious was the nature of Mark. He had been very secretive about why he was here, what's his concern and who was funding his travels.

For now, Sam left it. There were other things to worry about.

After Mark's friend called him last evening, he told only one thing.

'We need to go to Delhi.'

****

There was nothing more to tell.

When Eva called last evening, she was very cryptic.

'Mark. Is it a treasure hunt?' Eva said from the other side.

'Huh!!!'

'It seems the person who was writing this note, has put his next clue in Delhi.' Eva told. 'We need to go to Delhi.'

'Wha.... oh!!...We? Why?'

'Yep. You know you can't keep me out. I have leaves left for the year, and I am taking it now.'

There was nothing Mark can tell her, plainly because he is not able to understand what's going on.

'Good.' Eva said after a moment, enjoying his silence. 'I will meet you at Delhi International Airport. There's a flight going today evening to Delhi. I will tell you the details once I reach and meet you there.'

Now, Mark felt he could have averted this. Eva didn't need to come here. But he could understand her excitement. Days on, she had just been decoding encryptions, providing relevant information for the nation's defense, but never was able to go in the field.

I want to go into the field Mark. What's the point of all the field training in NSA if I can't go out there, and physically work out there. Now she got a chance to get out of her office and feel the excitement out in the field. Though she was not sure what was there to do in the field.

Everything seemed still in the dark.

Was Alexander Penbrose responsible for the death of the Professor? What's with that note? Was it okay to follow a trail of an Old man's note before death? Maybe that's nothing, or perhaps Eva is wrong. No, Eva had never been wrong in the last six years. If she has told to come to Delhi, then she might be on to something from that note. She hadn't told the details of the note yet, but from her call, it was evident that coming to Delhi was an important part.

****

It took her precisely an hour to get out of the customs in the Airport.

'Hey, Eva.'

She heard the voice and looked at her right.

There. Mark was waiting for her as promised.

She felt exhausted, though she felt a little respite seeing her friend there. It had been a long flight for her, traveling for nineteen hours with only one stop in between. She desperately needed a shower to loosen herself up.

It was then that she saw the Indian young man standing beside Mark and for the first time in her life, she felt an emotion she had seldom felt.

Attraction.

<u>CHAPTER TWENTY-TWO</u>

Those hazel eyes.

That was the first thing Sam noticed about her. When Sam had first heard of a lady friend of Mark, he had thought that it would be an elderly lady working in NSA. There was no expectation at all for a young twenty-something female working in the National Security Agency.

So, it came as a shock to him.

The person approaching them felt to Sam like a mermaid coming out of the water, dripped with beauty instead of water in every single cell of her body. Sam remembered a story his mother used to tell when he was starting his schooling. The story was about a fairy.

Today, after more than two decades later, that story came back into his mind, afresh. Only this time, Eva was the fairy.

To him, it felt like something special radiating from her. She was the perfect girl he has ever met. She was tall, nearly five six. The burgundy hair straightened, and unlike most of his fellow classmate girls whom Sam has noticed to keep short hairs, hers were long. The hairs continued through her shoulders and flowed down till near her waist. Her perfect body seemed to be that of a Leonardo Da Vinci model instead of a cryptographer. The slender neck, the perfectly curved shape, and long white legs together accentuated her beauty. The Greek nose, the round face, and the stylized Gigi Hadid haircut made her the perfect female anyone could desire.

But the most prominent feature was her eyes. At least to Sam, they seemed to be hypnotizing. The hazel colored eyes seemed to be energizing the whole world.

'Hey, Mark.'

Eva's voice broke him from his reverie.

****

'What the fuck?'

Both Eva and Mark got surprised by the outburst of Sam.

'This was *mlechhita-vikalpa*?' His voice was reverberating in the McDonalds just outside the airport.

The trio was having dinner there with burgers and happy meals and exchanging pleasantries among themselves. Sam had recounted the events of the last two days to both for the first time, starting from the Prof's call two nights ago.

On cue, Mark told that he had been appointed by someone high enough in the United States to look into the issue of the death of his friend, the Professor. His employer seemed to have been fond of the Professor for some reason and needed Mark to see till the end.

And then came the big revelation.

'It's not just gibberish.' Eva had said. 'It's a code.'

'Oh great!' Was Mark's reply. 'So, he wanted to play Kryptos before dying.'

Sam understood the humor behind Mark's words along with the reference of the famous code – Kryptos, created and kept outside the CIA Headquarters in Langley by the former CIA Cryptographer Ed Scheidt with the help of artist Jim Sanborn.

He had studied these as parts of language and code verification during his first year in research.

It was then that Eva told the nature of the code the Prof has written.

'It's *mlechhita-vikalpa.*'

CHAPTER TWENTY-THREE

10:00 PM

'Ma zaluu yatahadathun.'

They were still speaking, noted Ahmed. He was seated just three tables away from where the trio was sitting with three of his men. Though he couldn't hear anything that they were saying, from what he could see, the lady was telling them something and showing something in a diary.

For last one day, he and three others have been tracking the Indian and the American. It was difficult to know the path of the Private jet from Cambridge, but ten minutes with the Air Marshal in the airport made sure that he gave the flight path to Ahmed without any trouble. That person won't be able to tell anyone anything due to a sudden 'accident' that happened to him resulting in an unfortunate death. After that, a call to Sabir, and the arrangement of a private plane to India with the help of his employer was all that required Ahmed to track their prey again.

Now the duo was joined by the beautiful American lady in the Delhi Airport, and they have been sitting for the last half an hour now.

One thing that bothered Ahmed and Sabir alike was the fact how the Americans were connected to all this.

Sabir seemed to have the idea of how Sam was connected in all this and shared with him yesterday.

'His name is Sameer Rawath.' Sabir said. 'Surely you remember.'

'Yes, I do.' Said a surprised Ahmed.

'But we need to know why and how the American is connected. Its disorienting for our employer to have them involved.' Said a certainly unnerved Sabir. It seemed to him that Sabir never loses his cool. Not that he has ever seen in last twenty years he has been with the Syrian.

He still remembered the time in Germany. It feels like yesterday. Only if they were co-operative......

'Follow them.' He had said. 'Find out what they know and what they are doing. And Ahmed...' He paused for a moment to stress his next words. 'If you find the package, get hold of that at any cost.'

Now the only thing was to follow the trio wherever they were going and hoped for Sam to find the package from the Professor.

Ahmed still didn't know what this was all about even after so many years. Their employer had always been too much secretive about the thing he had been searching for nearly two decades. Sometimes Ahmed still wondered if there was any value in the search. Only Sabir seemed to know what this was all about.

What if there was nothing to find, or what if the thing which his employer was searching for might not be so much of value as he thinks.

But one thing was for sure. His employer had gone through a lot for so many years and had taken significant risks to achieve what he wanted.

And he would not stop until he got what he wanted.

CHAPTER TWENTY-FOUR

'Feels like studying the pre-school again.' Mark said in an airy tone. Both he and Sam have been looking at the alphabets Eva had written for them in her diary.

A B C D E F G H I J K L M
N O P Q R S T U V W X Y Z

I Agree.

It felt like the nursery class to Sam too, looking at the alphabets divided into two lines.

'You have heard of *Mlecchita-Vikalpa*, right?' Eva said, looking at him.

'Yes, I have heard of it. It's one of the sixty-four arts described for women in ancient Kamasutra.' Sam said sheepishly. Mentioning Kamasutra, the ancient Indian Hindu Text by the Brahmin scholar *Vātsyāyana* was not something people do in the open here in India. This book was widely considered to be the standard work on human sexual behavior in Sanskrit literature, and a portion of the work consists of practical advice on sexual intercourse.

'The forty-fifth on the list is *Melcchita-Vikalpa*. But to be honest, I have not pondered on it more to know the details on it.'

By now both Mark and Eva were grinning like children on seeing the hesitation in his voice while speaking about Kamasutra, making him visibly blush.

From what he had gathered information about Sam, Mark knew that he has never been with a girl, let alone discussing sex and Kamasutra. So understandably, this hesitation.

'Stop blushing like an idiot.' Mark said to him. 'Nobody's asking you to go into the details of Kamasutra. We are studying English,' he said, looking at Eva, 'from our teacher.'

Eva started laughing and playfully hit Mark on his shoulders. The act made the Indian a little relaxed.

'It's something like a substitution cipher.' Eva continued, now that the blushing and playfulness gone, 'where we substitute letters to their corresponding partners. We were shown different kinds of ciphers and cryptology processes when we joined the service, so it was easy for me to decipher this.'

'Normally the *Melcchita-Vikalpa* consists of the pairing of letters at random, but when I checked it, I found a complete English message by dividing the alphabet list in half, like this.'

'Ok.' Sam picked up the diary, 'So according to this, N should be replaced by A and M to be replaced by Z, right?'

She nodded in agreement. 'The Professor had left the clue at the end of his note as Mlechh, which helped to understand the code quickly.'

'So, let me check it then myself.'

It took two minutes for him to decipher the message and write it down beside the diary, and......

And in a flash, he understood why Eva asked them to come to India.

Hemanth room, Delhi,

basement locker seven.

CHAPTER TWENTY-FIVE

FRANKFURT, GERMANY
6:10 PM

'There has been a development *Rabiy*.'

The man stared at the screen with a stony gaze. Such was his unwavering gaze, piercing through the wall mounted video screen, that Sabir had to take his eyes away.

The room was dark, at nearly 30 ft below the sea level, where one side was entirely a glass wall and outside that green sea water can be seen where occasionally the sharks seemed to be roaming around. The man whom Sabir was speaking with, had been sitting with his back towards that wall on the couch and looking straight at the opposite wall where Sabir's face could be seen from his hotel room in Frankfurt. Though the other walls couldn't be seen, Sabir knew they were all dark brown in color.

It's the same room where……..

Sabir shut down the memory.

There was not a single light in the room, except for the projector which was showing the video. In that light only, the Syrian could see the spectacles of the man he knew very well. Though the features of the person were not clear at all in this low light, still he understood the ferocity with which this person was looking at him right now.

'The Indian boy is joined by two Americans.' Sabir said again, swallowing his nervousness. 'One man and a woman. And they all are in India.'

The eyes behind the spectacles narrowed a little, posing curiosity to him. The Syrian knew about this person's lack of empathy, and moreover his dislike of failures. For the last twenty years that Sabir knew this man, he had never seen him speak too much.

Except when……

However, this man liked to create fear with his silence and malevolent features.

And that is working.

'I have dispatched Ahmed to shadow them 24/7.' He said again, 'They should be updating me soon.'

'They better.' The man from the other side of the video call said at last. The voice was more like a whisper, something that could chill a person to his core. 'I need to know what Sam is doing, and who his new friends are.'

'Yes, *Rabiy*. We are anticipating news soon.'

'I don't pay you to anticipate Sabbir-in-Ahzah.' The man said in the same tone, indicating Sabir's full name. 'I pay you to improvise. Sam is critical to my plan, and until we know more, there is nothing much we can do. So………' He paused for a second to emphasize his next word – 'Improvise.'

Sabir looked at his tablet for a few more seconds after the call got disconnected. This man was someone who could induce fear in anybody's mind whenever he wanted. And the cunning plan of his was the ideal way to get things done now.

Now the only thing that needs to be seen was……...

What Sam finds.

CHAPTER TWENTY-SIX

DELHI, INDIA
10:20 PM

Again, that tingling sensation. Mark could still not shake the feeling away. It's like his Spidey senses have gone haywire.

It had started the moment he came to the airport. For last one hour, this sense had been troubling him. It was like in the field, when he had been discovered, or someone had him in his scopes. Years of battle and field experience has taught him one thing.......

Trust your gut.

And that had saved him a number of times. Once in Iraq, twenty years ago, during the Operation Desert Storm, an Iraqi soldier had him in scopes, the Dragunov was pointed straight at his temple. It was this feeling that made him jump a split second before the trigger was pulled.

And that feeling was coming back now. As if he was discovered, being followed, being watched.

But Mark was not someone who worked irrationally.

If I look everywhere to check who is watching, they will be alerted. I don't want that.

That meant doing something which they didn't expect him to do. The only possible explanation of being followed right now could be because of Sam. Someone was watching every move he was making.

That means they haven't got hold of the package yet. That's good.

So, Mark thought and made a decision.

'You guys carry on to Sam's home.' He said looking towards Eva and Mark. 'I have to go somewhere.'

'Where are you going?' Sam asked, curiosity in his eyes.

'Somewhere I need to be.'

Then without waiting for the answer, Mark turned and dashed out of the McDonalds.

'What the hell was that?' Sam asked looking at Eva.

Eva was as surprised as Sam, but she knew Mark better. If he has decided to go somewhere, then it must be important.

She looked at Sam and just shrugged.

****

The roads didn't seem that much empty as she would like. At this time in Maryland, there were scarcely any cars moving in the street, except the odd one taking the freeways. But here, as Eva could see, many cars were driving to the city. It seemed like the town was still lively even at 10:30 at night.

The sedan soared through the roads of Delhi. She could see the silhouettes of the building created nearly a century ago, like the shadows of time standing guard in the city. Some forts and buildings could be seen with lights coming from other parts of the city, and some were deranged in shadows at this time of the night. She liked the city. The stores and shops were open even this late. People could be seen walking on the roads, speaking to each other. She felt a sense of belonging here after looking at the streets of India.

'So, you know Mark for a long time?' Sam asked from her side.

She looked at him. He was young, really young. But there was a brightness in his eyes, a flash of brilliance that held promises of a bright future. Eva had never been attracted to someone like this before. He seemed to be looking towards a distant object from the cab window.

'Been a few years that I know him.'

Sam looked towards her this time.

'I still don't know how you two got dragged into this. But I am glad that you are.' He said with a warm, genuine smile.

'I feel likewise. I have worked with Mark, helping him to point out the attacks and other details always, but this is the first time I am entering in the field with him.'

'Hmmm.' Sam breathed.

'Your stop is here sir.' The Uber driver reported.

That made Sam stop. He gave some cash to the driver and quickly came out of the car.

It's still the same. The house on the left. The duplex house was standing right there.

His childhood home.

CHAPTER TWENTY-SEVEN

11:01 PM

The black cab stopped twenty meters away from Sam's Uber. From the driver's window, Ahmed could see Sam and the American woman coming out of the car and moving towards the house. He saw the nameplate on the gate from his position.

MR & MRS HEMANTH RAWATH.

Sam's house.

So, this was why they were here. It seemed that the good Professor somehow had led his Indian student here, or somehow Sam was trying to unravel the mystery of Hedley's death here.

He smiled.

Whatever the Professor had done, somehow has led Sam here. And if he was back to his home after all these years, then he was sure to find something here.

Maybe a clue.

It seemed that Sabir was right to send him and his mates shadowing Sam. Whatever his employer and Sabir wanted could be found only by following the Indian. Sabir had suspected that the Professor might lead Sam to some clue regarding what he was researching on.

And here Sam was. Maybe Sabir was right.

The only issue is the American man. Where had he gone?

Ahmed thought about the two men, whom he had sent to shadow Mark.

Where can the American be?

CHAPTER TWENTY-EIGHT

Blam.

Mark was in hell. The bullet just hit the wall of the pillar and showered him with plaster and concrete.

After leaving Sam and Eva at the McDonalds, he decided to go to another quieter part of the town, but not far away from Sam's destination. So, he took a cab and reached this place in Delhi where most of the apartments are under construction, courtesy of the cab driver whom he had instructed to take him to a place nearby as such and came to the fourth floor of one of them.

As he had suspected earlier, just after the cab left him there, he saw two people out of the four he had seen previously from McDonald's, leaving a Maruti Swift, and coming towards the apartment he took shelter in.

So, they divided and sent two to follow me.

And, he was ready. The Px4 Storm Deluxe glinted in his hand due to the low lights coming from the streetlights up ahead. This particular Beretta pistol was the most refined PX4 model ever, made unique through the goldening of the central metallic parts and the exclusive polished finishing. By using corrosion-resistant techno-polymer reinforced fiberglass, Beretta had developed a light and technically advanced pistol with an extremely modern, ergonomic line. The rounded, snag-free surfaces of the gun ensured trouble-free insertion, and holster extraction and the rounded trigger guard provided correct hand firing position. Right now it contained 17 rounds plus one chambered.

Let the games begin.

At least that was what he had hoped for.

But things suddenly changed when his pursuers understood the trap he has laid for them and started shooting.

He could see how the two of them have him pinned down while leapfrogging each other and closing the distance. One person was giving cover fire while the other covering the gap.

Need to do something. Something that… …

There.

The pillar beside the wall he was stranded had a gasoline container. No time to think how a gasoline container could be here in a new building. Mark fired towards the oncoming goon and quickly vaulted from his cover to leap towards the pillar.

Blam.

A bullet from the man further down the next room missed him by mere centimeters, but he had already somersaulted and reached the next pillar.

'Bloody Amateurs.' He said through ragged breaths.

Now to wait for the perfect opportunity.

The two bad guys couldn't be seen now. Must be hidden behind some wall or pillars.

There.

They have tried to hide very cleverly behind two consecutive pillars some ten feet away from Mark, but the shadows betrayed them.

'God. I like streetlights' Mark whispered to himself, grinning ear to ear.

Quick in a flash, he took the gasoline container and threw it underhanded aiming towards the pillars where the bad guys were standing and at the same time aimed and pulled the trigger.

Blam.

The result was instantaneous.

A withering ball of flame ignited covering its surrounding of nearly 5 feet on each side with a massive bang in the confinements of the under-construction apartment.

Mark, being away from the blast was not affected much. But the two-people attacking him were not so lucky. The goon standing nearest to Mark was hurled out of the open balcony on his backside from where he plunged to his death screaming all the way down. The other person was also hurt, but since he was standing behind a pillar when the blast occurred, he was just hurled back towards the open door where his shoulder collided with the door.

Craaak.

A horrible crack sounded when he collided to the side of the door, marking the dislodgement of his shoulder.

'Aaaaaarghhh.'

The sound satisfied Mark. He sprinted towards the man, and before the goon knew what happened, a kick from Mark's boot on his right temple put the person in a deep sleep.

He then searched the person's all pockets, but there was nothing. No identification, no cards, no wallet, no phones.

'Great.' Mark sighed. 'I can't play Sherlock Holmes with you now. Got work to do.'

As with the mercenaries all over the world, this person had not carried any identification with him.

Mark quickly tied him and put him on his shoulders to carry out. This guy's car should be outside.

CHAPTER TWENTY-NINE

WASHINGTON DC
12:30 PM

Mark's employer was sitting in his private chamber. A person of his stature gets very less time to enjoy himself.

Despite the fact that he was one of the busiest people on the face of the planet, this rare moment came for him today where he just got a few minutes to relax.

What's happening with Sam and Mark?

The last he heard from Mark was they were en route to India. Something regarding a code from Hedley that have led them there. But that was nearly 12 hours ago. Now in his free time, the anxiety suddenly kicked in. He opened the drawer and took out the bottle holding his anxiety pills and popped it open. He then took two pills out and swallowed both with water.

For his work to go smoothly, the doctor had prescribed the pills to be taken every day. He waited for a minute to digest the pills and then took the phone in his hand.

The automated call connected to the operator.

'Put me through to Mark.'

****

'We have to go to Sam's parent's house.' Mark said while driving the car.

The Maruti left over by the person who currently lay unconscious on the rear passenger foothold, was now his car to drive.

'And how about others? Have anyone followed you?'

Mark looked behind himself, checking the tied body of the goon he had knocked out earlier and carried with him in the car.

'Yes.' He said in his phone. 'It seems there were four hostiles following us.'

'And?' Was the anxious question.

'Two of them are neutralized, and two others to be dealt with.'

'Do you need help?'

'No.' Mark said, smiling to himself. 'They can be handled.'

'Ok.' The voice from the other side said. 'Keep me updated.'

CHAPTER THIRTY

COPENHAGEN, DENMARK
7:40 PM

Alexander paced back and forth in his penthouse.

The meeting with Bill Gates was a good one the other day. But that was not what was keeping him agitated right now. It's the news from Frankfurt that was making him anxious. Nothing new coming up yet. The news was precisely that, nothing new.

And he was not a person who liked to wait. According to him, the greatest strength comes from knowledge. It's like what Tom Clancy has told once: *The control of information is something the elite always does, particularly in a despotic form of government. Information, knowledge, is power. If you can control information, you can control people.*

So that was what he was trying to do. To gather knowledge. A piece of knowledge that was lost two centuries ago. A knowledge of the world that can make him more powerful than anyone can ever imagine. The power of money was nothing compared to the knowledge he hoped to achieve from this errand.

But, right now, there was nothing. After a long time, there seemed to be some clue as to the whereabouts of the knowledge, but it seemed that destiny had put him on hold again.

And he despised that.

First, it was an Indian couple, and now it's their son. It seemed like this family was determined only to stop him.

But enough is enough. This can't go further.

He took out his phone and dialed a number from his speed dial.

Triing......Triing.

'What's the news?'

He waited for the answer from the other side.

'That is not acceptable.' His icy voice said over the phone. 'I want to seize control of it as soon as the Indian finds it.'

He paused for a moment.

'Do whatever is necessary. It's been a long time.'

CHAPTER THIRTY-ONE

SOMEWHERE IN THE WORLD

The snows were everywhere.

The room was lit with only fire torches. There were eight of them on each side, total sixteen, as always. The snows were falling outside, and a blizzard seemed to be happening.

However, that was no concern for the people inside the room. The fireplace was lit fully now. But if one observed closely, a weird sight would greet them. The people inside the room are wearing only dark blue robes, devoid of any other clothes below the robes. With a temperature of -20 Degrees Celsius, it seemed impossible for anyone to survive by just wearing a robe, but the men in the room did not seem to care at all.

All they seem to do was wait. Waiting for someone to enter the room. The room was on the far western side of a five-story building, a temple in fact, with an area of nearly a thousand square feet. The people in the room were sitting on their knees, with the robes covering half of their faces, looking towards a makeshift platform created just in front of them. The vast glass window behind the platform looked out towards the godforsaken village outside.

Creeeaaak....

The door opened with a loud sound in slow motion.

A single person entered the room wearing a dark blue robe, a shade darker than the others were wearing.

Everybody stood up in unison with respect to the newcomer, bowing their heads. The man seemed old, really old. In fact, it seemed like he was a bit hunched due to the weight of age.

'Knowledge is ultimate; knowledge is immortal.'

He said in a hushed tone, but such was the structure of the room that his voice reverberated throughout it.

'Knowledge is ultimate; knowledge is immortal.'

The others in the room repeated his words in chorus.

The leader, or the Grandmaster, as he was known here, put his both hands up and gestured for everyone to kneel again. Once everybody was in position, he followed suit.

'I bring news from another part of the world.' He said in his same hushed voice, 'It seems others are searching for our haven.'

Everybody started looking at each other, look of concern showing up on their faces.

'Yes, my fellow members.' The leader said, looking at them, 'We must be ready.'

CHAPTER THIRTY-TWO

DELHI, INDIA
11:10 PM

'Nothing has changed.'

Eva looked at him. It seemed like Sam was in an ecstatic mood. The return to his childhood home had made him much more excited than what she had seen for last hour or so.

She could see the dust-covered furniture in the room like nobody have entered the house in the last few years.

And that seems correct.

From what she heard from Sam on the way to here, it seemed that the house was under lock and key for last 13 years or so, after the death of his Granny. He also told about his time here with his parents and the way Professor Richard Hedley used to visit.

'Everything is the way I remember it.' Sam said looking everywhere. They had just entered the house a minute ago. The living room was dark, and there seemed to be no electricity available. It was then that Sam lighted some of the candles available in the chandeliers and the room lit up. The shadows seem to run away with the advent of the lights and hide behind the chairs and sofas in the room.

For the next ten minutes, Sam just roamed around. He went to the bedrooms on the ground floor and the first floor, he went to the kitchen, he went to the balcony and checked the garden in the backyard. The garden was overgrown with the bushes here and there, but he still seemed to be happy seeing it again.

'Sam.' Eva called slowly to him. 'We need to find whatever Professor has hidden here.'

That made Sam turn. It was as if he was in a different world for the last few minutes, and her words pushed him back to reality.

****

'How can a room be a basement?' Eva said, curiosity evident in her voice.

Sam looked at the page of the diary where he had translated the Professor's note.

Hemanth room, Delhi,
basement locker seven.

A thin smile materialized in his lips.

It can be confusing.

'It is something most people who have ever visited my house does not know.' He said to Eva.

By now they have climbed the stairs to the first floor and came to the first bedroom on the right of the stairs. According to the Indian, this was his parent's bedroom. A door to the left of the room took them to a study room. Sam explained to her, how his father used to stay up at night and read various books here. This was the place where his father Hemanth spent most of his time at home. More specifically – *Hemanth room*. As the Professor had mentioned.

Excitement coursed through his veins. Now they would know what Hedley wanted to tell him, and why he was murdered, or at least some clue for that. Sam felt a pang of sadness remembering the Professor's death.

'Focus Sam.'

He looked and saw Eva looking at her. The sadness must have been showing in his face, his attitude.

Sam composed himself.

'This wardrobe here in the study.' Sam told her showing a wardrobe on the right side of the study table, just below the last shelf of the books. 'I used to play inside it.'

He looked at her, squarely in the eye.

'This wardrobe has got ten lockers and is a way to the basement. It is basically a tunnel.'

'That's it, then?' Eva breathed.

'Yes, this is what the Prof meant.' Sam said excitedly. 'In the seventh locker of this tunnel, is something that the Professor has kept.'

A pause.

'And that is the reason for all these. That's the reason for his death.'

CHAPTER THIRTY-THREE

Sam opened the door to the wardrobe.

A nasty smell should generally come from these kinds of spaces which had been closed off for so many years. But that kind of smell never came to Sam. It was a clear sign that somebody was explicitly here, inside this place itself. A quick look inside by the duo revealed that there was not much dust as was supposed to be in a space being closed for more than one and a half decade, an obvious clue of the Professor being here.

'I have to go inside.' Sam said to the American woman.

Eva nodded in reply. She was a little worried that if there could be any snakes or insects there but didn't voice anything. If Hedley had entered here and remained unscathed, then there was nothing to worry here.

Sam entered the tunnel slowly.

The first thing that came to his mind was how different it felt than that of his childhood to enter here. It was the greatest adventure of his life at that time to enter here and making his parents nervous. They kept searching for him for hours sometimes, and it was he who surprised them suddenly coming out of this place. It felt to him now that sometimes Hemanth and Rita were feigning to search for him for his own pleasure, knowing the whole time that he was inside this tunnel.

Sam pictured the Prof entering in this cramped space and keeping something at the Seventh locker, just to keep away from everyone else and making sure that only Sam learns of it. To the Indian right now, it felt cramped space too. Good that he was not a claustrophobic, or else it would have been challenging. However, to enter the tunnel, he had to kneel on his knees and use all four of his hands and legs.

****

Eva looked towards all the books in the study. It looked like this place was a small library, dedicated to the history of the world. She could see lots of books related to different eras of History. She saw the books like - The seven wonders of the ancient world, a masterpiece written on 1988 by Peter A. Clayton, The Rise and Fall of the Third Reich, a book on the total history of the Nazi regime during the World War II, by William L. Shirer which was written around 1960.

After a careful looking at most of the books, she thought she got an idea on the interests of Rita and Hemanth. It seemed more than half of the books present in the room were related to the Nazis and the Second World War.

Thwack.

A sound came from somewhere. But before she could make out the details of the sound, something pricked her neck at high speed.

She looked back and thought for a second that she had seen a couple of people entering the room. But then everything blurred, and she started to wobble on her legs.

Someone is there. They followed us, and now they have drugged me.

Oddly the first thought that came to her mind was to warn Sam, instead of helping herself.

She tried to scream out to him, but before that, she fell back on the floor with a *thud*.

Darkness enveloped her.

****

Ahmed smiled at his triumph.

Last twenty minutes he had been looking through different windows from outside and following the Indian-American duo. Now that Sam went inside the hidden tunnel in the study room, it seemed to be an excellent time to capture the woman, and then to pressurize Sam with whatever secret he was trying to unearth from the depths of the tunnel hidden in the study room.

The other person with him, Steve, an Australian by birth, but spending most of his time in Germany, came behind him.

'*Kein anderer ist hier.*' He said.

Good. Ahmed wanted to make sure no one else was there in the house, and so, he had sent Steve to survey the house.

'Go to the basement.' He wanted to be ready when Sam came out of the tunnel to the basement.

The only thing was, his two men following the other American, have not checked in yet. They were supposed to tell him the whereabouts of the other American guy. Last he heard from them was that the American has got off to an under construction building and they would be following him.

Anyhow, now that the lady was incapacitated, it would be easy to overpower Sam.

****

Thud.

Sam heard a sound of something heavy falling on the carpet in the study room. He was crossing the third locker when the sound happened.

'What's that Eva?' He asked without turning. In that cramped space, it was anyhow not possible for him to turn around.

Oddly, even after a minute of waiting, there was no reply from Eva.

Maybe she is moving to the other part of the room.

He continued towards the next locker, unaware of the danger looming.

CHAPTER THIRTY-FOUR

11:31 PM

The car seemed to just stand outside Sam's house. The tail lights glowed in the low light of the approaching midnight of Delhi, with a fog slowly building up.

It had been a minute now that Mark was watching the car.

There seemed to be not a single person present near the car.

They must have gone inside the house. Need to hurry.

Both Sam and Eva have not driven the car to his house, which he knew for sure. Moreover, the car did not seem to be damaged. These and the fact that there was no person available near the car gave him all the answers he needed.

Two people have followed him, while the other two followed Sam and Eva. And they have now gone inside the house. There was no other house nearby where the occupants of the car could have gone.

He quickly left his car, and its unconscious and tied occupant on the next block.

Coming through the main road would not be safe. So, he did the only other thing he could. He jumped through the boundary wall of the house and entered the garden from behind.

Too many bushes would cover his advance.

He could see some lights in a room on the first floor.

Probably that's where everybody is.

He quickly covered the distance and took cover and climbed a bigger tree, just outside the study room window. Carefully he looked inside the room.

What he saw was not a pleasant sight.

Eva was slumped on the couch, and she seemed out cold. A man, Middle Eastern by his features, the same one he had seen earlier tonight at MCD, with his trimmed beard and crew cut hair, was standing by her side. And from where Mark was looking, it seemed like the man was looking towards an open wardrobe on the left side of the room.

Where's Sam?

Where's the other man?

He must find them.

It was then that he saw through the corner of his eye the other man, a Caucasian by his looks, another one he had seen earlier sitting with the Middle Eastern man, in the basement on his right, a little above the floor. Till before that, Mark did not notice the small window on the garden floor level, which gave a view to the basement from his vantage point.

Now that he had seen it, it was time to do the worth of his employer's money.

CHAPTER THIRTY-FIVE

What happened to Eva?

Everything suddenly seemed too much silent. That was what nagged Sam the most. The sound he heard a few minutes back was suspicious.

Anyhow he carried on forward. The fifth locker he could see just in front of him. He was able to see the toy car still there, broken from his childhood. He still remembered when he had set it there, and his mom was searching for him.

Pushing the memory away, for now, he urged on.

After a minute, he came in front of the seventh locker.

Hemanth room, Delhi,
basement locker seven.

So, this contained all the answers. The answer to the Professor's death.

****

Mark entered the basement from the window through the garden.

Nimble as a cat, he jumped into the room without a sound. The goon was standing just a few meters away in front of him, with his side towards him.

Mark positioned himself behind some storage cartons in the room, just a foot away from the window he made his entry, making sure the guy waiting for Sam have not seen him.

Yes, it must be Sam for whom he is waiting.

Mark had deduced this by a simple fact. Sam was not there in the upper study room. And if the guy here is waiting in the basement, it was surely not to play hide and seek.

Moreover, he couldn't use the gun in these confines of the room. It would sound like a bomb here, and the guy above guarding Eva would be alerted.

That cannot happen.

Mark shifted a carton, and suddenly he stumbled upon a nail.

Cring.

The guy looked towards the cartons, alerted by the sound and started coming here, drawing a Desert Eagle in his hand.

Have to do something.

Mark looked everywhere, to find somewhere to hide, something to use in his advantage without alerting the goon above.

Cartons here, nail on the floor, and the wall behind him.

Nothing to use.

The man kept coming towards him. Mark only looked helplessly with the nail in his hand.

Not a good weapon.

Before he could think more, the pistol and the hand holding the pistol appeared in his view, though the man himself was out of view, thanks to the cartons where Mark was hiding.

Can't give him the opening.

Without wasting any more time, Mark crossed the distance in less than a second, and before the goon knew, Mark collided with him in full force. The Australian, Steve, was not at all ready for such an attack and was thrown to the ground, causing to lose his gun in the process. He saw Mark coming towards him, and without wasting time to get his gun from the floor, the Australian stood up and blocked an incoming punch from Mark.

However, that did not stop Mark from landing a perfect kick on his stomach, causing Steve to double over and fall again. Now Mark, without giving any opportunity to his opponent, landed another blow on his face, causing the goon to lose a tooth in the process.

Steve spat blood from his mouth and stood up in a quick motion, and threw a punch towards Mark, which the American allowed to sway high over his head and continuing his motion, Mark landed a perfect uppercut on Steve's chin. That caused the man to wobble a bit on his legs, and the second punch on his nose made him land hard on the floor for the third time in the last few seconds. Knowing that he couldn't win the fight with his bare fists, Steve got a Ka-Bar knife out of his ankle sheath and in a swift motion jumped up on Mark, causing the latter to fall on the floor.

Must not allow him to pin me down.

Mark caught the goon's attack with the knife on his face, just an inch above the eyes. The Australian started to apply his full body pressure, taking advantage of his weight, causing the knife to come down, nearing Mark's eye every second.

'You thought you could surprise me?' The goon said, while still applying pressure on the knife.

'No…... but…... I…. want…. to…... do…... this.' Mark said in between ragged breaths, trying to avert the oncoming knife.

Mark hit the man on his temple hard with his hands. Surprisingly, a trickle of blood started flowing from the goon's temple where Mark had hit, and after a second, the Australian stopped applying pressure. Getting the opening he needed, Mark just got hold of Steve's hand, and without wasting another second, drove the goon's own hands, still holding the knife, through the latter's Adam's apple.

Steve's eyes bulged out at this sudden attack, and slowly he started falling down on the floor, on his right-side temple, driving the nail inside his head that Mark had used to attack a second ago inside.

'Serves you right.' Mark said while standing up.

****

When Sam came out from the tunnel and reached the basement, he saw a mess at the end of his line.

Cartons were fallen everywhere, a pool of blood and a body on one side.

His astonishment reached its end when he saw Mark standing and smiling towards him.

'Hello, Sam. You took a long time.'

CHAPTER THIRTY-SIX

'I got this satchel from the locker above.'

Sam showed the satchel he got from the locker number seven above to Mark. After a brief update from the American on what's happening, Sam also showed him what he got there.

However, Mark had other things in mind.

'We will look at it later Sam. We need to......'

Blam. Blam.

The sound of the gun took both of them by surprise.

Sam and Mark looked at each other for a second, the same thought crossing both their minds.

Eva. She is up there.

****

They came up to the study room, running from the basement two steps at a time and reached the study room at the same time.

'Oh, no.'

Sam was the first to enter, and the sight that greeted him was not a good one.

Books were fallen on the floor and the air smelled of petrol. The room looked like a war had been fought here.

The gunshot now became clear. Someone have burnt down the whole room using the petrol and gunshots.

Creeeeeeeeeechh. Spiiiiiiiiish.

They both heard the screeching of the tires on the main road. In a split second, everything became clear.

The goon must have heard the fighting downstairs and understood that he was outnumbered. So, he had now set a fire in the room and kidnapped Eva.

'Come with me Sam.' Mark said while running towards outside.

They both ran to the main road without delay. Mark opened the driver side door and hopped inside quickly, while Sam vaulted over the bonnet and opened the passenger door.

Vrrooooooom.

The car started and shot off the mark.

The game, it seemed, was really on.

CHAPTER THIRTY-SEVEN

The Delhi roads shoomed past Sam in a blur.

The car was doing eighty miles and still going up. Mark seemed oblivious to that fact and kept his scopes on the fleeing car half a mile in front of him. In November, the temperature of Delhi was starting to go down, and at 11:40 PM it was nearly 12 Degrees Celsius at night.

The result was that in a crowded city like Delhi, right now, there were not as many people as would be on any summer night. Some cars here and there were on the roads, and a few pedestrians could also be seen. But that was nothing compared to a typical day in May-June in Delhi.

Sam was thinking this when suddenly …...

Whooosshhh.

The car zoomed through the tunnel following the other car, and suddenly the street light was lesser here, plunging the tunnel into twilight darkness. The main reason for this is the under-construction road in the tunnel. Sam remembered hearing the news of this proposed tunnel for ease of traffic in the first half of the year, and the work had started on it.

The other car also slowed a bit, realizing its mistake.

Blam. Blam.

It was when it seemed that the fleeing car was slowing down, that two bullets were fired from it. One bullet hit the side view mirror on the driver's side, whereas the other hit the front windshield, shattering it into a thousand pieces. Sam and Mark were showered with a volley of glasses everywhere. The wind rushed through the open front of the car.

However, Mark didn't slow down.

'Son of a bitch.' He swore.

'What the hell are they doing?' Sam said in a near panic as another bullet just missed him.

'Don't know, but it feels like a trap.' He said, while still driving at eighty miles per hour in the undulating road in near darkness now. They have crossed around one mile inside the tunnel, and as per Sam's idea, they should cross the tunnel in next few minutes.

He conveyed the same to the American beside him.

It was then that the unthinkable happened.

The end of the tunnel suddenly came into view, and as the fleeing car was about to cross it, a sudden sound could be heard.

The sound seemed a little distant to Sam, but Mark suddenly slowed a bit hearing the noise.

Chuff.chuff.chuff.....chuff.chuff.chuff.

'Son of a God swearing bitch.'

Sam looked at his driver after this outburst from him, when suddenly out of the corner of his eye, he saw something looming on the tunnel exit.........and his jaw dropped.

'What the......'

It just looked like a monster looming in front of them.

A Boeing AH-64 Apache just hung in there, in front of the exit of the tunnel. With its four rotor blades, twin-turboshaft, the 30mm articulated cannon, it just looked like an ancient monster from his childhood coming to life and hanging in the air.

Add to that the 70mm missile launchers behind them and a particularly hellish monster's look gets completed.

And the last but not the least feature of the Apache were the Hellfire missiles attached below the wings.

Although Sam didn't know it, the Boeing AH-64 Apache was one of the best attack helicopters in the world. It's an American made, but different countries of the world were now starting to use it, India among them.

But Mark knew.

And that made him slow his car.

Now they could see a ladder coming out of the cockpit ramp of the chopper. Then they saw the lead car stopping just below the chopper, and in a flash, all became clear.

The goon on the other car had called in support, and they got it in the form of the chopper, and now they were planning to flee away.

****

Sam saw all of it.

'What are we going to do?' Sam cried, over the sounds of the rotor, now just more than twenty feet away from them. 'He is going away with Eva.'

'I'm thinking, I'm thinking.'

Mark desperately looked around himself. He needed something, something he could use.

The goon on the other car has already leaped out of the car, carrying the unconscious form of Eva slumped on his shoulders and started towards the helicopter, firing wildly behind him towards the waiting car behind him.

The bullets whooshed past Sam and Mark in quick succession while the American fired two bullets in rapid succession back to Ahmed.

But the Middle Eastern had already reached the ladder and climbed two of its steps when suddenly, the chopper turned in a fluid motion……

Towards Sam and Mark's car.

And its cannons came to life.

'Oh Shit.'

Mark shifted the car in reverse and then slammed the accelerator to the floor. The car moved like a bullet, backward.

Bullets shockingly started raking all around the car, but it seemed they were not trying to harm the car itself. It was more like warning shots, rather than killing shots.

'They want me alive.' Sam breathed.

Mark was impressed with the boy. Not only was he calm and composed during such a life-endangering situation, but he could use his mind as well.

He smiled….and did something nobody anticipated.

He changed gears and lunged forward…. towards the chopper.

* *

'What the hell is he doing?' The gunner said.

The pilot, Clark, was wondering the same thing while keeping the Apache in a hanging condition. He has reached within ten minutes of the call from Ahmed and Sabir to give back up to the Middle Eastern here in Delhi.

But there was one condition.

It seems they have called our bluff. We can't kill Sam, not now.

Therefore, he did the only thing he could right now.

He turned the Apache and started going away.

* *

Mark smiled.

'What on earth are you trying to do?' Sam asked, all the while watching Mark's maniac smile.

'Getting back Eva.' Was all he said.

He floored the accelerator, and the car sped behind the flying apache.

<u>CHAPTER THIRTY-EIGHT</u>

The car made for ninety miles an hour in a few seconds.

The Apache turned on itself and started going the other way already.

'Sam, get out of the car.' Mark cried above the sounds of the rotors.

Before Sam knew, Mark moved his left hand and opened the

passenger door and threw the Indian out. Sam, not being ready for

such an act, fell on his elbows painfully and then rolled onto his butt.

He looked at the speeding vehicle in front of him, which Mark was

driving, following the chopper.

'Oh No…...'

He looked straight ahead and understood the plan of Mark.

****

'He is still following us.' The pilot of the chopper said on his

earphone.

Ahmed looked behind and saw the speeding Maruti behind them and

smiled inwardly.

The fool. He thinks he can catch us on this four-wheeler.

'Don't worry.' He said in his earphone, 'He will never be able to

catch us.'

He looked at the pilot in the cockpit and asked – 'How much time before we go full speed?'

'Need a minute more to pick up full speed sir.'

'Good. Let's get out of here.' A look at now immobile Eva. 'We got the leverage.'

****

Mark looked at the ongoing work of the flyover just a few feet away. It seemed like the work had been stopped in the middle. Probably the labors have gone for the day after a whole day's work. He could see some tents on the far side of the road, where probably the workers have retired for the night.

Fortunately for him, the work of the bridge was completed until the part where the elevation had started, near the middle of the bridge. The place where the bridge's work was stopped seemed to be nearly thirty feet above the ground.

The plan will work.

He looked at the Apache, running away, still fifteen feet away from him and nearly ten feet above him, and would cross the end of the bridge in less than a minute.

He sped the vehicle at full speed.

****

The four-wheeler shot through the bridge and jumped over the bridge in a near slow motion…...

At which point, the driver's side door opened, and a small figure jumped out of it…. towards the chopper, which was now just four feet away from the falling car.

From his vantage point, Sam saw it all.

He saw the speeding car falling in a slow motion from the bridge, saw Mark coming out of the driver's seat and making his jump for the last few feet towards the helicopter, and a person looking out of the helicopter, whose mouth fell open, as if he had never seen anything like this before in his life.

Indeed, nobody has ever seen anything like this.

****

'Take up speed, you moron.'

Ahmed cried above the sounds of the running helicopter.

This man is crazy.

He just saw the American following the helicopter doing something that he had never thought anyone would ever dare to do.

He just flew off the edge of the bridge and jumped to reach the helicopter. This man is desperate.

But a thought crossed his mind, and a wicked smile appeared on his face.

We can't kill Sam, but nobody told us to keep this American alive.

****

Mark sloshed through the air at breakneck speed.

'Oh Shit.'

At the last second, it felt like he was falling short of the flying helicopter which just took off speed. However, at the very last moment, when he was about to plunge to his death, forty feet below to the ground, his right hand touched the lower skid of the Apache, just above the left landing wheel and held on to it.

The jolt he felt nearly took his right shoulder out of its socket.

'Shocking landing.' He said gritting his teeth.

CHAPTER THIRTY-NINE

Chaos.

Mayhem.

The Maruti crashed on its front bumper forty feet below the speeding up Apache. It just crumbled on itself, disintegrating the tires on every side. Then the fuel pump ignited, causing the car to explode with a ball of fire above it.

The Apache itself lurched on its left with the sudden weight of Mark on its skids.

'Losing altitude. We are losing altitude.'

Ahmed could hear on his earphones the frantic cries of the pilot in the cockpit.

'Speed up you fool.'

After a few seconds, the pilot was able to adjust the weight and sped up. The altitude started to rise gradually.

'Now to get that bastard.'

****

Mark was still trying to get his legs up on the skid and balance himself.......

Blam.

The bullet just missed him by inches.

He looked up and saw the Middle Eastern just reaching outside the helicopter door, with a Desert Eagle in his hand.

Blam. Blam.

Ahmed fired two more rounds towards the American, but by then, knowing his intentions, Mark has placed his legs on the right skid, the other one, away from the reach of the door from where the goon was shooting at him and hung upside down.

'Great.' He said while the rushing wind gushed his face. 'Now what Mark?'

He looked around himself and saw the rear Sikorsky S-76 Tyre, just beside the lower ramp and swung himself to catch it.

Ahmed, now not able to see the American, came back inside.

'Lurch the helicopter, Clark. We need to shake this bastard out.'

He tried to go beyond the unconscious Eva, to open the other side door of the Helicopter when suddenly, the ramp below burst open and the metal door of the ramp hit him awkwardly on the knees.

'Awwwww.'

Ahmed's cry was drowned out entirely with the sound of the rotors and just as he was about to come out of the shock on how the hell the ramp opened....

A kick.

A severe kick with two heels of the boots came out from below which Mark used to haul himself up inside the chopper. The heels connected the lower jaw of the Middle Eastern and....

Krack.

The sound of breaking teeth came out.

Mark reached the arc of his flight and …... and landed awkwardly on his butt, just an inch beside the ramp.

'Well, that was a good landing.' He called out to himself.

He saw a punch coming on his way through the corner of his eyes, and in the last split second moved his head out of the way, causing Ahmed to lose his balance and…….

And his right hand and head plunged into the now open ramp, the same one which was used ten minutes earlier for his escape with Eva.

Now losing all control of itself, Ahmed's body came out of the ramp in a flash and plunged towards the ground, now more than sixty feet below.

He cried all the way to his death.

****

Mark looked about himself.

He could see Eva slumped on the rear seat of the helicopter. How on earth the Middle Eastern was able to sit with the slumped form of Eva in this cramped place, he had no idea.

'Doesn't matter.'

However, before he could save Eva, he has to do deal with the other…….

Klang.

The metal rod hit him hard from behind.

Mark saw colorful stars while his vision got blurred. But his other senses were working perfectly.

Hearing the sound of a rod cutting the air around him, he turned back in a flash and saw the pilot attacking him with a metal rod, and before he knew what was going on, he put his left elbow on the way.

Klang.

The metal hit hard on his arm, nearly shocking his senses.

'Ahh. You little shit.' Mark cried on top of his voice, which in turn suddenly woke Eva up.

* *

The first thing she saw was Mark standing in front of her, on her right.

The next thing she saw was a man attacking him with a rod, and looking at Mark, he had not fared well.

Need to help him.

Without thinking, she just lunged out her left leg which caught the attacker's knee from the front…...

Crunch.

The hideous sound denoted the dislocation of the kneecap of the attacker, causing him to lurch back into the cockpit behind him….

And falling into the controls with the metal rod in his hand, while he himself fell on the co-pilot, who tried desperately to keep the chopper in the air.

The result was instantaneous.

The Apache was running on full speed when the pilot attacked Mark, but now, thanks to the rod and the falling body of the pilot himself, some of the controls broke immediately, causing the helicopter to lurch in all directions.

Inside, it felt like a roller coaster ride to Eva and Mark. The dazed Mark and now conscious Eva, both tried to understand their predicament.

And it doesn't look good.

The now incapable pilot, the damaged controls, the confused co-pilot, and the lurching helicopter...... all denoted the same thing.

It is going to crash. Any second now.

'It must be somewhere here.' Mark said while starting to search behind the rear seat.

'What must be somewhere?' Eva asked frantically. 'Mark we're gonna die.'

'No, we won't.'

Mark said coming back up with a smile, holding a black bag in his right hand.

A minute later, they both jumped out of the helicopter, Eva holding Mike in an awkward hug, from nearly a hundred feet from the road below.

Mark opened the sling on his chest which in turn opened the parachute on his back from his newly acquired black bag, slowing their pace, and they started flying towards the road below.

For its part, the helicopter ran for another thirty feet, before it hit a building, the Civic Centre of New Delhi, one-third of the height of it, and crumpled on itself, blowing the top half of the building in an explosion. The fireball exploded everywhere, and rain of glasses from the commercial building's windows fell all the way through to the road below.

For their part, Mark and Eva reached a junction of a road, flying in their parachute where they landed safely and looked around.

A taxi was standing just fifteen feet away from where they landed, and a young driver looked at them with his mouth hung open.

Mark just shrugged off his parachute and came running to the driver with a broad smile on his face.

'Hi. Can you take us to an address?'

Minutes later, the driver was speeding off the road, wondering who the hell these people were and hearing all sort of sirens-

Ambulances, Police, and Fire Engines all going in the opposite direction of him.

CHAPTER FORTY

FRANKFURT, GERMANY
10:10 PM

'And Ahmed is dead?'

'Yes, *Sir*.'

Alexander seemed fuming in rage hearing the news, which was expected.

It was some time ago that Sabir got the news of a Helicopter crash in Delhi and the death of Ahmed in the process. At first, it was unbelievable, owing to the fact that Ahmed had been a soldier for more than two decades, specializing in combat and rescue operations.

But then he came to know about the perpetrator of the death of his loyal comrade.

'And how was that?' The anger could be felt even over the other side of the phone, from countries apart.

'The American, his name is Mark Brent.' Sabir said, looking at a still picture of Mark in front of him in his laptop. The profile of the American soldier was open beside the picture. 'He is Special Operations officer of *MARSOC*. And from what I can gather from his profile, very dangerous.'

'And the woman?'

The voice of Alexander Penbrose from the other side seemed calm this time, but Sabir knew that he was anything but calm.

'The woman is a Cryptologist in *NSA*.'

'And how these two are related to Sam?'

'I am still working on it, sir.'

'Work on it quickly.' The Danish said. 'And Sabir, come back here. We need to find a solution to this.'

'Yes, sir.'

CHAPTER FORTY-ONE

MARYLAND, US

November 13,

6.50 P.M

Sam,

I am making sure that you are the only person who can read this. In the event that I can't meet you for some reason, maybe even murdered, this is the way that I can tell you what has happened.

You have always been my best student. You have shared my interests in archeology for all these years. Though I believe that interest is in your blood. Your parents were one of the most knowledgeable archeologists I have ever met in life.

Both your parents and me were obsessed with the Archeological history of the Nazis during the Second World War. It was during that quest that I had met your parents in the historical Concentration camps in Poland. It was before your birth.

However, we pursued the different angles of the Nazi history. While I was more interested in the routes taken by Heinrich Himmler, your parents were following the path of Ahnenerbe, the archeological division of the Nazis itself. You might remember the book – 'Ahnenerbe history of the Nazis', that your parents wrote.

During that path they came to know about Hans Schleif, the head of the Ahnenerbe during the end of the Nazi period. They tried to find the notebook of Hans and the reason of his death. However, they seemed to have got the notebook but there was someone else who was also behind the notebook.

Your parents had told me during their visit to Germany that they have got a location on the notebook, but someone powerful is behind them. However, after their unfortunate death, when I tried to find that notebook, I have been unable to do so for so many years. But it was just a week ago that I was contacted by a labor from your parent's detail.

I went to meet him and found this notebook with him.

Yes, the notebook of Hans. I still don't know why people are behind this notebook, but I fear that I am in danger too. So I made a digital copy of it and destroyed the original notebook.

In this quest I also came to know about another thing. Your parents didn't die of drowning. They were murdered.

Sam, this is the legacy of your parents and you need to think what to do with it. But I must warn you, people are behind this for many years, and you might get in danger too. Better to leave it here Sam.

God bless you Sam.

Yours Truly,
Professor Richard Hedley.

P.S. : So sudden is the Advent of Mother and father.

Perhaps this was the Hundredth time that Sam was checking the letter.

Some of the alphabets seemed like English, but most was gibberish.

'Are you sure that Hedley was a Professor, not a spy?'

Sam also wondered the same.

He looked towards the kitchen. Mark was jokingly speaking while fetching milk from the refrigerator. Eva had gone to the NSA office to complete some of her works there.

It had been nearly 12 hours they reached here, and she said she needed to do something at the office and rushed off.

After the events of Delhi, both Eva and Mark suggested they are better off from India. Though Sam was not so sure at first, after a lot of convincing from both the Americans, he reluctantly took the satchel retrieved from the basement tunnel and kept in hiding in his basement and headed here with his companions.

The private jet was at Safdarjung Airport, and it was in the morning of 11th that they started for Maryland.

'Let's go to my place.' Eva had suggested to her male companions once they all boarded the jet.

After a nap for a couple of hours, they all huddled together to get a good look at what was in the satchel. The first thing that came out was a letter, rolled inside the satchel. The other thing that they found was an iPad, out of charge.

The letter looked like the Prof had made a joke out of them.

'Seems like the Professor has made another code for you to solve.' Eva said seriously, looking towards the Indian.

Sam, on the other hand, seemed like he could do with a little rest. So, they all decided to take rest in the flight, though everybody was thinking about Hedley's letter in their minds. Once they reached

Eva's home in Maryland, she went for office, letting the boys figure out the puzzle by themselves.

Unfortunately, for both Sam and Mark, they were getting proved to be incompetent to solve this one.

One thing was clear. The Professor was somehow sure that he would be in danger, or even be murdered. There was no other explanation of going to such lengths to keep an iPad away from prying eyes. And whatever was in it, seemed worth killing for. And for the same reason, Hedley had to die.

'What was he trying to tell me?'

'ummmm...' Mark replied from the kitchen, 'That he is an ultra-secret spy?'

Sam nearly laughed at the way Mark said that out loud.

Ever since they found this letter with all weird looking alphabets, Mark had been sure that the old man Professor Richard Hedley was actually a spy. He even went ahead and established his own thought about which spy agency the Professor was working.

'He might have worked for the Mossad.' He had said in the flight.

Sam felt tired. It had been a long few days. Ever since the Prof had died, it had been a roller coaster ride for him. First a bomb blast at the old man's home, then Mark's arrival, coming to India, Eva's arrival, the car chase and helicopter fight to get her back, and now this letter. It was all too much to take in for him.

'I should go to the washroom.'

****

The splash of cold water made him feel better.

The last few days have been really stressful. He looked at the mirror and saw a ghost of himself looking back at him. It felt as if his age had increased ten years in the last few days.

The letter was really baffling. What made the Prof create such a code? What was he trying to hide? And from whom?

Sam never knew that the Professor traveled back to India a week before his death, nor he was aware of the fact of how Hedley could create codes. First was the *Mlechhita-Vikalpa* and now this. He wondered what else he didn't know about the Professor.

Maybe he really was a spy, as Mark was suggesting. Sam laughed in his mind. No, that is not possible. The Professor was a historian, an archeologist.

Suddenly something clicked in his mind.

Yes, the Prof was a historian. An excellent historian.

He looked in front of him and smiled.

He knew how to crack the letter of the Prof.

CHAPTER FORTY-TWO

COPENHAGEN, DENMARK

November 14,

12:55 AM

Alexander was sitting alone in his room when the call came.

He looked at his screen and smiled.

Sabir.

He must have got hold of them somehow. Or else he wouldn't have called at this hour. The threat worked it seems. Sabir knew if the trio was not found then what could happen to him, and it was made clear to him as well.

It's been more than a day that Sabir left from here, in search for the Indian and his new acquaintances.

He must have some news.

'Yes, Sabir.' He spoke in his usual ice-cold voice picking up his phone.

'There's been a new development.' Sabir's voice came from the other side.

'What is it?'

'They are in Maryland.' Said Sabir. 'In the NSA woman's house.'

Sabir had gone for more than a day now and kept his associates to keep an eye on the houses of Mark, Eva, and Sam. Sooner or later, one of them should turn up in their own houses. There were a couple of people who were keeping an eye right now on the Cambridge campus. Though there was very less chance of Sam going to his campus, still Sabir's people were there in case he returns.

So, it seemed at last their spying on the houses was successful. But Sabir himself was in Washington. And instead of him traveling to meet the guys spying on Eva's home, he had called him right now means there's something he wanted to tell.

Alexander had told him to do anything to retrieve Sam or whatever the Professor had found.

'What is it?' Asked Alexander, his curiosity piqued.

'They have most probably found something from the Professor.' That held his interest.

'What is it? Has it been retrieved yet?'

'Not yet sir. But the guys are moving in. You will have it within the hour.'

'No delays this time Sabir.' Alexander said, his voice like steel. 'I want whatever is found.'

'Yes, sir. You will have it.'

CHAPTER FORTY-THREE

KATHMANDU, NEPAL
November 14,
5.00 AM

Ballav Sang didn't get too much sleep nowadays.

For the last twenty-five years, he has been an informant for an ultra-secret organization or more accurately a Brotherhood in one of the most isolated parts of the world. And he did that willingly, not forced by someone.

Sometimes he still wondered if it was a dream or reality.

Criiing. Criing.

His phone rang. The sound of the phone ringing suddenly made him jump. At this time of the morning, everything was sleeping, and contrary to the whole day, there's not a single sound anywhere. It's as if the whole world was at peace and everything have stopped. In this silence, the ringing of his phone naturally made him jump.

He was having his morning tea while sitting on his favorite couch on his balcony when the phone came.

He took the phone in his hand and saw the number.

Must be important news.

'Yes, tell me.' He answered the call.

'Sir, I think the boy got the package.'

'Hmm. Then the Professor must have left it somewhere before his death.' A smile crossed his face.

'Yes, sir. The boy is helped by two Americans who seem competent enough to always save him from dangers.'

'Good. Then we don't need to worry.' He said. 'At last the package has gone to him. Just keep an eye on him.'

'Yes, sir.'

Ballav kept the phone and smiled.

At last, the death of the Indian's parents has not been gone in vain.

He took the phone and dialed another number and waited for it to be picked up. This was a number only he knew in the whole world.

'Grandmaster.' He said once the phone was picked up. 'Sam has the package from the Professor.'

CHAPTER FORTY-FOUR

MARYLAND, US

November 13,

6.00 P.M

The door was opened by Sam when Eva entered.

The joy on his face told her everything.

'Let me guess. You found the key to crack the code.' Eva said.

'Yes exactly.' Sam said excitedly.

'Is it the mirror image?'

Now Sam got surprised. He thought he was the only one to have cracked the Prof's code in the letter. *How could she know?*

Eva had seen the surprise on his eyes and understood his thoughts.

'Cryptologist, remember?'

She said, smiling while sitting on the living room couch.

Now it was Sam's turn to smile. Yes, he had forgotten entirely that Eva was a cryptologist in NSA. So, understanding this type of code would not take much time for her. She must have searched through the different types of encryptions to understand what type of code the Professor might have written.

It was then that Mark entered the room having completed taking the milk and saw both smile and talking about the code.

'Anyone going to tell me what's going on?'

'We cracked the code of the professor.' Both cried in unison.

146

'Well ok.' He said, looking about himself, and in the process making himself look more awkward than he already was.

****

The dinner now over, they all sat in the living room. Mark had made himself comfortable on the couch with Eva sitting beside him. Sam took his place on the chair opposite to them.

In the middle was a large coffee table with black glass. All their attention was towards it, or rather what was on it, except one.

Eva was unaware of Sam looking at her. Her full concentration was based on the letter in front of her, placed on the table.

'Can anyone explain me the details? And quit the sarcasm.' Mark said to his companions, exasperated with the smiles of both for last half an hour as if they were the smartest person on the planet sitting with the dumbest one.

His voice broke Sam from his reverie. He needed to check himself. This was not the time for daydreaming.

'Certainly.' Sam said, looking towards the others, a smile on his face. 'Let me explain first.'

The others looked at him with their full attention. He certainly looked very enthusiastic, the most in last few days.

'First, to understand this letter and the code, we need to know a few facts.' Started Sam. 'The first person to write this kind of texts was one of the most notable persons of medieval history. Leonardo Da Vinci.'

He stopped for a second to let the words sink in.

'Leonardo the Vinci! The artist?' Mark said. 'As in *The Monalisa*?'

'It's not Leonardo the Vinci.' Corrected Eva, laughing. 'It is *Leonardo Da Vinci.*'

'Yes.' Sam continued. He seemed happy to be in his turf first time in last few days. The murders and running and fighting have never been his turf, this was. The history, the archeological wonders of the world. 'And to tell you, Mark, Leonardo was not just an artist. He was an Italian Renaissance polymath whose areas of interests included invention, painting, sculpting, architecture, science, music, mathematics, engineering, literature, anatomy, geology, astronomy, botany, writing, history, and cartography. He has been variously called the father of paleontology, ichnology, and architecture, and is widely considered one of the greatest painters of all time. He also is known as the creator of modern parachutes, tanks, and helicopters. He later came to be known as a Universal Genius and one of the greatest minds during the Renaissance period.'

'Well, that's all good.' Mark said; still the words sinking in and clearly lost. 'What has that to do with the Professor's letter?'

'That is the most interesting part. You see, this is a part of his genius. He is the creator of this code you see in front of you right now. This is the language he used in his notebook to write down about his inventions, about his works. And to this day, his notebooks are still on display in the British Library.'

That made both the others look at the letter in front of them.

'It makes sense.' Said Eva. 'A process by which one of the greatest historical minds have written his notebooks, and the Professor following that path. It's another old code which he knew surely.'

'Yes.' Sam continued. 'And he knew that I can always decode it anytime if I knew what I was looking at. Every archeological student has been taught about this.'

'As a Cryptologist, we too are taught about this style at the early stage of our study.' Eva commented.

'That's outstanding folks.' Mark said this time, clearly out of patience. 'But can anyone tell me exactly what language or what code it is?'

'It's English.' Said Sam, surprising Mark. 'Just not the way you are used to seeing it.'

'It's Mirror writing.'

CHAPTER FORTY-FOUR

Chuck 'Scotty' Rielly nodded and hung up his satellite phone. The order was clear enough. He looked at his two partners and gave them a silent command.

He had to eliminate the threats and retrieve the package and the Indian with it. Sam was key to everything.

It was an easy task. He looked at the house through his night vision binoculars. The world turned into a shade of green.

He could see the American guy leaving the living room towards the restroom. The other two were talking something among themselves. But the most important thing could be seen clearly on the black table in front of the Indian in the middle of the room. The package which his boss wanted him to retrieve. A paper and an iPad could be seen here. He could not see the details, but his instincts told him that these were the items that were to be retrieved along with the Indian guy.

The last few days have been really tiresome. Though earlier he had worked for the militias, for the last decade he had been part of an army employed by his Danish master Alexander. However, the orders always came from Sabir. On his orders, they had been keeping a lookout here in Maryland, in the hopes of the trio coming here after the proceedings in Delhi.

Two other teams were looking out for the same trio in Washington DC and Delhi. Keeping an eye on the houses of Mark and Sam.

After what happened in Delhi, the two Americans and the Indian had disappeared from Delhi. But Sabir had assumed correctly that sooner or later they would turn up in one of their houses thinking to be a safe haven for them. As a result, the three teams were created with few militia people in each team, looking out for them.

And now here we are.

He knew how hostile Sabir could be, and he couldn't be on the other side of that rage.

He looked at the bag of weapons in his disposal and smiled. An SR-25 semi-automatic sniper, few M-21, a couple of Heckler and Koch assault rifle and an RPG-2 rocket launcher. Having Danish employment for one of the billionaires of the world has its advantages. They were able to get the weapons without the checking of the customs, thanks to Alexander's private jet, which they landed in the Private airfield of Maryland.

Now to action.

He gave hand signals to the other members of his team.

We go out there. Silently. Kill the Americans, get the Indian alive. But most important is the package. Look out for that. We need to retrieve it.

The team fanned out quickly and started leapfrogging each other. It would take them two minutes to reach the house. And then in next two minutes, they would retrieve the package and Indian and then leave.

The authorities would have a hard day finding out what happened.

CHAPTER FORTY-FIVE

COPENHAGEN, DENMARK

November 14,

1:00 AM

The man with the specs stared hard at the screen.

'So, Sam has found the package then.' A rare smile started to show up on his face.

'Yes, sir.' Sabir's voice came from the other end of the screen.

The big screen loomed in front of him. Except for the light from the screen, there was no other illumination in the room. The room looked devoid of any feeling, devoid of anything else in this world. But Sabir knew better.

This man was as ruthless as anyone he had ever seen. He remembered an incident from a few years back when one of the associates of this man had disagreed on a simple fact. After a day he was found dead with most parts of his body missing, eaten by sharks. Though nobody found any evidence, it was clear to Sabir who was responsible for this death.

Not many people know what this man's agenda was. Except for Sabir. And that made him afraid of this person. Any day he might think that there is no need for Sabir for his agenda to work, and that would be the last day of his life. Over the years, he had seen many people who opposed this person vanishing from this world.

152

Though this person didn't have much financial backing, his genius had kept him ahead of others in the game.

'Right now, our people are acquiring the package as well as Sam.' Sabir said.

'Good.' The man said. His eyes were glinting in the low light. 'Once you bring Sam and the package to Alexander, our work can begin.'

'Right sir.' Sabir's voice trembled a bit. He has no idea what this person was going to do once the package comes to the Danish billionaire.

'I have waited long enough for this moment.' Said the man. 'Many of the people in history has tried to achieve it, but none came close.' He paused for a moment. 'Except the German archeologist Hans. Now I will be able to achieve it.'

'Ri……right sir.'

'The wheels are set in motion Sabir. Once two Indians had stopped me from getting what I want, and now their only heir will help me to get it.'

With that, the man ended the video call.

A smile crept across his face. A rare one. A smile of triumph.

Hemanth and Rita had stopped me nearly two decades ago. Now their son will help me to find it.

CHAPTER FORTY-SIX

MARYLAND, US

November 13,

7.04 P.M

'Well?'

Mark's question came out feeling much dumber than he had actually intended, drawing smiles from the other two.

It was easy to understand his confusion. Most people didn't have any idea what Mirror writing was. The people who might understand had difficulty to acknowledge the fact that someone really can write that way. They had to admit; it was a nice play by the old Professor.

Even if this one fell into some unwanted person's hands, he would be unable to read it, unless he was an absolute genius.

But what's the big secret? Why murder him? Why are the people behind them? Who was trying to kidnap Eva?

The questions really nagged Sam. His gut was telling him that there's much more he didn't know, or many things he was yet to understand. It's not always that people chase in helicopters in Delhi roads. *And Cambridge professors don't get murdered every day.*

He still couldn't fathom the fact that the Prof was dead.

And then there are these two.

Sam still found it difficult to understand why Mark was helping him. The American had not yet offered some good reason to justify that.

Granted, this guy had helped him after the bomb blast at Professor's home, and then in his home in Delhi, but still, that doesn't prove him to be his friend. Right now, it was merely an acquaintance. Mark have his uses. Moreover, it seemed that this guy has a lot of things at his disposal, like the Private Jet used to travel to Delhi and then here. Sam had seen him speaking in his satellite phone couple of times, giving updates to someone.

When asked he had said – 'Someone of importance who wants you safe and also this issue solved.'

He had not offered anything more, and Sam had not asked for anything more.

Also, then there was Eva. It seemed her beauty and brain were in perfect alignment. She was a cryptologist in NSA, beautiful, with an aura around her. Not many people can break the wall she had around her. However, the thing that nagged him the most was that he didn't know anything about her yet.

I don't know a thing about both of them.

'It's a way to write something which can only be legible when held in front of the mirror.'

The answer to Mark's question came from Eva.

At the same time, Mark started fiddling with the iPad, which was still being charged near the kitchen.

Sam was also looking at the letter in his hand. He could see the iPad's light being turned on, as Mark switched it on.

'So what doe-----'

Blam. Blam.

Crack.

****

The door burst open after the twin gunshots and combined kick of two people.

Sam saw some people storming into the room, guns in their hand. He was about to jump when a bullet grazed inches past his left ear, deterring him from taking one more step.

'No one moves.' A muscular guy among the attackers said. This guy seemed to be the leader of the band of gun-toting people.

'We want the package.'

Sam saw them all looking towards him and the letter he held in his hands.

So, they want the letter and the iPad.

'Ok.' He said. 'You can have it.'

He held the letter in front of him and started taking steps towards the guy. He could see the guy tightening his grip on the gun, tensed and ready to fire. Eva was still a little left of him, looking straight at two of the goons just a few feet away from her, holding their guns on the ready.

Sam was the one facing most of the gun trotting goons in front of him, but Mark was just out of reach as he was standing on the far right, just near the kitchen and the glass door to the garden behind him.

After two steps Sam tripped on the coffee table in front of him and fell to the floor, releasing his grip on the letter, which fell in a kind of slow motion.

All the gun dwellers looked towards him, distracted for a split second.

A split second very much needed for Mark and Eva. And at that moment all hell broke loose.

One moment all the mercenaries were looking at the letter falling, and the next suddenly Eva jumped like a spring doll and threw a mighty blow on the gun hand of the man in front of her with her right leg, whereas her other leg connected to his gut, winding the man. The blow struck the wrist of the man, resulting in losing his grip on the gun, which flew away and landed just a few inches away from Sam. The man who got hit tripped on his legs and fell on his mate and both tumbled on the floor together.

Blam.

At the same time, suddenly Mark got his gun out while trying to put the iPad in his pocket safely with his other hand, and without losing a single moment, fired at the guy in front of Sam, the one who seemed to be the leader.

The SIG Sauer P226 blasted a 9 mm bullet, but the guy was much more cautious than his mates. At the same time that Mark fired, the guy just dropped flat, resulting the bullet soaring just above him, missing his head for mere centimeters and lodged itself in the head of the man standing behind him.

In the same fluid motion, Mark pocketed the iPad and started firing blindly, all the while taking cover behind the kitchen sink.

The others also jumped into motion. A volley of bullets fired towards the kitchen, also breaking the glass door now on the right of Mark in the process.

Sam took the opportunity and without so much of a second thought, gripped the fallen Heckler and Koch assault rifle, put his finger on the trigger and started firing blindly. In his inexperienced hand, the gun trembled violently, resulting in missing most of the mercs, but multiple cries proved that some of it had hit its marks.

'Come on; we need to leave. Now.' Eva's voice came, while she started running towards the now broken glass door to the garden. Most of the goons have scattered all over the living room, running into cover from the mad cluster of bullets from Sam.

Blam.

Mark had started to follow, but a single gunshot made him turn. What he saw made his blood cold.

CHAPTER FORTY-SEVEN

7.07 P.M

'Aaaahhh.'

Sam cried in agony. He had never felt anything like this before. The bullet had lodged itself in his left shoulder, just below the collarbone. A line of blood came out, soaking his shirt red within a matter of seconds.

Just a moment ago, while he was firing blindly, the leader among them, the one who had evaded the bullet from Mark, fired a single bullet towards Sam with clinical precision.

The moment it hit the Indian, he flew a few feet away and fell on his back. It felt like a truck had hit him with a force he never knew could actually be possible. Fiery agony spread through his body, every muscle paining beyond imagination.

'SAM.'

Mark's cry from behind made him focus. He opened his eyes and saw the six remaining goons bring their weapons up as one, saw Mark taking a step towards him.

In that single moment, several thoughts crossed his mind.

They will kill Mark. I need to save him. They can't kill me. If they wanted to kill me, they would have put the bullet in my brain. They need me, and they need……….

In that single terrifying moment, he made his decision.

'MARK. RUN.'

At the same time, he pulled the gun which he was somehow accidentally still clutching in his hands and jammed his finger on the trigger.

Trat. Trat.

Only two bullets were left which were spent in a heartbeat, but that did the intended result. The goons ran back for cover, giving Mark the opportunity to run away. But before going away, their eyes met.

You can't save me, Mark. Save yourself and Eva.

Mark understood the emotion, and tactically that was correct. He also came to the same conclusion as Sam.

They won't kill you, Sam. I am sorry, I couldn't save you right now. I am sorry that you got hit by a bullet. But I make a promise to you. I will come back for you and save you.

With that, he ran. He ran and crossed the shards of glass and jumped onto the garden, followed by bullets chewing up the soil behind him.

****

'Dimitry and Serov, go behind the Americans.' Said the leader. 'Find them and kill them.'

With that, two of the mercs started running towards the garden.

'But be careful, the MARSOC guy is nasty.' Said the leader, by now whose accent Sam could make out that to be of an Englishman.

Thud.

The kick from him made Sam lose his grip on the gun, which fell away a short distance.

Thud.

'Awww.'

Another kick on his gut and Sam saw stars in front of him.

'You think yourself as a nasty little bustard, Sam?' The man seemed to fume with anger. 'You made me lose three of my guys here.'

With that, he picked Sam up clutching his collar and made him stand up in the swift flow.

This man is strong.

'Be sure that I will avenge them, you little fuck.' Spittle came out of his mouth as he was speaking, fuming with rage.

'Y…you a…... re messing with the wr…wronggg people.' Sam replied with the last ounce of strength he had left.

And with that, his head lolled to a side, and his body gave up. His unconscious body fell with a thud on the couch.

'We'll see 'bout that.' Chuck said while taking the fallen letter of the Professor and pocketing that.

'Pick him up.' He said to the others standing. 'We need to take him to the Boss.'

Ten minutes later, the living room of Eva looked like a place where a war had happened. Shards of glass, broken table, bullet casings, and bullet marks reigned the room.

However, there were no bodies.

CHAPTER FORTY-EIGHT

'Run Eva.'

Mike was running with his full might in the garden. By now, Eva had crossed the garden and was waiting for her male companions to join her. The plan was to evade the mercenaries and run away from this place until the authorities were here.

She had called 911 for help, but it would take at least ten minutes for the police to reach here.

So, she had decided to run away from here. With a single handgun of Mark, it would be tough to fight so many men with automatic rifles. She even saw one of them carrying a rocket launcher.

It was then that she heard another gunshot.

After a long minute of wait, she saw Mark coming up, and a couple of goons following him a little behind, exchanging gunfire. Mark saw her a little away from him and called for her to run and changed direction to join her.

'Where's Sam?' Was the first question she could ask him when he reached, pursuers following hot.

'They shot him.'

'Wha---'

'No time.' He clutched her hand, and both started running. 'He'll live.'

I have left him alone there.

'But how could you-----'

Blam. Blam. Blam.

Before she could ask fully what happened, three bullets chewed up the grass near her foot, and without a second thought, the Americans ran.

'Don't…ah…. worry.' Mark said, running hard, all the while clutching her hand and practically dragging her.

'They…wont…kill…. him.'

In that instant Eva discovered something.

Sam is alone with the enemies. They have shot him. What if…....

She couldn't think anymore. The worst could never happen.

Moreover, with crystal clarity, she knew one thing at that moment.

I care for Sam. I love him.

'We…should…. go…help…. him.'

They crossed the boundary of the house and reached the garage.

Eva's BMW was parked there, and the keys still in the garage.

'Don't worry. I know where they will take him.' Said, Mark. 'Or at least where I can get news of him.'

That startled her.

'How?'

Blam. Blam.

Mark fired two bullets towards where the goons were coming from, scattering them to take cover while crossing the boundary. In the meantime, Eva found the keys and got inside the car.

Mark also got inside, all the while firing, so that the enemies were more intended to take cover rather than following them.

'I will tell you. But first, let's get out of here.' Mark said while getting inside the car, on the passenger seat in the front. 'I have only a bullet left.'

Vroom.

The engine started, and the car sped out of the garage, onto the road.

BOOM.

Just as they crossed the building, the sound of a blast came from behind them. From her living room, a billowing cloud of fire and black smoke erupted out.

'Guess they have put use to the RPG Launcher.'

Destroying all the evidence of the fight.

The car sped away, leaving the smoking house behind.

CHAPTER FORTY-NINE

'What's all this about, Mark?'

It's been more than half an hour that they were driving and just reached Baltimore. Mark had decided to go this way, as going to Washington was not safe anymore. They surely would have people looking out for them near his apartment. Going there would be a drastically lousy idea. So, to be safe, he had decided to hole up in a motel somewhere near Baltimore/Washington International Thurgood Marshall Airport and had already called up his jet there. Now the next step was to get through the night and decide what to do next.

But Eva seemed to be pissed off leaving Sam alone in the hands of the enemy. However, most of all, she seems to be more upset with Mark, plainly because he knew more than he was letting out.

'We will find and get him back.' Mark said, in an apologetic manner.

'What are you not telling me?'

Eva's eyes narrowed, and she watched Mark suspiciously.

Ok. I have to give her something.

'Ok stop.' Mark said. 'Let's get somewhere quiet, and I will tell you.'

****

Fifteen minutes later, they were sitting in the Woodberry kitchen, in a quiet table.

'Ok, tell me what the hell is going on.'

Mark sighed. He has to tell her.

'I can't tell you everything.' Mark started.

'But let me start.' He said, looking into the eyes of his companion before she could protest. She didn't seem too happy about the prospect.

Understandable. Secrets have a way to make things worse.

'The Professor, Richard Hedley, was interested in the Nazi history and went all over Europe searching for the different experiments they did or finding the different concentration camps they had. When he went to Denmark, he was searching for some of the historical experiments the Nazis performed there during the World War II. I am not sure what he found there, but as far as I know, he was approached by a Danish Billionaire there to provide input to him on his research. The good Professor declined the offer. Mind you; the offer was most probably a very lucrative one. Nonetheless, he had declined the offer. I am not sure what he was searching for, or what he found, the next day he declined, he came back to Cambridge and worked on his studies there. After a few days, he had received a package from Denmark. Again, I am not sure what it was, but whatever he got, it was essential. And it seemed to be related to Sam's parents – Rita and Hemanth Rawath.'

He saw the look in Eva's eyes on the mention of Sam's parents.

She is surprised.

'Yes, that's correct.' Mark continued, seeing the surprised look in her eyes. 'Somehow the package had something to do with them. And from what we know now, the Professor indeed felt that it was something significant, and so he called one of his friends, a person who was an archeologist himself, and told him about the package, and that this same package has something to do with Rita and Hemanth's research. Now, we know he was afraid that something might happen to him, and I am guessing it's the same Danish Billionaire who he was afraid of. From what I have learned about this person, he is one of the most dangerous persons in this world and can go through any means to fulfill his needs.

He also has a private security firm appointed entirely in his payroll and from the last few day's adventures, it seems he can go to any limits to receive the package. My employer and I believe that it is him, who has orchestrated the death of the Professor. He is the same person behind the attacks in Cambridge, Delhi and now here in Maryland. But we don't have anything on him to have a legal action on him. Now, since its related to Sam's parents and the professor, the next person who can help him achieve whatever shit he wants is Sam. As a result, I concluded that they wouldn't kill Sam, only subdue him, so that he can help them to find whatever they are after.' After speaking for a few minutes, Mark stopped.

'So, who is this Danish?'

'You know his name very well. We all do.' Mark said. 'His name is Alexander Penbrose.'

The look on Eva's face gave him the answer. *She indeed knows the name.*

Eva really got shocked hearing the name. Alexander Penbrose was a well-known name in the European continent and outside too. He was a self-made Billionaire and a ruthless businessman. Just two days ago he was in the news for making a partnership and going into a joint venture with Bill Gates.

But there was another question which nagged her right now.

'Who is your employer? Who asked you to help Sam?'

'He is the friend the Professor called on receiving the package.'

'So, he has a name?'

'I can't tell you the name, Eva. He has asked to keep his name a secret.'

Eva sighed. *No point trying to get his employer's name now. Mark is really good with secrets.*

'So, what to do now?'

'From what I know,' Mark replied, 'They will take Sam to Alexander and give him proper medical help.'

A grin spread on his face.

'Alexander is going to get a surprise visit from us.'

CHAPTER FIFTY

COPENHAGEN, DENMARK
November 15,
8.34 P.M

'Hello, Sam.'

The sound of the footsteps had already alerted him. Last two days he was in and out of consciousness. It was only today a few hours ago that he had regained full consciousness. Still, the shoulder throbbed in pain. Just sometime back a nurse has administered a heavy dose of painkiller, which made the pain a little better. It was only a dull ache now.

As soon as he had regained consciousness, Sam could see the Little Mermaid sculpture at a distance from his window. Not that he had tried to get out of his bed, the head still felt heavy, and the whole body felt like a truck had hit him.

So all he could do was watch the sculpture from here. The floor to ceiling glass window provided a good view of the sea. He could see children coming near the sculpture, tourists posing for selfies with the mermaid. But all the people looked like ants from this distance. The moment he had seen the sculpture, he knew where he was.

I am in Copenhagen, Denmark now.

Mark had told him about the *Kastellet*, that Alexander owned here in Denmark. He had also seen the picture of the Danish Billionaire too, inside the jet after Mark had told him about the Professor's venture in Denmark. Sam, not being a regular follower of news, was not familiar with the appearance of the great Alexander Penbrose.

But it didn't come as a surprise that the business tycoon himself came to meet him. Ever since he came to know that he was in Denmark, Sam had an inkling that the Danish would come to meet him. After all, he was the one who was behind all the attacks and playing a game of cat and mouse with Sam.

'Hello, Alexander.'

Sam said while shifting himself in the bed to sit up straight and get a good look at the orchestrator of all the pains he had faced for last week.

'Oh!' Alexander seemed a bit surprised hearing his name from Sam. 'So you know about me?'

He was surrounded by three black-clad figures with holstered pistols with them, making the threat explicit.

No one can attack Alexander.

'What's there to know?' Replied Sam, making his irritation clear in his voice. 'A billionaire who likes to kill people and kidnap is hardly anything for a surprise.'

The leftmost bodyguard was about to take a step with his fist closed to show that nobody was supposed to speak to his employer like that when the Danish raised his left hand to stop him.

'Well, it seems you are quite comfortable here.'

Alexander seemed to find the sarcasm in Sam amusing. He sat down on the only couch available in the room, adjacent to the plush bed that Sam was sitting.

'As comfortable as a prisoner can be.'

The anger in Sam's voice was quite clear.

'Well Sam, I think I would call it an arrangement for partnership, rather than imprisonment.' Alexander answered, smiling, though his voice suggested that he was not accustomed to being spoken like this by someone. 'If you help me with what I want, I would help you gain your health faster and additionally…. A good fortune for you.'

'Well, thanks for the offer.' Sam replied, sarcasm plain in his voice. 'But no thanks.'

'That's very unfortunate.'

With that, Alexander stood up and, in a flash, got his ZIGANA M16 pistol out of his own holster and pointed directly towards Sam's head.

'It seems, in that case, I have no need for you anymore.'

CHAPTER FIFTY-ONE

8.40 P.M

Sam stared straight into his eyes.

Alexander held the pistol in his hand, pointing straight at the middle of his eyes. He stayed that way for half a minute more. Both stared at each other, holding each other's gaze unblinking, each getting a measure of other.

After a full minute, a minute which Sam thought would be his last, Alexander sighed and put his gun down. For a second, the Indian had really believed that the tycoon might pull the trigger. It had been a gamble, albeit a calculated one. And it paid off. Somewhere in his mind, he was sure that the Danish won't kill him. He was still needed, and Alexander wouldn't have gone through so much trouble in different parts of the globe just to kill him.

'Well, I see you are brave.' The appreciation in his voice clear, Alexander holstered the weapon. 'Braver than Richard Hedley, but I can see that you have the same adamant behavior as your parents.'

That held Sam's attention.

'You knew them?' His voice raised, not sure if it was due to the anger that such a selfish man had met his parents, or that somehow, he could be related to their death. Anyhow, Rita and Hemanth died in Germany, not far from Copenhagen, in mysterious circumstances.

'Yes, dammit.'

172

The frustration suddenly burst out of him. It seemed like there has been a frustration and anger boiling up inside him for a long time.

'Yes dammit.' He repeated, this time with less anger. 'I have met them, before their death. They were in Germany, investigating on the Ahnenerbe.'

He sat back on the couch, holding Sam's gaze.

'No, I had nothing to do with their death Sam.' He said, shaking his head, seeing the question in Sam's eyes. 'I just wanted the diary.'

'What diary?'

'The diary of Hans Schleif.' He said with a resigned voice. 'I had offered them a million euros. Can you believe it? A million euros. And they refused.'

'Yes, that seems like my mom and dad all right.' Sam said, smiling. The pride in his voice must have been apparent.

'Oh, you think that's funny?' Fumed the Danish. 'I had asked them to give me the diary repeatedly, even after they refused me twice. I had met them in Germany itself. But before I could convince them, I heard the news of their death.'

A genuine sadness crossed his face.

But that was for a moment only. Again, that cold hardness spread all over him, and he looked straight into the Indian's eyes.

'I had tried to find the diary for the last eighteen years Sam.' He said with surprising calmness. 'Eighteen years, I have traveled everywhere, checked wherever possible for that diary. But you know where I found it?'

The question in Sam's face must have been clear.

'Yeah. Your parents had given it to some person on their detail, a guide of some sorts. He had kept it for so many years, without anyone knowing. And when I find him, he is already on his deathbed, an old fool.' He said with regret. 'But when I had found him, I come to know that he had given the diary to a Richard Hedley of Cambridge.'

He shook his head. Sam was not sure if it was due to regret, or due to the fact that Alexander thought that the guide had missed a good deal.

'I gave Hedley an offer of five million euros.' He said again. 'That old fool. He refused. You all are of the same category.'

'On that, I can agree.' Sam said, smiling.

Though somewhere inside he felt sorry for his parents, that guide of them and for the Prof. They had all held their positions till death. He could now join the dots of this mystery. But one thing was still not clear.

'He went back to Cambridge.' Said Alexander, before Sam could finish his thought and voice it out loud. 'And the diary was kept in an airport locker for few days. He had made arrangements to receive the diary a few days later, and when he did, he called a friend of his. Lucky for me, I was monitoring his calls, and immediately decided on what to do.'

'And so, you got him killed and ransacked his place.' Sam spoke.

'Yes. But that old Professor was no fool.' The Danish spat. 'He was ready for it, and somehow he has given it to you.'

He spread his hand forward.

'I need that diary Sam. I know you retrieved it from your house in India.'

Now it was the turn for Sam to be surprised.

There was no dairy in the package.

'There was no dairy in the package.'

'I don't believe you.' Alexander said. 'Where have you kept it?'

Sam voiced aloud the thought he was having.

'Why do you need the Diary of an Ahnenerbe leader?'

Alexander laughed out. Very few people knew about it.

'Because Sam, it contains the location of the Library of Alexandria.'

CHAPTER FIFTY-TWO

ATLANTIC OCEAN
November 15,
3.45 P.M

'Ok. So, make things ready. We will be landing in a few hours.'
Mark disconnected the call and took the seat in front of Eva. They
have started an hour back from Maryland on the jet, on their way to
Denmark. Alexander's people would be sure to keep an eye on the
nearby airports of Copenhagen. So, the plan was to land in the *Karup*
airport of Denmark. After that a short trip of half an hour to reach
Copenhagen.

The American was just getting the things ready using his contacts in
Denmark. They would hit the road hot, so everything needed to be
ready. Already too much time has gone, nearly two days.

'So, everything ready?' Eva said sourly.

She's got a point. It might be already too late.

'Well, is there still a need to be so....' Mark searched for the correct
word and failed to find one.

'Oh! Now you think I am overreacting, right?'

Mark could literally feel the anger boiling in her head. It felt to him
that if he could pay a little more attention, he might feel the heat
radiating from her mind.

Pushing the thought away, he started speaking on the matter on hand.

'I know Eva. But you must understand---'

'Understand what Mark? That you lost time to get new gears?' She said pointing to the bag sitting on the seat beside him.

That's true.

'I had to speak to my employer Eva.' He said apologetically. 'We need to be ready.'

After being holed up in the motel that night, Mark had called his employer and updated on everything. Eva tried to hear what he was speaking, but he went to the other side of the road, being too much secretive. Once he was back, his face said everything that Eva needed to know. From his sour expression, it was clear that the call didn't go well.

He later explained that his employer had been upset that he had failed to save Sam and got him injured. Worse, Sam was captured and taken by the enemy. Now, to rescue Sam, he needed some essential gears and also required to include help from a friend with whom he had worked earlier in Iraq during the Desert Storm. As a result, he had to call and tell his employer.

Now, all the arrangements done, everything was ready for the oncoming rescue mission.

Alexander would not know what hit him.

'So, you were helped in Iraq by a guy named Helper Dixido?' Eva asked quizzically, raising an eyebrow, also changing the topic.

'Dixido was a Delta Force specializing in hostage rescue.' Replied Mark, smiling. 'He had worked with us to save hundreds of civilians during our mission in Iraq. Later he started his own business in 2015 and settled here in Denmark. Now he works with private security firms to provide consultation and gears for their work. I have called him to get some things ready.'

'And what's the plan exactly?'

'We go in, kill any bustards stupid enough to interfere, and get Sam out.'

'And what of this?' Eva said, showing the screen of the iPad. It still showed the same thing that it showed last evening when they had tried to unlock it the first time.

━━   ━━   ━━   ━━   ━━   ━━

ENTER THE PASSWORD.

3 CHANCES LEFT

Mark sighed.

'Well, you are the technologist one.' He said. 'Can't you, I don't know, hack it or something?'

'Nope. I tried last night when you went for your call.' Eva replied sourly. 'There seems to be a build in a feature where if someone tried to hack the iPad, a self-destruct mechanism would be triggered, which is attached to the microchip and will fry it.'

'So, no hack.'

They became quiet for a few moments.

'You know, this Richard Hedley guy,' Mark said again, 'Seems to me like he was more a code creator than a simple history professor.'

Eva also thought about the same thing. Who would write code in the tissue paper of a café? Or write a mirror image letter? On top of that, the Professor has ensured that anyone without knowing the correct password, cannot open the tablet at all. Seemed like paranoia was all over him. Though on second thought, considering his mysterious death, attacks all over and Sam's kidnap, the professor, was correct to be paranoid. He had to go through an awful lot to keep his secret safe, to keep this away from the Danish billionaire.

'Yeah, you are right.' She said at last. 'But considering all the circumstances, it seems like he did a good thing.'

'You think Sam will have knowledge on how to open the iPad?'

'Richard has gone through a lot to keep this thing out of the hands of the unwanted people and ensured that it reaches to Sam, and Sam only. So yes, I think Sam will be the one who can figure out how to open this and get whatever information the professor wanted him to have.'

'Ok.' Mark breathed. 'So, we have to get Sam back. Mission Sam on the go.'

CHAPTER FIFTY-THREE

COPENHAGEN, DENMARK
8.45 P.M

'The Library of Alexandria?' Sam nearly laughed out. 'The burnt down Library of Alexandria?'

'Yes Sam.' The answer came from Alexander. 'The same one. It's somewhere out there. And I will get it.'

Sam, now for the first time, thought about the sanity of the man. *This man has lost it. He thinks he can find the Library which was burnt down repeatedly.*

'You have gone mad Alexander.'

'No, I am not.' The anger seemed to surge through his veins, but after a moment he controlled himself again. *I can't lose my temper now.*

'So you want to find a library which was burnt when Julius Caesar came after Pompey in 48 BC? Which was again burnt by Emperor Theodosius I in AD 391 and then again by the order of Caliph Omar in AD 642?' Sam said, now laughing sarcastically.

But the Danish seemed to be impressed.

'You certainly know your history kid.' He said, eyes shining.

At the same time, another person entered the room. He seemed a little overweight, somewhere around his fifties and German by nature. The round wire-rimmed glasses sat on his pudgy nose a little awkwardly. The moment he saw this man entering, a memory triggered somewhere in Sam's brain. The Indian felt like he had seen this man before but couldn't remember right now. He was followed by a Middle Eastern man, with features of that an Arab, and the eyes as cold as ice. Then his gaze went into the hand of the German man. The bespectacled man was holding ----

'That's the Professor's letter.' He cried out seeing the letter in the man's hand.

'Indeed.' The man said, his German accent thick. He then looked towards Alexander. 'This letter is written in a language used for coding by Da Vinci himself. It's a mirror writing.'

'Wow.' Alexander replied, contemplating the fact. 'But first, I want you to meet this young man.'

He then took the man by the hand and waved towards Sam.

'Dr. Berthold Weber, meet Sameer Rawath.'

****

Dr. Berthold Weber. *Yes, that's how I know the man.*

'You are Dr. Berthold Weber.' Sam said, shocked. 'You worked with my mom and dad on their Nazi project.'

'Yes.' The historian said with a smile. 'Yes, I worked with the Rawaths. But when your mom and dad didn't respect the offer of Alexander, I did.'

That shocked Sam more than anything. *How can a historian like him join a ruthless businessman like Alexander Penbrose?*

The Danish saw the question in his eyes and replied.

'Sam, your mother, and father denied my offer of a million, but Berthold showed more compassion, and came to me for that same offer. And for last eighteen years, we have been trying to figure out a way to find the diary of Hans and the Library of Alexandria.'

That insanity, again.

'First of all, that Library was destroyed more than two millennia ago. There can't be any trace of anything there. Second, the ruins are still there in Alexandria for all to see. Third, a true lover of books will never kidnap or murder anyone to get his hands on a ruined library.'

'Sam, you misunderstand me.' Alexander said. 'I am not a book lover. We need something very specific in the Library. And believe me when I say that the Library is real.'

'How do you know?'

'Because Hans mentioned it in his diary.'

'And how do you know that?' Said the Indian.

'Let me tell you that.' This time said Berthold. 'I was working on the life and works of Julius Caesar when I came to know about his true nature of travel to Egypt. Do you know that Pompey was his son in law?'

Sam nodded. Indeed, Caesar's son in law was Pompey.

'Ok. So, let's start there.' The German started, with a meticulous interest, as if he was teaching a class. Once again, Sam was reminded of his parents as well as Professor Richard Hedley. *All the historians and archeologists seem to like teaching history to others.*

He pushed the thought away. He needed to understand what was going on. And how everything was connected to the Library of Alexandria.

'Now, from the records of history on the different discussions that Caesar and Pompey had one thing always came up first. Whether it's a message sent through Caesar to Pompey or some of his army person listened or stumbled upon their conversations and recorded it somewhere, but the details were still the same.' The historian spoke excitedly. 'It always spoke about some scroll, a scroll with each and every detail of an awesome power among other historical facts. Something to do with limitless energy.

So the story goes like this. Caesar tells Pompey that he has heard about a scroll from someone working on his uncle Gaius Marius's detail. After that, he had researched for nearly twenty years and found that a person named *Callimachus* had written certain scrolls or texts which has details on many of the historical facts. Among them--'

'Is that *Callimachus of Cyrene?*' Asked Sam, stopping the German.

'Yes, yes exactly.' Berthold nearly jumped in his excitement. 'You are good Sameer.'

Sam just stared in reply.

'Ok, so continuing the story.' Said the historian. 'Among those scrolls was one which described something with unlimited power and limitless energy. As Caesar was not aware of where the scroll was, he asked his son in law Pompey to locate the scroll.'

'Hmm.' Sam took over, understanding the concept. 'So, let me get this straight now. Would like to check if I understood it correctly.

Pompey then started to search for that scroll and finally found it in Alexandria, Egypt in a Library. The Library of Alexandria.'

'Yes. And then he went rogue. He did what everybody does in greed of power. He wanted the scroll for himself. He starts the civil war with Caesar and then himself flees to Alexandria in search of it.'

Sam nodded. Except for the scroll part, everything else he had already heard or read earlier.

'But he didn't expect one thing.' Sam said, going forward with the history. 'Being murdered by a Military officer of Ptolemy XIII.'

'Right. And here is where the legends begin. As per some of the records from different sources who have researched either on Pompey, Caesar or the Library of Alexandria, Pompey was murdered by a man named Septimius who in turn was helped by Achillas and Savius, the two assassins. But it was Ptolemy XIII originally who had appointed them. Now some believe that Ptolemy actually found out about Pompey's actual intention and had him killed.

He also suspected that Julius Caesar would be coming in pursuit for the same thing in a few days and as a result ordered all the books and scrolls to be moved away to another location, leaving only a handful of books, which were not needed anymore, just to create the illusion of the library being there, when in fact, it was moved to a secret location.

Anyhow the final touch was a brilliant one. Many of us archeologists have visited the ruins of the ancient Library, and there are signs which suggest that the fire was actually intentionally started in the library when Julius Caesar came to siege the library.'

'How can the fire be intentionally started?' Asked Sam. 'According to the history, the fire was because Caesar had lit up one of his ships to start a chain reaction in order to escape the siege, which in turn caused the library to burn actually.'

'Well, Sameer.' The historian said. 'Isn't it suspicious that the fleet of Julius Caesar which was lit more than a mile away from the library can cause it to burn? With all the water and Alexandrian soldiers between them?'

Berthold gave him a minute to contemplate this. When he first thought about it, he was suspicious too, all those years ago.

Sam seemed to give it a thought. Then he looked back at the German, urging him to continue.

'So, when Caesar actually came to take the Library, he found all the books are gone and the library on fire. He was shocked at the outcome and didn't live more than four years. Till his death, he wondered what exactly happened to the Library.

Then nearly four centuries later Emperor Theodosius I tried to find the books, suspicious of the fact that the Library existed somewhere outside Egypt. So he orchestrated the hate for paganism, which gave him an opportunity to search throughout the city for the books or anything related to the Library. Failed after months, being infuriated, he started destroying the building.

Again, the same thing repeated itself three hundred years later when Caliph Omar tried to find another holy copy of the Quran.'

'But how does Hans know about them and wrote down in the diary?'

'Well, that's another story.' Said the historian, looking back towards Alexander. 'Which I think Alexander can tell you.'

'Enough of the history lessons Berthold.' Alexander said, his patience wearing off. 'What's in the letter of the Professor?'

Sam also wondered the same thing.

The German took out a translation from his pocket and shoved it towards the Danish when suddenly, Sam with his uninjured hand snatched it out from the historian in a flash.

And he started reading it.

<u>CHAPTER FIFTY-FOUR</u>

Sam,

I am making sure that you are the only person who can read this. In the event that I can't meet you for some reason, maybe even murdered, this is the way that I can tell you what has happened.

You have always been my best student. You have shared my interests in archeology for all these years. Though I believe that interest is in your blood. Your parents were one of the most knowledgeable archeologists I have ever met in life.

Both your parents and me were obsessed with the Archeological history of the Nazis during the Second World War. It was during that quest that I had met your parents in the historical Concentration camps in Poland. It was before your birth.

However, we pursued the different angles of the Nazi history. While I was more interested in the routes taken by Heinrich Himmler, your parents were following the path of Ahnenerbe, the archeological division of the Nazis itself. You might remember the book – 'Ahnenerbe history of the Nazis' that your parents wrote.

During that path, they came to know about Hans Schleif, the head of the Ahnenerbe during the end of the Nazi period. They tried to find the notebook of Hans and the reason for his death.

However, they seemed to have got the notebook but there was someone else who was also behind the notebook.

Your parents had told me during their visit to Germany that they have got a location on the notebook, but someone powerful is behind them. However, after their unfortunate death, when I tried to find that notebook, I have been unable to do so for so many years. But it was just a week ago that I was contacted by a labor from your parent's detail.

I went to meet him and found this notebook with him.

Yes, the notebook of Hans. I still don't know why people are behind this notebook, but I fear that I am in danger too. So I made a digital copy of it and destroyed the original notebook.

In this quest, I also came to know about another thing. Your parents didn't die of drowning. They were murdered.

Sam, this is the legacy of your parents and you need to think what to do with it. But I must warn you, people are behind this for many years, and you might get in danger too. Better to leave it here Sam.

God bless you, Sam.

Yours Truly,
Professor Richard Hedley.

P.S.: So sudden is the Advent of Mother and father.

The letter ended here.

It made Sam feel multiple emotions at the same time. He felt empty, sadness, rage, and confusion at the same time. The Professor had never told him much about how he had met the Rawaths. He never said to him that they were all looking in the Nazi history, into the World War II. But out of all of that, the one thing that stood out to Sam was the most difficult thing to comprehend.

In this quest, I also came to know about another thing. Your parents didn't die of drowning. They were murdered.

He had always known his parents drowned at Markkleeberger See near Leipzig. They were searching for something there, and accidentally they fell and drowned, though their body was never found.

And now the Professor wrote him a letter saying that his parents were murdered. This is not true.

If it's true that means......

'You killed my parents?' He asked, staring straight into the eyes of Alexander.

188

The Danish was about to ask one of his bodyguards to get the letter from Sam when the Indian asked him this sudden question. The red-rimmed moist eyes looked straight at him, looking for answers.

'Rita and Hemanth were killed?'

The confused expression on Alexander's face seemed genuine.

Along with confusion, Sam thought he saw something else, surprise.

This man doesn't have anything to do with my parent's deaths.

'Give me the letter Sam.' Alexander said placing his hand in front of him.

'No, you killed them.' Sam said, a drop of a tear running from his left eye.

'I didn't kill your parents Sam. I never knew they were murdered at all.' Alexander kept speaking, but with his eyes, he ordered the bodyguard nearest to Sam to approach him silently. 'I would have never harmed them.'

Sam looked at him, his eyes moist with fresh tears.

'Think about it, Sam. If I wanted to kill them, I would have never offered them a million euro.'

The bodyguard reached his side and, in a flash, pounced upon the Indian, causing both to tumble on the ground, with Sam below the man. With Sam overpowered now, Alexander snatched the letter and started reading it.

Unable to do anything, Sam just watched.

'Where's the digital copy of the notebook?' Alexander said, after two full minutes of reading.

By then, Sam has returned to his bed, under the watchful gaze of the two bodyguards in the room and Dr. Berthold. The Middle Eastern man also stood in the corner.

'It's out of your reach Alexander.' Sam laughed. 'Mark and Eva are already on their way to wherever the Library is and taking every step to keep it safe.'

'THEY WILL FAIL.' The cry reverberated through the whole room. 'I am the blood of Hans' family, who took his own as well as the life of his children and wife so that nobody else can find the library and the scrolls. And I will fulfill his legacy.'

'You are an heir of Hans?' Asked a surprised Sam.

'Yes boy. I am.' Said the angered Danish. 'Hans went to Egypt and Alexandria in 1936 for the archeological excavation on Olympia, Greece. During his way back to Germany, he had stopped for a week at Alexandria and there he found the evidence that the fire in the Library was initiated from inside rather than the outside. So, he followed through the discovery and in the end, he found the final resting place of the scrolls after years of research. He wrote down the details in his diary in hopes that he would visit it someday in future in order to get a good look at all the different scrolls. But destiny didn't allow him. Heinrich Himmler came to suspect during the fall of Reich that Hans had found something. Fearing that they would be tortured to discover what it is, he killed his sons, his wife and then himself because he didn't want the Nazis to find the Library. They would have plundered and destroyed everything.

But before death, he kept his diary in a secret place and sent a letter to his brother in Munich saying that he has found the legendary

Library of Alexandria and the details are in his diary and how it can be found. Nobody in the Reich actually knew that Hans had a brother, so their search ended with the death of Hans. But the legacy was passed on to my dad Ulrich from my grandfather Jurgen, who was also the son of Matthias, the brother of Hans.

Now, you see Sam, this diary belonged to my family, and I will get it. Now tell me where the digital file is.'

Sam laughed, annoying the Danish businessman more.

'I have no idea, Alexander.' The Indian said, stopping his laugh. 'But I am sure my friends are going to find it and reach the Library much before you do.'

'Very well.' Alexander replied. 'I see you don't want to do this the easy way. Fine. I am giving you tonight to think. Tomorrow you better tell me where the copy is, or I will find your friends and then kill them slowly.'

With that Alexander stormed out of the room, followed by his bodyguards and Dr. Berthold.

CHAPTER FIFTY-FIVE

KARUP AIRPORT, DENMARK
November 16,
12.45 A.M

'Welcome to Denmark.'

The owner of the voice had to shout for his words to reach the recipients. Mark and Eva were coming down the jet when they heard the sound. The plane was still powering down, so the shout was understandable.

The man who welcomed them was still in the shadows, coming from behind the tail lights of the jet. So the features of the man were not apparent, though Eva noted that the man was well above six feet tall, maybe six-four. The man's features got cleared once the Americans landed their feet on the ground of the *Karup* Airport.

He seemed to Eva to be a giant of a man. Up close it looked like he was easily six-six of height, with well-built a physique. The muscles were bulging out, even when the guy was wearing a battered old brown leather jacket. The way he carried himself, to Eva, it looked like that the guy must be spending a lot of time in the gym.

Currently, he carried a small backpack behind him and was rubbing his goatee.

Once he came near them, he put his backpack down and stared hard towards Mark.

'How are you, old man?' The person asked the American.

'Like I have just banged your wife.' Mark replied stoically.

Eva watched with growing horror as the man's expression changed to one of total hate and rage, and then suddenly without giving them a time to think, the man burst out laughing. From her side, Mark also laughed out loud, and both embraced each other with open arms.

'Hello, Dixido.' Mark said while being under the embrace of the big man.

'Hello, my friend.' Dixido said smiling, 'you haven't changed a bit.'

'Neither have you.'

Then Mark introduced Eva to him.

'You look like an Irish beauty to me.' Dixido said while shaking her hand.

'Tha…... thanks.' Eva said, attempting to release her hand from the big man's palm without getting crushed.

With all the pleasantries done, they started to move away from the parked jet.

'So, I understand you want to rescue a hostage from the *Kastellet*?' Dixido asked once they were away from the jet.

'And I need gears and your help to do that Dixido.'

'Yes, I know.' The big man spoke while moving towards another part of the airport. 'I have checked the plans for the *Kastellet*, and it seems to be heavily guarded. I will show you the plans once we are aboard the helicopter. Also, it seems to have a good level of securities.'

'Then it's good I asked for your help.' Mark said smiling.

'Ha! Yes.' Dixido seemed happy to join their rescue mission.

Eva instantly became very fond of the guy. It seemed he was a friendly guy with a big heart and body.

It was nearly five minutes later that they reached for their helicopter.

'Wow.' The first word came from Mark. 'That's a sexy bitch.'

'I bet it is.' The big man replied, beaming with pride.

Eva also got mesmerized by the beauty of the helicopter. It was easily the sleekest helicopter anyone had ever seen. The name was emblazoned just near the tail section of the aircraft. Bell's FCX-001. Mark remembered hearing of it being displayed in the Heli Expo 2017, christened as the sleekest helicopter in the world. Indeed, it seemed to take the same amount of space as the newest two-person electric cars, just a little longer in length. The front half of the helicopter was entirely covered in tinted glass, whereas the other half was covered with reinforced steel white in color. The cockpit had got a single seat for the pilot, and behind that there were two rows of two seats each, making it look like the interior of a van. The only drawback seemed to be there were no weapons hold to carry any guns or missiles. But considering the sleek figure and the interior, it seemed to be made only for passenger travel, not for a fight.

'I remember this one.' Said, Mark. 'It's the FCX-001. But are you sure it would fly?'

'The original prototype was made not to fly. However, my employer here, the Macro Industries CEO, had bought three of these and upgraded them to fly.' Said Dixido. 'So yes, it will fly.'

'Let's get inside.' Eva said, excited.

'Yes.' Mark said, a smile creeping on his face. 'Let see how good the security for Alexander is.'

194

THE THIRD ORDEAL

THE RESCUE

CHAPTER FIFTY-SIX

COPENHAGEN, DENMARK
12.55 P.M.

Sam was not able to sleep. Not after what happened.

Every time he closed his eyes, the conversations with Alexander and Berthold came back haunting him. It felt like a never-ending nightmare. And to think of his parents somehow involved in this, it was all too much to take in.

And what had everything got to do with the Library of Alexandria? The whole world knew that it's been burnt to the ground due to Julius Caesar's siege. And now, according to this Danish tyrant, it seemed that the person believed sincerely that the library existed somewhere else. But to Sam, it still felt like farfetched.

How could a group of people have lived somewhere else with so vast a collection of scrolls and books? And indeed, even if the library existed somewhere else, why does Alexander want it?

The scrolls talk about an immense power, and absolute energy.

That's what he had said. Alexander wants that power, that energy. And he was willing to kill for that. If indeed that kind of power existed, it would be foolhardy to hand it over to a person like Alexander. From the brief meeting that Sam had with the billionaire earlier in the evening, it was clear that the man was a psychopath. To have such power in his hand, there was no saying what he would do with that.

But Sam still couldn't believe it. The Library of Alexandria. To have such a vast collection, to gain knowledge of the ancient world, it's a dream come true for any academic. If considered only about the discovery of such scale, it's an archeologist's dream. And Sam felt no exception. The moment Alexander told about the library, Sam in his mind started to piece the things together.

'Ok.' He said to himself. 'So, mom and dad were searching for the Nazi Ahnenerbe when they stumbled upon the diary of Hans. When Alexander wanted, they tried to keep that away from him, suspecting correctly that the tyrant will misuse the scrolls. Then they kept it somewhere safe with one of the persons in their detail, and after all these years, the Professor found the trail of the diary and recovered it. He also tried to keep it away from Alexander.' A cold determination crossed his face.

All his close people have always tried to keep the details about the Library away from the Danish, and he would also do the same. He won't help Alexander get his hands on the Library or any of its scrolls. He would fight until his last breath to save them.

'So, Hans got info on the Library's location and kept it with himself in his diary. In order to save the location from the Nazis, he hid the diary and committed suicide, after killing his family. Why does everybody keep doing that? Either getting killed or killing others to keep the secret safe?'

Maybe there's some truth about the awesome power in a scroll.

197

Sam always believed that the ancients had superior knowledge than the modern people to create such marvels in the world. His study on archeology and history through the years have made him believe that the ancients somehow had knowledge on constellations, on solar energy, on other different kinds of scientific knowledge that the modern scientists were still struggling to find. Some of the examples were the Stonehenge, the Pyramids.

So, it was not a surprise to him that a specific scroll might contain the knowledge of remarkable energy. The ancients were indeed capable of that.

But in order to keep Alexander out of the Library, he had to find it first. And that couldn't be done staying as a prisoner here.

Time to find out a way out of here.

CHAPTER FIFTY-SEVEN

01.25 A.M

The *Kastellet* seemed like a crude pentagon from the top. From the FCX-001, it looked like a sketch made by a child who tried to make a pentagon, but something in between had gone awry. Though the symmetry of the plot was stunning. Northern and Southern parts of the plot concluded with two endpoints of the Pentagon each, whereas on the western part the fifth point stood. Instead of any point on the southern side, it was totally flat, giving the occupants an uninterrupted view of the beach and the famous iconic Little Mermaid Sculpture by Edvard Eriksen, one of the most visited tourist attractions in Copenhagen.

However, the building itself was in the middle of the plot, covered on all sides with lawns. And in each point, Mark saw two persons covering the entry and exits. The main hall on the southern end held a museum that Alexander owned and hosted free concerts and events there. However, from a birds-eye view, at an elevation of 14,000 feet, and through the night sky, even with the US Night Vision (USNV) PVS-7 Gen 3 Auto-Gated Military Spec Goggle – latest among the night vision binoculars used by Delta force and the United States Marines, and supplied by Dixido for this operation, Mark was having difficulties to see all the security personnel covering the ground.

'So, what do you see?'

The question came from his front. Mark looked back from his window towards from where the question arose. Eva was not looking at him; instead, she was looking in front of her.

How is she flying the helicopter?

For the few years that Mark had known her, Eva had never told him anything about flying helicopters. Today after seeing this sexy chopper, Eva insisted that she would fly and that she had been trained in NSA for the flying lessons. Though wary at first, Mark could now see that she really was a fantastic pilot.

'Not much.' Replied Dixido, while checking his own gear. 'Guards are securing the perimeters. They are outside on the lawn and covering the area, so I would estimate them to be total ---'

'Twenty people outside.' Mark completed for him. 'We have to assume that there would be a minimum ten people more inside. So that makes around thirty people.'

His face suggested the odds were not good, but all the occupants knew that they have handled more in the past. Eva gave hold of the chopper to the other person in the team, Evan, the original pilot of the helicopter and gave the correct coordinates for the helicopter to land. Before leaving the cockpit, she gave some more specific instructions to him.

The men looked at each other and smiled.

'Looks like it's Beirut again, old man.' Dixido said, looking at Mark, smiling.

Mark also smiled, remembering the two of them along with ten more people rescuing more than fifty hostages from the American University of Beirut nearly a decade ago.

Indeed, it's the similar texture.

'Yeah, the only difference was we had more firepower with us.' Mark said looking at his own gears.

A bag was donned on his back, same as others. Other than that, there were three SIG SAUER Mosquito with suppressors attached to them for stealth with loads of reloads, few AR-15 or the Armalite Rifle-15 as its more commonly known, again with suppressors. There was also a Wildey and few Desert Eagle 50 present, but those would create too much sound for his liking. As a result, Mark had discarded those. Dixido even brought an M24 sniper too. And along with all these, there were the knives. The most eye-catching among them being the Ontario MK 3 Navy Knife, the most used blade for close combat by the Navy Seals. Along with that, there's also few Ka-Bar knives and Mark's personal favorite Strider SMF.

It took them another two minutes to holster their weapons and get ready for the upcoming action.

'You sure you will go too?' Mark asked Eva this time.

'Yes, I am.' The determination in her eyes told Mark everything he needed to know. He nodded.

'Well then, I think we are ready.'

'Ready we are.' Shouted Dixido.

'Switch to comms.' Said Mark and switched to the 3M Peltor MT90-01 headset. He had always been impressed by this type of headset, mainly because it's a throat microphone. As a result, it absorbs vibrations directly from the wearer's throat by way of single or dual sensors worn against the neck. So, this kind of microphone was right for both noisy places such as on a motorcycle or in any covert operation like this, where silence is a necessity.

'Comms Check.' He said, speaking in a hushed voice. 'Everyone able to hear?'

'Yes.' Eva's voice came into his ear.

'Yo. Loud and clear' Dixido's voice boomed in his ear.

He looked at his companions to see them give him thumbs up.

With that, Mark opened the door on his side, and the three of them jumped out of the chopper.

CHAPTER FIFTY-EIGHT

For the first few seconds, to Eva, it felt like a dream come true.

I am flying, soaring through the clouds in the air, like a bird.

It's really one of the best feelings she ever had. She felt like a bird, free and careless of anything happening in the world. The wind blasted at her face, despite the fact she was wearing the flight navigator snowboard goggles. Her burgundy hair was tied in a bun, but still, a lock of hair floated in front of her eyes. The bag on her back felt very light, though it contained everything needed for the mission.

She looked at the duo on her both sides. Mark was on her left while Dixido on the right side. And then she looked down. And that's when the realization hit her.

It's so much high. I am free falling.

The city of Copenhagen seemed to be far away, only the lights showing up. The body of water below looked like a void, with nothing but blackness. From up here, nothing could be seen except the lights and the darkness in between the two parts of the city.

The vertigo set in. And a cry started to leave her mouth.

'Aaaaaaa…………aaaahhhhhhh.'

'Oh Wow.' Mike's voice came into her earpiece. 'Stop that. You are blasting our ears.'

'B…. but…... but…. I…..will…..fall.' Her words came out of fear, in different installments.

'Nope. You won't.' Dixido's voice intruded her earpiece. 'After a few seconds you have to deploy the suite, and then you can fly.'

Along with those words, another sound came into her earpiece, which sounded a lot like the Danish person laughing. That made her annoyed with herself.

She really had not been in the field ever. So, jumping from a helicopter had never been her thing, she just did that on instinct because she needed to be there on the ground, fighting and saving Sam. The man whom she felt attracted to, was down there in the *Kastellet*, among numerous guards and a billionaire psychopath. When Mark and Dixido try to save the Indian, she couldn't just sit by and watch. It was her instinct that dictated her to be there to save Sam, and she wanted to be there when the Indian gets saved.

'Deploy the wingsuit now.' Mark's voice interrupted her thoughts.

At first, she didn't even remember how to deploy the wingsuit. Then she remembered what Mark had told and shown her, just 15 minutes ago.

'This is the wingsuit.' Mark had said when they were on the chopper. He was carrying three neoprene suites in his hand. Over the next few minutes, he started wearing the suite and once done, he looked like a circus trapeze master in that jet-black suite.

He then had helped Eva getting into her own suite. It felt really light. 'The neoprene suite helps you not to get cold in extreme weathers, and it's also water resistant.' Mark said. 'When you land in water, the oxygen cylinder in your bag will be deploying itself, and the

204

oxygen mask will be deployed automatically when the heart rate increases with the initial contact with the water.'

Then he had shown how to deploy the wingsuit in order to fly and guide the body in the air.

'You need to press this button.' He said, showing the red button near the waist of the suite. 'It deploys the wingsuit to glide through the air.'

The wingsuit she and the others were wearing now, was sent by Mark's employer earlier, one of the items for which he got delayed in planning and executing this rescue operation. It's one of the new inventions, the light fiber neoprene wingsuit, lighter than any other ever created before. One of the latest inventions of DARPA, The Defense Advanced Research Projects Agency of America, responsible for the development of emerging technologies for use by the military, which somehow his mysterious employer was able to get him for this mission at Denmark.

She pressed the red button near her waist and then threw open her arms and legs just as Mark had shown. As a result, three flaps sprang opened, two for each of her hands and one for her legs. The arm flaps connected from her wrist to the waists on both her sides and the third from her groin area to the ankles. She looked at her partners, and both of them had deployed their suites the same as her. And from her vantage point, they both looked like Batman soaring through the air, only without the cape. The winds flipped through the flaps and as a result, they glided through the air in much less speed than a few seconds ago.

She remembered what Mark had said next.

Use your body as a fuselage. The flaps will work as your wings.

All three of them soared through the air, descending at a much slower rate than they were earlier. The speedometer connected to her wingsuit was attached as a wristwatch, and currently, it read 35mph. That means the fall rate is presently less than 60 kilometers per hour.

'Aim for the water between Trekroner Fort and the Langelinie.' Mark's voice came over the earpiece.

The altimeter read 6000 feet when she could see the city of Copenhagen and the water, albeit a little blur. But the outline could be made out now. But she could see right now, all three of them were way out of course, above the waters way away from Copenhagen. So, she glided herself more towards the Trekroner Fort and with a smile noticed the other two following her in the air.

'It seems you have picked on the wingsuit quite well.' Dixido said over the earpiece.

'It seems you had underestimated me Dixido.' Eva said laughing, all the while enjoying the view and her own flight.

'Indeed.'

After a minute, the altimeter read 100 feet when Mark's voice came in through the earpiece.

'Retract the wings in…. '.

Mark started the countdown.

'3'.

The altimeter in Eva's wrist read 80 feet.

'2'.

The lights and the city could be seen clearly now. The Trekroner Fort and it's V-shaped harbor could be seen with crystal clarity.

'1'

The altimeter read 65 feet. She pressed the red button again. Instantaneously, the flaps retracted, and she started falling with too much speed.

The water came rushing, and she suddenly remembered Mark's another suggestion.

While falling in the water, keep your head up and the toes down. Reduce your volume to break the surface of the water without making much noise and without hurting yourself. Falling from a distance in the water will hurt if the volume of the body is more while connecting to the water surface.

She did that, and a moment later her feet broke the surface of the water. Just before her head entered the water, she saw the other two men also entering the water with twin splashes.

Then her head entered the water, and everything became dark.

CHAPTER FIFTY-NINE

1:30 AM

Need to find a way out.

Sam was pacing in his room for the last few minutes, trying to devise a plan to get out of the hands of the Danish tyrant. He had tried getting out of the room 15 minutes ago, but saw a couple of guards outside, with Bergmann-Bayard M1910 pistols in their holsters. He had never thought that his interests in firearms would let him know the guns and other arms of his enemies, in such a situation.

The guards seemed to be always on their toes, with earphones in their ears and eyes on everything moving. It really was difficult to get out of the room, and the *Kastellet* in turn, without them noticing. From what he had seen, everywhere inside the installation, the guards were all crawling the facility, relentlessly.

I really hope Eva and Mark are already on their way to the location for the Library. The iPad should have all the information from Hans' notebook that should guide them to the Library's actual site.

Eva and Mark should have already opened the tablet, and it would be the logical step to follow Hans' path for them to get their hands on the Library than to try and come to this lion's den to save him. But somehow, he had to find a way to be out of this place, before Alexander again came back and decided that Sam was hiding something. Or, if he learned about the iPad that the Prof had kept.

As of now, it was only this night that he had got to get away from this facility. But in the daytime, when he was awake, Sam had seen that the lawn outside had been crawling with security people wielding guns. A lot of these guns were Heckler and Koch, but he had seen Kalashnikovs and few of the Russian Scorpions as well. The only thing that explained such a variety of firearms was that Alexander had employed mercenaries who worked for hire for him. But from what he had also seen inside the *Kastellet*, the guards outside his room and some others were not from any mercenaries, rather from some security firm. The suits they were wearing have the same logo, and they all carried the same pistols.

He remembered Mark's words, what he had told during their transatlantic flight from India to Maryland.

Alexander has a lot of thugs in his employment to do his dirty work. Some are mercenaries while some others are from a private security firm.

So, getting out of here wouldn't be easy in the daytime. Even if he got out from here, this was a completely different country where he knew no one. Sam also didn't have his passports and other documents with him right now, as those were in Eva's house when he was shot and kidnapped.

'The hell with passport.' He muttered to himself while stopping his pacing.

He looked outside through the window and saw the mercenaries all roaming around on the lawn. From his side, only the eastern part of the facility could be seen, where the beach and its adjacent area could be looked upon. At this hour, the road beside the beach seldom had any vehicles going. He couldn't be sure, but it seemed like something suddenly fell into the water a long away from where he could see clearly. But looking at that side, his mood dimmed a bit.

Even if I get out of my room, I have to cross all the security in the building, then I have to pass the lawn, crawling with so many mercenaries. Even if somehow, I manage to do that, the ocean is outside, which can't be crossed.

So, there's no way to get out of here.

There has to be.

He turned from the window and started towards the washroom.

A plan had started to form in his mind.

CHAPTER SIXTY

Silence.

Total and absolute silence.

It felt like as if she was in a tomb. Everywhere it was dark, and to Eva, at first, it felt like she had died. There was no sound, no sound at all. It felt like the world had come to an end, and everything, every living being on the planet have been eradicated from existence. Any side she tried to move her head, there was pitch darkness. Not a single light could be seen anywhere.

Is this what hell's like?

But the cold hit her a second later. The water all around her didn't get in contact anywhere in her body, except her open face. The pool was cold, really cold, colder than she had actually thought.

Am I going to die?

The thought was suddenly interrupted by a sound.

Hissssssssssssssss.

It felt like gas leaking from the tires of a vehicle. Before she could comprehend her predicament, a hose suddenly came out of her neoprene suite and attached to her nose, covering the nose and lips. At last, she could breathe.

It took her another few seconds to adjust her eyes and being brought back to reality. The automatic oxygenation in her suite had been deployed after she went into the depth of 30 feet underwater when her heart had started to beat faster than usual. The oxygen mask had deployed itself when the nanobots in the suite detected her heartbeat and the pulse rising, all the while sensing the presence of cold water and the depth she was in.

Mark had told about the phenomenon once he had got the neoprene suites sent to him by his employer from DARPA.

'Get your underwater helmets and the micro scubas.'

Mark's voice interrupted her thought. She looked at the altimeter in her wrist. It showed 60 feet underwater. The bag on her back was also waterproof, acquired by Dixido, on request from Mark. She opened the bag while being in underwater, aware of the fact that the other two were doing the same. Once the bag was opened, she inserted her hand and immediately found the underwater helmet but pressed on to find another thing. After searching for around ten more seconds, she got the thing out, and then ziplocked the bag again.

She donned her helmet, imagining Mark and Dixido doing the same with their helmets, all the while floating in the water, and keeping hold of the thing, she had just got out of the bag. Then she pressed a small black button on the side of the helmet, which illuminated the UV light on the thing, bringing light to the world around her, albeit a little. Next, she pressed a small blue button on her waist, in the suite, which suddenly started to fill suite with air only to her palms and feet. A minute later, both her palms and feet looked like flippers, for easy travel under water.

And then she looked on all her sides.

The inky blackness all around her suddenly became colorful. Mark had told them that it was better to use UV lights rather than anything else so that attention would not be drawn. The pinkish hue coming out of her helmet illuminated only a few feet in front of her, but what she saw took her breath away.

She had never imagined so many colors underwater. What looked like a fish with greenish tendrils, she understood after a second, was actually a plankton floating around her. Several fishes swam around her, curious to understand this new creature among them. There were all the colors among those fishes. Eva saw some of the fishes illuminated in yellow and orange, while some others gave a bluish-greenish hue.

She looked at the small bottle like thing in her hand. This was the micro scuba which Mark had got for this operation. Latest of the scuba tanks, the Triton Scuba tank was the most miniature sized scuba tank ever created. Though the original Triton scuba tank was constructed in South Korea, the American Harvard University had upgraded it to a better version. Now combined with the DARPA technology, this was the first scuba tank of its kind. Looking like a blue water bottle of half liter size, this scuba tank was capable of carrying a person of 500 pounds at the height of 700 feet below water at a speed of 60 mph. Truth be told, it was not a real scuba tank, but a cross between underwater jet ski and a scuba tank. While it looked like a bottle and easy to carry, the function of this device was the same as any underwater jet ski. It's ultralight and super-fast at the same time.

'Let's rock n roll.' Dixido said over the earpiece.

'Yup let's save a damsel in distress.' Mark said. 'Not…. a damsel though.' He said, reconsidering his words.

Eva smiled and started the engine of the Triton tank. She could picture in her mind the frown on Mark's face while calling Sam a *Damsel*.

Vroooooom.

With a sound, the engine started, and all three of them sped towards the Den Lille Havfrue, the Little Mermaid Island.

CHAPTER SIXTY-ONE

Sam felt claustrophobic.

Minutes ago, he came inside the washroom having an idea. A way to escape this prison, the Danish tyrant's domain. The ventilator on the top of the restroom felt to him to be the only way out of this place.

I didn't think it through.

It had taken him a better part of 10 minutes to open the ventilator standing on top of the sink, and then crawl into the ventilator itself. Dragging himself through the narrow opening proved to be the hardest thing to do, thanks to the bullet wound in his shoulder. And to make matters worse, the bleeding has started again from the injury. The shoulder felt burdensome to him. Though bandaged, the blood had made the shirt red in no time.

He had done the only thing he could think of. He pulled open his shirt and tied it tightly above the bandage, to staunch the flow of blood. In a way, it helped to dull the pain a bit as well.

Can't think of the pain right now. Need to get away before the guards realize.

It won't take them long to figure out that Sam was missing. And it would be easier for them to find out that the only way to get out of the room was this ventilator.

But that was not the biggest problem. Sam, at the age of 26, was not someone very skinny. His broad shoulders nearly touched both walls of the ventilator. And that was not the end of it. The place felt dusty,

215

with the smell of dust covered everywhere. Even his knees and elbows were covered with dust.

And it's cramped and hot here.

Sam was already covered in sweat. Sam wondered if the warm air from the Air conditioner was being flowed through this way and then shoved out from here somewhere.

Probably that explains the heat here.

The other problem that Sam faced right now was the darkness. It seemed to be pitch dark in front of him. There seemed to be no use of his eyes here. So, using his hands as his eyes, Sam urged on. A minute later, he reached a junction where there were two open sides in the ventilator. One going to the right side, whereas the other on the left. By now, his eyes had adjusted to the darkness here, though that didn't help much.

There's a light somewhere.

Looking to the right, he could see a source of another light, probably an opening into any other room or washroom. Squinting his eyes a bit, he tried to gauge the distance. It seemed he could reach there in the next few minutes, provided the claustrophobia didn't set in.

Twice in three days in tunnels. Way to go, Sam.

Being an archeologist will be fun. That's what the Prof had said to him.

Only if he knew that he would die to save an archeological site and that Sam would be crawling tunnels for the very same reason. And probably Rita and Hemanth Rawath were also killed for similar reasons. All the killings and kidnappings for an archeological site.

A pang of sadness came into his mind. Pushing the thought away, he urged on.

He needed to reach that opening.

CHAPTER SIXTY-TWO

1:42 AM

It took them exactly 12 minutes to reach the shore of The Little Mermaid.

The Triton scuba tank had lived up to its name. The trio reached the shore at the end of the line at the expected time. However, instead of reaching up and breaking out of the water, they did quite the opposite. They started swimming down.

'ETA 90 seconds.'

The voice of Dixido reached her ears. Eva tried to look up and check if she was able to see the Little Mermaid sculpture on the shore, but only inky blackness shrouded her everywhere. As a caution, just before reaching the coast, Mark had asked everyone to switch off their UV lights, resulting everything to turn into blackness once again. However, what she has seen in the last 12 minutes would be etched entirely into her memory for the whole lifetime.

The different fishes, the planktons, the colors, the rifts, the ridges – everything was so much colorful, so much full of life.

Now I know why Clark Mann talks so much about Marine biology.

From the time she has known Clark, a fellow marine biologist in employment with the Harvard University, and part-time helper in NSA for underwater travels and sonar experiments, he had always been telling her to visit the underwater life in Miami, Florida.

'You will not believe how much color and life you can see underwater.' He had always been telling her.

They have crossed some ridges in between, and behind one of them, she had seen a cluster of fishes, maybe a thousand of them in total, none more than an inch long. The UV rays fell in them making them glow in a whitish hue, in turn making the whole place alive. She has seen other different kinds of fishes which she never knew existed. The different types of squids, sea turtles and krill, were all new to her. At one point, she had seen an orange colored plank floating in front of her, which suddenly started zigzagging on her path. It was not until Dixido told her through the earpiece that it's a *Spanish Dancer*, a kind of snail, that she had really understood what was looming in front of her.

'We have reached, just a few feet ahead.'

Mark's voice brought her back into the reality and the work at hand. The altimeter in her wrist read 90 miles below the shore.

'Let's switch on the lights now.' Dixido said.

On cue, all three of them switched on their UV lights again, illuminating the water around them. After twenty seconds of traveling forward, they came face to face with an iron gate.

Not many people knew about this gate, except the harbor people. This gate was built on 1443 AD when the capital of Denmark was shifted from Roskilde to Copenhagen. But it was not until 1601 AD, during the reign of King Christian IV that this gate was rebuilt and opened. But it was not for the use of the public. It was built as a secret getaway in case the city was sieged by the Romans or Ottomans or anyone else who decided to take over the city.

The *Kastellet*, being built later at 1626 AD, sat on top of this tunnel ranging from the SMK or *The Statens Museum for Kunst*, as it's known publicly, to this gate. The other opening of this tunnel was on the easternmost side of the Museum, but it was closed entirely with concrete and bricks. However, what most people forgot was that the opening in the Museum was not the only opening for this tunnel. One of those openings was just inside the lawn of the *Kastellet*, which was now covered by a makeshift windmill.

And that was their way in.

The gate was bolted shut with a lock in place.

Mark opened his backpack and got a curious looking pistol out in his hand. The front half of it was green while the trigger side of it was black. This was the *Core Drill* used for underwater drilling and as a bolt cutter. Then he pushed the nozzle on the lock and pulled the trigger.

With a blue haze, the bolt cutter started sawing through the lock with ease.

Once the lock was released, all three of them started pushing the gate. After being shut for a long time, it took the strength of all three of them to force the entrance free of the hinges and the rocks on the ground.

Once free, the gate opened wide for them. But space hinted for a single file.

'Let me lead.' Mark said and started off.

With that, all three of them swam inside the tunnel in a single file.

CHAPTER SIXTY-THREE

'Fuck.' Muttered Sam under his breath. 'There goes my tetanus shot.' In the darkness, there was a steel plank jutted out from the corner that grazed his left arm a bit, drawing blood. Though he couldn't see it, the blood started flowing slowly from the gash.

The light he had seen earlier from the turning was from another washroom, but there was no way to go out once he was able to climb down. The door to the restroom seemed shut from the outside. As a result, it forced Sam to again crawl back up into the ventilator and move bit by bit through the darkness again.

'Yes, *Rabiy*.' Sam suddenly heard someone speaking just a few feet below him. 'We have to use Alexander's rage to our advantage.' Sam guessed there was a room just below him, and someone was speaking there. And judging by the way the person was talking, it felt like there were only two persons in the room chatting with each other.

He heard someone speaking in a hushed tone something, probably the second one present in the room, but he couldn't make it out, plainly because it was too low for him to hear.

'Yes. But Sam needs to co-operate with him.' Sam was stunned. It seemed someone was trying to coerce Alexander to do their dirty work and needed Sam to help the Danish to get whatever he wanted.

Probably someone else wants the Library for their own purpose. And in the process, using Alexander.

Again, the other person said something with too low a voice. He couldn't get much more, except a couple of words.

'Having killed.'

'Sure *Rabiy*. I had killed the Professor and thought that we have everything with us to find the Library and booby-trapped his house to get rid of anyone curious enough, but now it seems without Sam's help we can't get to it.'

Sam couldn't believe what he heard just now.

So, someone else was working behind Alexander's back and killed the Professor, with or without the consent of the Danish. Maybe they have convinced the Danish that it's the only way to achieve the Library. They had thought raiding the Prof's house would give them Hans' notebook but didn't count on Hedley being so much secretive and code obsessed. After that, they had tried to blow up the house of the Prof and get rid of Sam or anyone else investigating his home. But why?

The only logical explanation was, the person who wanted the Library for himself, didn't have the resources or finances to arrange the search for the Library. So that person must have found out the connection between Hans and Alexander and used that knowledge to convince Alexander that his family legacy was connected with the Library. And that's how that person had been using the Dane to his own means.

Sam laughed out in his mind.

No good comes out with allying yourself with the bad guys. There will always be someone to stab you on the back. Everybody works selfishly for their own means. Too much is going on. Need to get out of here.

Sam started crawling again. He needed to find a way out of here, to be free, to be ready for what was coming, and to alert his friends.

But most of all, he had to make sure that these selfish bastards never get to the Library of Alexandria.

He started crawling again.

CHAPTER SIXTY-FOUR

1:55 AM

'Dammit. This place is cramped.'

Eva looked behind her. Her male companions were standing behind, head to head. The place really was small and dusty. There were two windows and two doors, and all of them were shut except for a sliver of an opening on the window facing the first building of the *Kastellet*. And that was where Eva is standing right now, trying to get a good look at everything, while the others started arranging the weapons and getting out of their wingsuits.

Eva looked outside. Today seemed to be a new moon night, and therefore, the whole area didn't have too much light, save for the lights coming from the buildings itself. The street and other buildings were further away from the *Kastellet*, thanks to the moat surrounding the star-shaped Castle on all sides. That suited fine for the trio inside the windmill, as the street lights were not coming into the lawn and the late night meant less interference. However, few lights were still coming, from the backside of the building facing the windmill and from the adjacent ones.

But, that was not enough at this time of the night to illuminate the whole lawn and the *Kastellet* itself.

And that was the advantage Mark, Eva and Dixido have decided to take. The darkness would be the best cover for them to enter and rescue Sam.

'Yup, that's fucking true.' Dixido said, his head bent at an awkward angle for not being able to stand fully upright.

Eva looked at the ceiling of the windmill.

It really is very low. Can't be more than five feet.

She had felt this the moment she got inside the place and stood. It was tough to get rid of the wingsuit for her without standing upright. So, she could feel the pain for the both.

'So now comes the hard part.' She said once the others had got out of their neoprene suits and arranged the weapons for them to carry. 'We need to find where Sam is kept here.'

The first two parts of their mission – Jumping out of the helicopter and landing in the water, and then traveling underwater and infiltrating the *Kastellet* have been successful. But now came the third part, which none of them had any idea on.

'That we have to find out.' Dixido said, and before anyone could say anything, he opened the door near the window where Eva was standing and came out of the windmill.

'*Hvor var du?*' A guard coming from the northern side, perimetering the area, asked seeing Dixido.

'*Jeg lettet mig selv.*' Dixido said in a gruff voice.

The guard looked at the Danish man a few seconds suspiciously and then started off on his way. Dixido waited for the man to get out of the sight and signaled his mates to come out.

'You are a madman, you know that?' Eva said in a very low voice, looking at all sides, in case any more guards came out.

'That's what I have been telling him for a long time.' Mark said, grinning.

The trio looked at each other, appreciating their appearances. In order to blend into the environment, they had dressed in black clad, same as the other guards in the Castle, before they had jumped off from the helicopter. That was the reason a minute ago that the guard didn't get too much suspicious of the fact that a perfectly unwanted person was among them. Moreover, all three had Kevlar plates inside their dress, which helped them in two ways. Firstly, it would cover them against any firing, and the second and most important was that it covered the features of Eva.

No guard would be dumb enough to believe that their master had suddenly recruited female mercenaries among them.

The faces being covered with a balaclava, same as the mercenaries guarding here, made their facial features also covered, ensuring that the guards would not be able to learn their identity.

'We need to fan out and search for Sam.' The NSA agent said, looking at the security camera near the light on the back of the first building in front of them. Currently, it was looking at the northern side and making the turn very slowly. But it would see them within next 30 seconds if they didn't move away.

The three of them moved in three directions in a flash. Eva started her march towards the north, Mark on the south, whereas Dixido straight towards the building.

'Be in the comms.' Eva said, before disappearing on the northern side, the right of the front building.

'We will be.' Mark said, looking back, after which he also disappeared on the southern side, left of the front building one, entirely opposite to that of Eva.

'Righto.' Replied Dixido, while he reached the light and the camera.

'Let us dance.'

CHAPTER SIXTY-FIVE

'Is it done?' Eva asked in a hushed voice.

She had taken refuge behind some bushes on the front side of the building they had seen from inside the windmill. Before her, just after crossing the bushes was a pool of clear water, covering the distance between the first building they had seen, and the second building just opposite that. The area seemed to crawl with guards roaming around. She has been to this place, almost twelve years ago with her parents, when it was only used as a museum and tourist place. Not much of it she remembered, but what she was seeing right now was entirely different from what it was at that time. For one, there was not so much security, and the place looked very different than before.

She could see on her side, two big buildings, looking like storehouses standing apart from each other with a distance of fifteen feet among them. And on the extreme left, stood a building, looking like a right-angled triangle, with the right-angled side facing the first of the storehouses.

It's same on Mark's side as well.

The specific feature of the *Kastellet* was its symmetry. She had remembered that part, and now she could relate it.

I had seen it last time when I visited but forgot.

Both of its sides were a mirror image of each other. The storehouse kind of building actually looked like a high school hostel to her at this time of the night.

'Just a minute.' The hushed voice of Dixido came in through her earpiece.

'We don't have time for you to jerk off, Dixido.' She heard Mark saying.

'Ha ha, very funny.' Said Dixido. 'There Eva, it's done now.'

'Good.' She said. 'Thanks.'

She opened a handheld GPD Pocket, known as the smallest laptop in the world, and connected it to the network. She opened the Command prompt and typed few commands. Dixido has attached the handheld micro camera to the external camera on the first building's back.

'There.' She said in a hushed voice. 'I have hacked into their network.'

'Ok good.' Mark said, in a similar hushed voice. They could see a total of four people around the pool covering the distance between the two buildings and two more sentries roaming around. 'How much time do you need?'

Eva typed in her laptop and said her words at the same time.

'I…. need…just…a…few…. seconds.' She continued typing for a few more seconds. At last, she hit the enter button.

'Ok, now I am into their camera feed network, and recording.' She said. 'Stay put for at least a minute, you guys.'

'Sure Eva.' Dixido said, from the back of the building. 'Just my back is itching standing below the camera…. oh no.'

'What happened?' Eva asked, hearing his distressed voice.

Dixido looked at his right and saw the man coming from the northern side of the perimeter towards the windmill and stop a minute. And then the thing happened that he dreaded.

The man saw him from the corner of his eyes and turned towards him directly.

Dixido kept himself calm, and spoke very slowly, just enough for his partners to hear from his voice box.

'Guys, I am in trouble.' He barely heard his own voice and was not even sure if Eva or Mark could hear. But he spoke the next words carefully too. 'The guard from the north is back, and he has seen me.'

****

'Eva how much time?' Mark asked in a panicked voice.

The whole plan might be broken down in bits.

Their whole plan was based on their anonymity. If Dixido got caught somehow, Mark was sure that he could fight the guys out without any hassle, but if the camera catches any glimpse of the fight or anything suspicious, Alexander would be quickly notified. And also, all three of them would be captured.

If that happens, then Alexander will move Sam out to some other secure location where we won't be able to find him, or we all will be trapped.

'Calm down you two.' Eva replied. 'Dixido, I need you to hold on for 15 more seconds.'

She could see the camera feed on her laptop from the backside of the first building. It was looking right now at the southern side, where the silhouette of another guard just disappeared, and the person started reappearing on the left security camera on the front of the building, far behind where Mark was hiding right now.

The laptop screen was divided into several smaller screens, all showing the different feeds from the various cameras in the Castle. 'I am holding on, but not sure how much the guy would want to hold on Eva.'

Dixido could see the man coming his way, but not too fast. He seemed to be just curious about the fact that why would someone on his entail be near the camera when there was nothing to guard.

'Just 10 seconds more.' He heard Eva's hushed voice on his earphone.

This guy would be onto me in 5 seconds.

'*Hej! Hvad laver du her?*' He heard the man asking while coming his way.

Dixido looked around himself, to find something, to say something to keep the man at bay for at least a few more seconds. He looked at the camera and saw it turning from the south towards the windmill very slowly.

'*Jeg...Jeg er bare....*' Dixido started saying and looked around himself.

'7 seconds.' Eva's voice entered his ears.

Without thinking, Dixido did the only thing that came into his mind. He turned towards the wall of the building, just below the camera, and started opening the zip of his pants.

'6 seconds.'

'*Hej, kig ikke der.*' The guard said and started running towards him.

'*Jeg ... Jeg kan ikke vente.*' Dixido said, all the while opening the zip.

'5......4......3.' Eva said in his earpiece.

The guard came near to him and put a hand on his shoulders.

'Don't attack the guard now, Dixido.' The voice of Mark could be heard, over the earphone.

'*Bror ... gå i vaskerummet.*' Dixido heard the man saying from behind him.

'2......1.' Eva stopped counting. 'The cameras are now hacked and in the loop.'

He was about to turn and hit the guard, now that the cameras were all hacked and looped with the same footage, there was no fear of cameras recording or seeing anything when he heard the unexpected voice of Mark.

'Dixido, don't hit the man. We might have got a chance here.' Mark said in his earpiece. 'Go inside the castle. We can find Sam inside.'

'*Ok, lad os gå til vaskerummet.*' Dixido said while turning back and at the same time closing his zip.

The man gestured for him to follow and started to take Dixido to the first of the storehouses on Eva's side.

CHAPTER SIXTY-SIX

2:00 AM

Sam was drenched in his own sweat.

It took him nearly 20 minutes, and a zigzagging crawl through the ventilation system to reach an open hatch at last. By the time he found it, he was thoroughly drenched with sweat and dust. The blood flow had already staunched, thanks to his now battered shirt.

At last, I am out of there.

He found a hatch lose on the top ultimately and climbed through that into yet another washroom. It was dark in here. The only light seemed to be coming out of an adjacent building just a few yards from the window of the toilet. And when he looked through there, he could see two sentries making rounds in the space between the building he was in and the adjacent one.

Sam guessed he was in a kind of a building which was long and straight, judging by the path he had taken in the ventilation shaft. The rooms were on both sides, like that of any good hotel, and as a result, he had to take a zigzagging path to negotiate his way to find an open hatch to one of them.

He had seen the architecture of the *Kastellet* before, during his second year studying the European architectures, and now judging everything, it seemed that he was in the second-long building on the northern side of the plot. He could see the Little Mermaid sculpture from his bedroom window, and he was in a long building. So, it didn't take him much to do the math.

Now to find a way out of the building.

That was the difficult one. But first, he started by freshening himself up, cleaning himself off the dust and sweat in his body. He dared not turn on the lights of the washroom, as it might catch attention. It took him five more minutes to clean himself up and then come out of the restroom.

I need to find something, something which can help me get out of the place.

The room looked similar to that he was in earlier, the only difference being the room he currently was in, was a little smaller than earlier one and from the bedroom window, there is an uninterrupted view of the sea and The Little Mermaid statue.

I am in one of the last rooms of the building.

He opened the only wardrobe in the room and smiled at what he saw.

At last a little bit of good fortune.

Two sets of the costumes wore by the sentries outside was neatly kept there.

Sam started changing his clothes.

Boom. Boom.

It was then that he heard the consecutive explosions.

CHAPTER SIXTY-SEVEN

SOMEWHERE IN THE WORLD
5:45 AM

Everybody was gathered in the main hall.

Like every day, it was time for their prayer. Outside, there was a snowstorm happening from last evening, and everything was covered in snow. Not that it mattered to the residents of the place. At this height in the mountains, the snowstorm was a natural phenomenon for nearly two millennia for the residents here. What they do here, what they were all sworn to protect holds much more value for them than the environmental crisis.

The Grandmaster was sitting on the middle of the platform, and the attendees were all gathered in front of him, all praying silently. The prayer had always been the same for the last 2000 years. They were all peace-loving people, nothing to do with the outside world. But the threat still kept coming. Time and again, people were always searching for their haven, trying to disturb their peace.

Like now.

Grandmaster opened his eyes to see all his people in front of him, praying with their eyes closed.

It will not be the same anymore. Dire times are ahead.

He waited for a few more minutes for everybody to complete their meditation and prayers. Once everybody opened their eyes, he spoke –

'My friends, my most loyal people. It seems the time is nearly upon us to come to the light of the new world.'

He stopped for a moment and let his words hang in the air, building the tension in the room.

They need to know, they need to understand.

'This new world is a dying world. The people here are all consumed with machines, technology, websites. The problems for food, energy, and water are consuming this world day by day. The rich are becoming richer, and the poor are becoming poorer. Everybody is busy either on their phones, their laptops or their Televisions and all the fancy gadgets and websites. A new kind of warlord runs this world now. They call themselves tech giants. They play with the people's money, they play with their information and daily lives.'

He paused a moment to catch his breath. At the age of nearly a hundred, it was difficult for him to speak continuously.

'But,' He said, raising his index finger in the air, 'There are people in the world who try to do good. Who wants the world to be a better place, who want to share knowledge, who want to understand our history and the past.

And now one such person will be coming soon, as was foretold by our forefathers. As was told by the Oracle a long time ago. But from what I have heard, he is in grave danger now, which was also foretold. For that reason only, we will also be facing great threat ahead, people with insatiable greed will also be visiting us, and will try to destroy everything we stand for. And though it pains me to admit it, it was me for whom this person is in great danger now, and maybe we too.'

A low murmur echoed through the room. The others, nearly fifty of them, all started speaking with each other in hushed tones.

He could almost read their lips, their minds.

How can this be his fault? How are someone in danger and he is responsible? Why do we bother if someone is in danger? And why do we have to reveal ourselves to the world? Why now?

The Grandmaster raised his right hand to stop the murmur. Instantly all the speaking stopped.

'You all must be wondering how it is my fault, and why we should be bothering about that?'

Someone from the back raised his hand respectfully. The Grandmaster saw that it was a young boy, was eager to ask something.

'Speak my boy.'

The man respectfully bowed his head and asked the question that was in everybody's mind in the room right now.

'Who is this person in danger?'

The old man sighed.

There's no easy way to tell this. I have to face what I have started.

He looked up and smiled. A sad smile.

'His name is Sameer Rawath.'

CHAPTER SIXTY-EIGHT

COPENHAGEN, DENMARK
2:02 AM

'What the hell just happened?'

Alexander was trying to sleep, and plainly failing to do that, when he heard the twin explosions. The night had been hard already. Speaking to Sam brought back the unpleasant memories of how Rita and Hemanth had denied helping him even after the promise of a million dollars at their disposal.

Such arrogance.

And the trait had apparently been passed down to their son. Sam would not be helping him, and that was clear when he spoke to him. The boy got the same attitude as his parents. But there was something else that bothered the Danish Billionaire more.

Rita and Hemanth Rawath were killed? How is that possible?

He remembered the first time he had heard the news of the death of the pair in December of 2000. They were supposedly searching for something that Alexander had assumed was the same diary of Hans that he was searching too, when the ice above the *Markkleeberger See* broke, and they were trapped in the water below, not finding a way out of the water and drowned.

He had checked the letter from the Professor a dozen times after it was taken from Sam, forcibly, by his bodyguards.

How did the Professor come to know about their death being a murder?

But those answers have to wait.

Less than a couple of minutes ago the twin blast rocked the place. It was just a minute later that Sabir came running to his aide and faced his outburst.

'Who is bombing the place?' Alexander asked again.

'I…. We…we are searching for that sir.' Sabir stammered while replying.

He was also dumbfounded by the fact that someone could really dare to create a blast in such a massive security compound.

'Search faster.' Alexander shouted at the top of his voice, in the process making the other man flinch.

'And why the hell alarms are not sounding, and the place is not on lockdown.'

Just then two of his personal bodyguards came running into the room and threw the door open.

'Sir.' They said matter-of-factly. 'There is two air to ground missiles that blasted in the compound. The signature seems to be that of ARMIGER missiles.'

That got his attention.

'What?' The Danish person's eyes nearly popped out of his face.

'Why would German Air Force attack us?'

'We are checking everything sir.' Said the other bodyguard. 'The first one landed on the security office on the northern corner, and the second on the southern side, taking out the radar.'

'Check it quick!' Alexander said, still fuming with fury. 'And why the hell no alarms are blaring?'

'Sir.' Sabir said, checking his phone. He had just received a message on his earphone, from the compound security. As the head of security here, it was always him that the first communication on the security breach came up.

Alexander looked at him.

'Sir.' Sabir said again, breathing deeply. 'It seems the security is breached. Our systems are hacked.'

CHAPTER SIXTY-NINE

2:05 AM

Mark smiled.

The tactic had worked like magic. He remembered what his commander, Brad Thor had told him during the Desert Storm mission many years ago.

A good tactic is like magic. Use that to your advantage.

And he had done exactly that now. The ARMIGER missiles or Anti-Radiation Missile with Intelligent Guidance & Extended Range, as it was more commonly known, were fired from an Island situated near Saltholm. Eva's instructions to Evan, the pilot of their chopper, was carried out precisely. Using the rangefinder and GPS lock, it was not difficult to pass along the coordinates of their strike to some of Dixido's friends located in the Island. The ARMINGER Missiles, being long range, had no problems to hit their target at all.

And it worked out perfectly.

All the sentries and security were running around everywhere. The distraction had worked out perfectly.

Now to find Sam.

****

'I am going to the northern building and scouring through them for Sam.' Eva softly said in her earphone. 'You take the southern side. I will find Sam and Dixido and meet you at the exit point.'

'Be safe.' Mark said and ran off towards the southern buildings.

'Don't worry, you trained me well for last few years.' Eva said with a smile, at the same time dashing towards to the second storehouse like building on the northern side.

For now, she knew that Dixido was on the other building and if Sam were there, he would surely be found there somehow. The other building, however, no one had entered. It was just three people who have exited from there only after the explosions.

One of them went to the security room, probably to check the security breach there.

The other two went together towards the southern building where their radar was situated.

So, none of them are Sam.

She ran and entered the building quickly------

---And came face to face with two security guards, wearing the same dress as her.

'Where are you going?' One of them asked. The balaclava was off from both of their faces, whereas she was still wearing it.

Eva searched for words.

They won't be particularly happy to hear a female voice behind the balaclava.

The immediate area didn't have too many lights, or it wouldn't have been difficult for the guards to see her features and identify her.

'Why are you not answering?' The guard's eyes narrowed with suspicion.

Eva looked at the other guard and saw him moving his hand to position the Heckler and Koch SP5K in his hand for the attack.

'Let me see your face.' The first guard said and moved a bit with his hand in front of her to rip off the balaclava from-----

Suddenly Eva lunged forward and caught the extended hand of the guard in her left hand, surprising him, while at the same time with her right hand she hit his elbow from below in a perfect Brazilian Jujitsu style with an open palm.

Craaack.

The breaking of the elbow joint made a horrible cracking sound, bending the guard's hand at the utterly opposite angle. But before the guard could cry out, she turned her own right elbow and hit his Adam's apple with crushing force, choking the guard in the process. The second guard, on the other hand, was just behind the first one, for which he was not able to open fire on her. She took advantage of her position and forced the already incapacitated guard on the second one, and both gun bearing guards tumbled on the floor. Without giving them a chance to recover, Eva struck the first guard on his face with her boot, drawing blood out. The guard finally succumbed to her attacks, out cold.

The second one, on the other hand, was below the first person, and before he could come out of the surprise, Eva hit hard with her boot on the hapless guy's jaw, making a couple of his teeth coming out clean from his face, followed by the crimson blood. A hit again on his nose made him join his mate.

The whole thing took ten mere seconds for her.

'I am going to find my friend.' She said, at last answering the question, while brushing her hands.

She looked at the passageway and headed off.

CHAPTER SEVENTY

Mark was trying to avoid any battle that would slow him down.
At first, that seemed easy when he entered the inverted L shaped building which appeared to be deserted for the most part. It was at the end of the smaller side of the L that had two guards covering. He guessed it was probably the security barracks here.

He tried to get away from the place unseen, but his shadow betrayed him in the end. At the junction of the L where he was standing, had a light behind him, which made his shadow fall on the wall opposite to him, while he was checking the other side.

And that was his mistake.

Gunshots followed him, guards being on their edge due to the missile attacks, and as many as four people came running out of the barracks.

'Bollocks.' He said while running. 'It's not fair, four against one.'
He looked back and saw one of the guards reaching the junction, some ten feet away from him, and turning this side.

Still running, Mark pulled out the SIG SAUER Mosquito from his back sheath, and in a swift motion turned his upper body, aimed and fired two shots towards the goon following him. The bullet hit squarely in between the eyes of the guard, and hurled him back a few feet, making his body fall on the next comrade who was just coming behind him.

Mark followed through his attack with two more bullets into the second person's chest and stomach and resumed his run.

I can't evade forever. This corridor is too long.

He saw a door on his right and lunged at it-----

Just as a bullet hit the top of the door, missing him by inches.

Following through his action, Mark used his weight and the right shoulder to break through the door, all the while bullets impacting around him.

'Fucking amateurs.' He said, hitting the floor of the room and grimacing. 'Can't hit even within 10 feet. They deserve to be underpaid.'

By the time the sound of the footsteps was beside the room, Mark was fully ready for what was to come. A bullet on the ankle of the first one, shattering his *talus* bone, in the process making him fall headfirst into the room. Another one on his temple to finish him off. The second guard didn't even get a chance to understand what happened when he was hit in the chest by a bullet, hurling him back.

'And that's how you hit the target.'

A minute later, Mark left the building with four bodies lying behind in the corridor.

CHAPTER SEVENTY-ONE

2:07 AM

Dixido's predicament was entirely different than his other partners. As soon as he had entered the building, he had directly stabbed the man who had brought him into the building gruesomely through his head with the Ontario MK 3 Navy Knife which was hidden inside his sleeve, in the wrist sheath.

After that, the next few minutes was a firefight on a full-frontal force. He had used the AR-15 on full auto to incapacitate the remaining guards, a total of twelve of them on two floors.

'Yeah, dance baby.' He cried once the last of the guards hit the floor. He looked around everywhere and saw his handiwork. Everywhere around him the walls were all colored with bright crimson. In between those, the brain matters were scattered everywhere along with their former owners.

The sight looked gruesome- bodies here and there, gaping holes everywhere in them, blood and brain matter everywhere. But Dixido didn't seem to care about them.

'Dah!' He said casually. 'Now let's find Sam.'

It took him a few more minutes to search every room in the building. 'That's a waste.' He said to himself, and then to his earphone, 'Mark and Eva, no one in this building.'

'Same here.' Came the voice of Mark from the other side. 'Moving to next building.'

Then with a pause, he said again, 'Dixido, the score's 4 here.'

'Ha!' Dixido laughed out loud. 'You should see here. Score triple than yours.'

'Boys, calm down.' Eva's voice came now in the earpieces. 'We have a job to do. I am searching in the building, but so far no luck.'

'Ok, let's continue the search. Mark out.'

'Yeah. Going to the other building. Dixido out too.'

With that, Dixido left the building and moved to the other L shaped building.

CHAPTER SEVENTY-TWO

Sam was in an entirely different situation by now.

Minutes ago, he came out of the room wearing a security guard dress and then moved quickly and swiftly towards the main gate of the building. After hearing the explosion, he had correctly guessed that the area must have been under attack.

Not surprising. A maniac like Alexander would have enemies. And one of them probably decided it's time to get a payback.

When he came out of the room, he had seen Alexander, along with Berthold, his two personal bodyguards and the Middle Eastern man he had seen in the evening. All four ran towards the first floor, whereas the last man dashed out towards the exit.

Through the ventilation shaft, he had moved to the other end of the building where he got the disguise. So, it took him some time to come to the middle of the building-----

-----And was suddenly greeted by a curious site.

One of the guards, wearing the similar balaclava as him, was fighting two of the other guards. *Seems they have a rogue guard here.*

The rogue guard was fighting fiercely. First, he took hold of one of the guard's right hand and kicked hard on his kneecap, breaking the joint with a sharp crack. At the same time, the guard flew his other leg and hit the chest of the second guard who was coming to attack him, causing that goon to tumble on the floor heavily.

'Aaaahhhhhhh…'. The first guard whose knee got broken was cut short of his cry by a powerful uppercut from the rogue one, who fell like a broken tree on the floor.

By then the second guard has started shooting on the rogue one, figuring out the truth at last.

The rogue attacker ran towards an open door on his left to evade the flowing bullets at which point Sam took the opportunity.

Enemy of an enemy is my friend.

From behind he came up fast and without any pretense directly hit the man with the heel of his boot on the spinal cord from behind. The force was so much that Sam's foot had a ringing sensation for next couple of seconds. The man was in worse condition. The hit had connected to his lower vertebrae, probably breaking one of them too. The rogue guard approached him cautiously seeing his attacker down in pain and quickly drew out his weapon, a Desert Eagle in his hand, pointing directly at the Indian's temple.

'Wait wait.' Sam said quickly, keeping his hands up. 'I am trying to help you.'

He was not ready for what happened next.

The guard hit the second and final guard with his boots, incapacitating him and opened his own balaclava-----

----At which point Sam saw that the person standing in front of him was not a *he* at all, but a *she*. And it was a person he knew very well.

'EVA.' The joy came out of his voice quickly. In front of him was standing Eva, who had fought for the last minute with two of the building's guards to get to him.

'Sam.' A smile came to her face, a smile of triumph, tiredness, and relief. 'Here you are.'

They embraced each other, and without thinking anything, suddenly they kissed each other. A kiss full of passion and relief. The involuntary kiss took both of them by surprise.

'Found Sam.' Eva said at last once they finished their kiss, looking and smiling at Sam. 'I repeat, I have got Sam.'

'Well, well, well.' The sound of clapping came from behind her, and with that came an accent, a Middle Eastern one. 'It seems a romantic reunion was underway.'

Eva, being on the other way from where the sound came, looked at Sam and saw a hint of fear in his eyes. Quick as a feline, she turned and pointed her Desert Eagle and ------

Blam.

The gun flew out of her hand. The Middle Eastern had been quicker than her.

'EVA. No.' Sam said and grabbed her. The bullet has just grazed her thumb, snatching the gun away.

'I am fine Sam.' She said, standing up on her feet. Blood flowed a little from her hand, but from the looks of it, the damage was not too severe.

'She's right Sam.' Alexander said now, standing behind the man who fired the pistol. 'Sabir here—' he said, gesturing to the Middle Eastern man, 'had been one of the best shooters in the Syrian army.'

Sam now saw them clearly.

Except for Sabir and Alexander, three more guards were standing with them, just beside the stairs to the first floor.

Sabir then spoke in his earpiece.

'It seems we have another rogue guard here.' He said looking straight at Eva and Sam. 'Guards, find him and kill him. Mark Brent should not be alive anymore.'

CHAPTER SEVENTY-THREE

2:15 AM

A few minutes later, Sam and Eva were sitting on the first floor of the second building of the Northern side of the compound. It was the same building where Sam had been held captive for the whole day.

'So tell me, Miss Eva,' Alexander said, smiling at his captives, 'How do an NSA agent gets involved with an archeological student and the Library of Alexandria?'

'Library of Alexandria?' A look of surprise crossed her face, and she looked at Sam.

'Long story.' The Indian said with a helpless smile.

'I am sure it is Sam.' The Danish said to him. 'But tell me where's Mark?' He said again looking at Eva.

The room they were sitting seemed to be a network room, where there were multiple computers at work, set in a desk a little away from them. Sam and Eva were seated on two chairs, with their backs towards the machines, facing Alexander and his four bodyguards now, two being joined a few minutes ago, and Sabir along with Berthold.

The last man was somewhere else in the compound and came here as soon as Sabir had asked a guard to fetch him here.

The four bodyguards covered the exits and the lone window in the room, two people for each. Berthold was seated a little behind Alexander, and Sabir was pacing, speaking on his earphone.

'What do you mean the whole building empty?' Sabir said, and then listened for a minute from the other side. Alexander also looked at him with a questioning look, hearing the anxious voice.

Sam guessed the news was not good.

'Sir, the other building on this side seems to be empty now.' Sabir said grimly, now gesturing at Sam. 'It seems his friend Mark has caused havoc there. 12 of our guards are found dead there.'

Eva smiled hearing the news, whereas Alexander's reaction was entirely different.

'What?' he said with a voice of absolute shock. 'What about the other buildings?'

Sabir heard the report for a few more seconds and looked at him with a grim expression.

'It seems there's more than one person in the compound who is running around killing our guards.' He said, all the while looking at Sam as if he was the one responsible for everything. 'As of now, except our 12 sentries outside, and we 5, no one is alive.'

'But.... But,' The Danish stammered, before regaining control. 'How can there be only 12 people alive out of 40 guards here?'

'I think the sound of guns we heard earlier, which made you suspect that they were here for Sam,' Sabir said, 'those were from two different people. One was heard from the next building from us, while the other was on the left corner of the compound, on the southern side.' A look at Sam and Eva, and he said again – 'So, I believe, we are dealing with two people, with hardcore military background.'

'Where are they now?' Alexander cried out, looking at Sam and Eva, in the process making Sam flinch.

But Eva looked tougher, sitting comfortably in her seat, and enjoying the show. The shout from the Danish Billionaire didn't even make her eyes flicker.

'Shout as much as you want Alexander.' She said, staring straight into the eyes of the Dane and smiling at the same time, 'You have no idea what Mark and Dixido can do.'

'Well in that case,' Sabir said, taking big strides towards her, 'Let's see if they can save you.'

He unholstered the Witness HTR .45 6in BL 10th pistol and pointed it directly at the cryptologist's head, right between the eyes.

CHAPTER SEVENTY-FOUR

2:10 AM

At the same time while Eva and Sam were kissing passionately each other, Dixido and Mark were doing their own battles.

Dixido had gone to the extreme eastern building after hearing that Eva had got Sam. He entered the building armed with an AR-15 and a Kalashnikov, which was taken from a dead guard earlier, in both of his hands. As soon as he reached the building, he wreaked havoc into the building with both his guns blazing. He looked like a crude version of Sylvester Stallone from Rambo movies.

It took another 2 minutes and nearly a hundred bullets for him to get the building enemy free.

'Dixido.' His earpiece crackled, and Mark's voice came in. 'What are you doing big guy?'

'Turning this place into a dead zone.'

'We should----.'

Mark's voice ended abruptly with a grunt, suggesting that he got busy with someone attacking him.

At that point, the big guy heard the scraping of some footsteps behind him, and before he could react, suddenly a strong hand gripped him from behind and started choking him with his arm. At first, he was so shocked, that Dixido was not able to fight back for himself.

Calm yourself. Calm. Calm.

After a few seconds, once his mind was calm, Dixido started fighting back. Taking his height and weight to his advantage, he began to bend down, and at the same time dropped the two empty guns from his hand.

'Dixido, we need to regroup.'

In between the fight, he heard Mark saying. But with his throat being chocked upon, there was no way for him to answer. Instead, he focused on the task at hand and continued bending. When his face came level to his muscular abs, he felt the other person being lifted on his back, owing to the fact that the man was much shorter than he was. And the other thing that he understood now was that the man didn't have too much weight.

Taking this into an advantage, Dixido then used his two hands to get hold of the person's shoulders and without much of an effort, threw the person out. The person cried out on impact with the wall and collapsed instantly, suggesting that it would take a lot more to fix his broken back.

'Yes, old man.' He said now in his earpiece. 'What is it?'

****

Mark was running towards the nearest wall, followed closely by the last guard in the southernmost building. The bodies of the other four people in the building were left behind in the corridor. The guard behind him was brandishing a brand-new Ka-Bar knife, running with anger and giving a battle cry. The man have seen this American kill four of his friends in front of him with just his bare hands…... killing one with just a karate chop and breaking his neckbone, whereas two of the others were killed by twisting their necks and the fourth one he had just cracked his head like an egg on the western wall.

And the reports coming in from other sides suggested that this American was responsible for many other of his comrades to die. Now he wanted to take the revenge.

But Mark did a curious thing after reaching the wall. He didn't stop near the wall. Instead, he put his right leg in the wall and followed his left leg a little above it as if running in the wall vertically. Now, without stopping, the American just used his momentum to perform a summersault and bring his right leg with tremendous force on the top of the head of the pursuer, kicking him hard and causing him to collapse on the floor below him. A nanosecond later, Mark himself landed on the floor, erect on his legs and brushing his disguised dress to get rid of some imaginary dust.

'Shocking fall, eh?' He said to the fallen guard, though it was clear that the man was totally unconscious.

'Dixie.' He said, touching his earphone. 'It seems that Sam and Eva are captured on the northern building. Can you give me an estimate of how many sentries outside?'

'Sure boss.' Came the gruff reply.

Mark came out of the building, albeit a little on defensive.

No knowing if they have people here to capture us. Can't have them leverage Sam or us.

'Mark.' He heard the gruff voice of Dixido in his earpiece. 'Seems there are a total of 12 people outside.'

'12 people.' Mark said, thinking out loud, 'And all of them are----'

'All are on the northern side, going towards the long building you mentioned.'

'Hmm.' Mark said, still thinking. 'How many there Eva? Morse code, a tap for each person.'

A few seconds later, four taps answered his question.

'Ok, so four guards upstairs there, and 12 outside.'

His eyes glinted as a plan formed in his mind.

'Dixido, be where you are. I will meet you. ETA 2 minutes. Mark out till then.'

CHAPTER SEVENTY-FIVE

Sam looked nervously at the gun pointed straight at Eva's temple. The man holding it seemed as ruthless as they come. Sabir's eyes looked like he enjoyed the killing and he would stop at nothing to kill her. He opened the safety catch and put his finger on the trigger to put a bullet in between her eyes-------

'Nooooooo.' Sam cried at the top of his voice, making Sabir pause. Alexander and Sabir both looked at the Indian with amusement. Sitting in the chair, bounded from behind, he was not in a position to do anything.

'Sam.' Sabir said. 'Your friends have done a lot of damage to us and-
----'

Whooooshhhhh. BOOM.

A loud sound, and a second later everybody in the room got showered with bricks, mortars, and dust. The two guards standing guard near the lone window of the room were hurled as dolls on the other side. One cracked his head open on impact to the opposite wall, causing blood and brain matters oozing out of it, whereas the other hit Sabir directly, causing the gun to go off and hit the guard on the back.

Both the guard and Sabir fell to the ground, in a heap of arms and legs, and were instantly covered with bricks from side and top. Alexander fared no better. The explosion created a hole in the room from the outside, and while the blocks flew everywhere, one hit him hard on the left temple, causing him to trip over from his chair and creating a bloody gash on his head.

Doom. Doom.

The sound of 2 shots from a sniper and the two furthermost guards near the door dropped dead, brain matters splashing on the door. In the mayhem, Sam and Eva were also hurled towards the desk behind them and fell on the floor along with their chairs, hands bound behind them. But that was the thing that probably saved them from any more serious damage. The L Shaped computer desk worked as a shade for them from all the showering bricks and mortars.

'Eva, Sam.' Mark's concerned voice came into Eva's ear. 'You guys ok?'

Eva tried to speak and immediately regretted that. There was a whole lot of mist being created in the room due to dust, and some of them entered her mouth, causing her to choke and cough.

'Eva, you fine?' Sam said, trying to unbind his hands. Both their chairs were broken on impact to the floor, making it easy for Sam to open his bindings and help Eva stand up.

'Yeah.' She said, both on her earpiece as well as to Sam. 'We are fine.'

'Ok, can you guys come out of the blown hole and jump?'

****

Two minutes later, all four of them were standing near the pool. Dixido and Mark were standing with their head tall, Mark carrying an RPG-32 Anti-tank grenade launcher in his hand, while his friend carried an M24 sniper in one hand and an M203 in another. They carried with them a winning smile.

The other two were not so much in good shape. Sam's pain on the shoulder had increased a lot after falling due to the blast from the grenade launcher in the room. Eva also had hit a corner of the desk, causing her a lot of pain in her left hand. And both of them looked like they have fought a war, being covered with dust and grits. The black disguise had been torn in few places and has turned into white now.

And both their faces looked tired.

'What the hell was that?' Eva cried out. 'Why you had to blast us out?'

'Well, we thought that was the best way, to use this RPG launcher.' Mark said, laughing. 'And Dixie here was using his talent to scatter the sentries in different ways using the M203 grenade launcher, and at the same time using the sniper rifle to get rid of the other two guards in your room.'

'So, a thank you will be good.' Dixido said, with a deadpan face. Sam nearly laughed out the way the big guy said it and patted both of them.

'Well, thanks to you guys I am alive.'

Right then all of them heard a buzzing sound from somewhere above.

'And that's our cue.' Mark said. 'Ride home is here.'

'You radioed Evan?' Eva asked, smiling.

'Yeah baby, I did.' He said, moving towards a hanging ladder nearby, coming out from the chopper. 'Now let's get going.'

'You bet.' Sam said, smiling.

'I would like to know what's with the Library of Alexandria.' Eva said to him, smiling back while trying to balance herself on the rope ladder.

'Sure.'

THE FOUTH ORDEAL

THE RACE TO RICH HISTORY

CHAPTER SEVENTY-SIX

KATHMANDU, NEPAL

November 16,

6:05 AM

Ballav was waiting for the call to connect.

He usually received the call from Grandmaster, not the other way around. But the information he gained just 15 minutes ago from his informant was an important one, and it needed to be conveyed to the Grandmaster. This was the second time this week that he was calling the old man, instead of receiving calls.

And this was the third time he was calling now consecutively today.

Has something happened?

The first-time call didn't connect, and the second time it was not picked up. The problem was that where the Grandmaster and his order was set up, it was tough for the phone network to be received. As a result, it was only the Grandmaster who called him up if deemed necessary.

'Yes Ballav.' The voice on the other side said in a monotonous tone after picking up. 'Any news?'

'Yes, sir.' The Nepalese said on the phone, maintaining his composure. 'As per the latest news from Denmark, Sam has been rescued from the *Kastellet*.'

'Good, it seems we had underestimated Mr. Mark Brent and Miss Eva Brown. Right?'

'Ye…. yes sir. It seems both are quite resourceful.'

There was a long silence on the other side, making Ballav nervous. A trickle of sweat started forming on his forehead, which was unnatural considering the whole area of Nepal was facing colder weather than usual in November this year.

He looked at the Ganesh mountain from his balcony. It stood a long way from him, and some parts of it were covered with clouds at this time of the morning. It would be only after 9 AM that the clouds would disperse, and the peak could be seen a little clearer. Named after the famed Hindu Deity Ganesh, the Elephant God, it clearly resembles the face of an elephant on the southern side, with a ridge that was reminiscent of an elephant's trunk. The whole Ganesh Himal or the Ganesh mountain range consisted of four peaks out of which, only one and a half were visible from his vantage point. But that was enough for him, as he was able to see some parts of the white peak, making him shiver for some reason.

I don't know why the Grandmaster is so concerned about the Indian. What has Sam got to do with anything?

'Good.' Grandmaster's voice came from the other side. 'Very good. It will be a pleasure then to make their acquaintance.'

'Acquaintance?' Said a surprised Ballav. 'You…. you mean----'

'Yes. Exactly.'

Ballav swallowed hard, careful not to let the person on the other side know about his nervousness.

The next words made his nervousness much more.

'Come here Ballav. I want you to be here when Sam arrives with his friends.'

'Y…. yes sir.'

CHAPTER SEVENTY-SEVEN

COPENHAGEN, DENMARK
November 16,
9:05 AM

'So, let me get this straight.' Mark said, sipping on his coffee.

'Your parents were searching for Nazi history, specifically on their archeological details when they came across Hans Schleif's diary, right?'

Sam nodded his acknowledgment.

After last night's rescue, the trio was holed up in the same base of Dixido's friends in the security firm near Saltholm, from where earlier the ARMINGER missiles were launched. Eva and Sam both were bumped up a bit after all the fight, and though the wounds have been patched up, still the shoulder was sore for the Indian. Mark had gone ahead and arranged for a tetanus shot for him as well, after hearing his little adventure in the ventilation shaft. A sleep for few hours have helped a bit for him, but still, it seemed like he could use a few more days of rest. Not that he wanted it right now.

Last night on his way to this island, he had told everything he came to know in the *Kastellet* to Mark and Eva.

'And then Alexander had offered them money to hand over the diary.' Mark continued. 'Now, they assumed correctly that he was going to try some evil thing and kept the diary away from him. Then they contacted somehow the Professor and told him everything about the diary, which the old man didn't believe.'

'And then your parents died.' Eva picked up from where Mark left.

'And they left the diary with someone they trusted, from whom after so many years the Professor found the diary. And that was bad, considering that he died transferring that information to you. So, he did the only thing he could and kept it hidden with clues leading you to it.'

'And now Alexander Penbrose wants it to go to the Library of Alexandria.' Sam finished for both of them.

'Here's what I don't understand.' Eva said, looking at both. 'Why would a Danish businessman want the Library for?'

'And that too the Library of Alexandria, which is believed to be turned to ash nearly 1500 years ago.' Mark said this time.

Eva and Sam shared a look at that and raised their eyebrows.

'What?' Mark said, raising both his hands to his sides, 'I read books.'

'Ok, yes.' The Indian replied now. 'So, Alexander believes that the Library exists somewhere else. All the scrolls were taken and kept somewhere. And according to the letter of the Professor, the Diary contained the location of the Library of Alexandria.'

'Yes, but that still doesn't explain his interest in the Library in the first place.' Eva still sounded skeptical.

'Well, from what he told me, Alexander believes that there's a scroll written by the master Librarian Callimachus which speaks about an ancient power, a power which he believes can give him the keys to be the ruler of the world or something. It's the same thing which the

Nazi Archeologist Hans believed and gave him and his family's life to keep the location of the Library safe from the Nazis themselves.'

'Ah.' Mark pitched in. 'Is it only me, or everybody here feels like that power should not be found, least of all by Alexander. If a Nazi historian committed suicide to keep this information away from his own regiment, that means its fucking bad.'

'I agree on that.' Eva said, though looking at Sam, it felt like he had some other ideas on mind.

'What is it?' Both the Americans asked him, after a few seconds.

'I agree on what you guys are saying.' Sam said, but in a thoughtful manner. 'But, as a student of archeology, as someone who studies and loves history, I want to see the Library of Alexandria.' Sam became excited speaking about it. 'Can you believe? Can you really believe that it existed? After it was burnt in 48 BC during the siege of Julius Caesar, then destroyed later in AD 391 by Emperor Theodosius I, and again on AD 642 destroyed by Caliph Omar?'

'I didn't know so much, I admit.' Mark said waving his hand in surrender. But he seemed troubled.

'But that makes me wonder. Why would so many people try to destroy the Library over different periods of history?'

'Yeah.' Eva said, looking at Sam. 'Why would so many people come to Alexandria and try to destroy the Library throughout the history?'

'There is no definite proof of that.' Said Sam. 'There is speculation about Julius' visit to Alexandria around 48 BC. According to conspiracy theories, he wanted his hands on something powerful.' He looked at his friends, with his eyebrows raised. 'And hearing Alexander's words, it seems that Julius was after the same power as our Danish friend. And as for Emperor Theodosius I, it is believed that he wanted to destroy anything remotely related to Paganism. And the Library of Alexandria contained too many texts on Paganism for his liking.'

'What about Caliph Omar?' Asked Eva.

'Ah.' Sam replied. 'Yes, Caliph. Well, according to history, he tried to destroy the Library and its books in the name of religion. As per him, anything that opposed the Quran should be destroyed.'

'Great. There we go.' Mark said with mock sadness. 'No short of tyrants.'

'But if so many times the Library has been destroyed, how can it have survived somewhere else?' Asked Eva this time. 'And if it was secretly transferred to some other place during the first fire on 48 BC, why it was attacked later?'

'Well.' The Indian said, nodding to himself. He was also thinking the same. 'My guess is, that the Librarians during Caesar's time didn't want anyone to know that the Library was being transferred. So they smuggled the most important scrolls, including the Callimachus scrolls to somewhere safe. And over the years and many generations, they kept smuggling the remaining scrolls, only keeping few texts there for the later tyrants to destroy, fooling the world that the Library was destroyed by repeated attacks, when the truth is that all the while, a small band of Librarians always kept the Library safe and set it up somewhere else, somewhere no man can think of.'

All three of them sat in silence for a few minutes, lost in their own thoughts.

'So.' At last, Mark said, looking at Sam. 'Since you want to see the Library, how do we find it?'

CHAPTER SEVENTY-EIGHT

All three of them looked at the letter.

Sam,

I am making sure that you are the only person who can read this. In the event that I can't meet you for some reason, maybe even murdered, this is the way that I can tell you what has happened. You have always been my best student. You have shared my interests in archeology for all these years. Though I believe that interest is in your blood. Your parents were one of the most knowledgeable archeologists I have ever met in life.

Both your parents and me were obsessed with the Archeological history of the Nazis during the Second World War. It was during that quest that I had met your parents in the historical Concentration camps in Poland. It was before your birth.

However, we pursued the different angles of the Nazi history. While I was more interested in the routes taken by Heinrich Himmler, your parents were following the path of Ahnenerbe, the archeological division of the Nazis itself. You might remember the book – 'Ahnenerbe history of the Nazis' that your parents wrote.

During that path, they came to know about Hans Schleif, the head of the Ahnenerbe during the end of the Nazi period. They tried to find the notebook of Hans and the reason for his death.

However, they seemed to have got the notebook, but there was someone else who was also behind the notebook.

Your parents had told me during their visit to Germany that they have got a location on the notebook, but someone powerful is behind them. However, after their unfortunate death, when I tried to find that notebook, I have been unable to do so for so many years. But it was just a week ago that I was contacted by a labor from your parent's detail.

I went to meet him and found this notebook with him.

Yes, the notebook of Hans. I still don't know why people are behind this notebook, but I fear that I am in danger too. So I made a digital copy of it and destroyed the original notebook.

In this quest, I also came to know about another thing. Your parents didn't die of drowning. They were murdered.

Sam, this is the legacy of your parents and you need to think what to do with it. But I must warn you, people are behind this for many years, and you might get in danger too. Better to leave it here Sam. God bless you, Sam.

Yours Truly,
Professor Richard Hedley.

P.S.: So sudden is the Advent of Mother and father.

'You are sure these are exactly the same words the Professor used?' Asked Eva.

Sam had written down the letter in notepad from memory. The words of the letter were etched in his mind forever, building up an emotion within him. So, it was not much difficult for him to write this letter remembering each and every detail.

'Of course, I am sure.'

'Ok great.' Eva said, looking back at the letter. 'So, this letter talks about how your parents found out the notebook, and how Richard himself got hold of it.'

'And it talks about my parents being murdered.' Sam's face was covered with grief. 'That son of a bitch Alexander had them killed.'

'I understand your grief Sam.' Mark said, from the opposite side of the table. 'But from what you told me, even Alexander was surprised to hear about them being murdered, correct?'

Sam remembered the surprised look on Dane's face when he had accused him of Rita and Hemanth's murder.

That was not acting. The guy didn't know my parents were killed.

'Yes.' Sam said, at last. 'But then who would kill him?'

'Sam, you also told us that there is someone in Alexander's team, who is trying to double cross him, right?'

'Yes.' Sam said, remembering the conversation he overheard from the ventilation shaft earlier.

'Then what's to say that whoever it was, he might have killed your parents to get hold of the diary himself?' Mark said pointedly.

That can be true. Whoever wants to double-cross Alexander might have already tried the same thing eighteen years ago as well. And tried to get the diary from Rita and Hemanth. When they refused, he had them killed.

'Yes, possible.'

'Ok, then let's think about the notebook, shall we?' Eva said now, looking at the letter.

'Sure.' Mark said, sarcastically. 'Oh wait! The good Professor has destroyed that one.'

'Good God Mark.' Eva said this time, looking at Mark, annoyed. 'Don't you read the full thing?'

Sam understood the point and smiled at Mark this time.

'What?' Asked an exasperated Mark.

'It says right here.' Eva said, pointing at a particular section in the letter.

I still don't know why people are behind this notebook, but I fear that I am in danger too. So I made a digital copy of it and destroyed the original notebook.

'The professor had made a digital copy of the notebook.' She said again.

'Yes but…...'. The American stopped.

Understanding dawned on Mark in a flash. He quickly rummaged through his backpack, searching for something. After a painful minute, at last, he found what he was looking for and held it high in his hand for everyone to see.

The digital copy of Hans' notebook was on the iPad that Professor Richard Hedley had kept safe in the tunnel, inside the satchel with the mirror imaged letter.

CHAPTER SEVENTY-NINE

'Shouldn't we go after them?'

Sabir had been fuming with rage after Sam's rescue. The whole compound was having a trail of bodies, and most of the security team were either dead or too much wounded to do anything. The late-night events have attracted the authorities, and a cover story of an outside attack on the Castle was prepared for the same. The whole city of Copenhagen and its outskirts were under watch, along with the surrounding water body. As per them, the perpetrators would not be able to evade the *Politi*, the Denmark Police Force for long.

But the Syrian had his own doubts. Among the people who died were some of his friends who had worked with him for nearly two decades and have been very loyal comrades. And the Indian and his friends were responsible for all the deaths. Even the same people were responsible for all his friend's deaths in India as well.

But Alexander seemed unusually quiet and calm considering the setback.

'We need to search for them.' Sabir said again. 'They will not be able to go far.'

The whole place has been cordoned off, and the cleanup was in progress in the *Kastellet*, and all the bodies have already been taken away. Still smoke was coming up from few places in the compound, reminding the defeat they had.

'Are you not going after Sam? And the Library?' Sabir was unable to control the temper. Seeing Alexander so quiet was not normal, more so after this attack.

Alexander looked at him. The Billionaire had few cuts on his face and arm, where small bandages had been put, whereas the Syrian person had his full left arm covered in dressing, due to a deep cut, thanks to the last blast, which was painfully another reminder of yesterday's failures.

But Alexander seemed not concerned with any of that. Instead, he smiled a bit and then looked at the third person in the room. Dr. Berthold Weber was sitting at the corner of the room, still contemplating the horrors of last night. Though, incredibly, he was the only one who had emerged unscathed previous night by some miracle. However, that didn't make him any less scared. For so many years he had been working with the Dane but never have this kind of thing happened.

'Don't worry Sabir.' Alexander said, looking at Sabir, and then looking back at the laptop screen in front of him.

'We will find them, and they will lead us to the Callimachus scrolls.'

CHAPTER EIGHTY

10:35 AM

Sam sighed.

The Professor really seemed to be well versed with codes. It was really a wonder that this part of the old man was not known to him at all during his lifetime. Professor Richard Hedley have proved himself time and again in last few days to be one of the best persons in the world to write things in codes and hide them from everyone. 'It's good that he was not a terrorist.' Were the exact words from Eva a few minutes ago. Mark had just laughed and gone out for some air and to get a cigarette with Dixido.

According to Eva, it was not generally that Mark smokes, sometimes just to clear his head he did that.

He looked at the iPad screen once again. It still showed the same thing.

H E D L E Y

— — — — — —

ENTER THE PASSWORD.

WRONG PASSWORD, 1 CHANCE LEFT

For the better part of the last hour, they have tried to give passwords with their guess. But that didn't seem to work.

First one that came to mind was ALEXANDRIA, which Mark had suggested, but it had too many letters to fit in the password box. Only 6 letters could be given. Next guessed password by Eva was HEMANTH, the name of Sam's father, who had found the notebook along with his wife Rita, but that didn't help much as the name had 7 letters. Again, a dead end. Next, Sam had tried giving RAWATH, the surname of the 2 people – Hemanth and Rita Rawath, who had found clues for the Library at first, the people who found the notebook of Hans. Moreover, Sam also have the same surname, to whom the Professor wanted to pass on the details of the discovery and clues that his parents had found.

This seemed to be a perfect fit, as it had 6 letters, as specified in the password box.

ENTER THE PASSWORD.

After entering the letters as a perfect fit for the password, the words '3 chances left' was replaced by ENTER.

With a look at his friends, Sam had hit the enter button. All the enthusiasm of the three disappeared seeing the next screen.

'Well.' Mark had said while looking at the screen. 'It seems the Professor has not made it easy for us.'

Sam and Eva also felt the same.

R   A   W   A   T   H

ENTER THE PASSWORD.

WRONG PASSWORD, 2 CHANCE LEFT

'Remember, the last wrong password would fry the circuit.' Eva had cautioned.

Still, next time it felt after a lot of thought, that HEDLEY might be the correct one. But entering that password also proved them wrong. Once again, the screen flashed the caution message showing that only 1 chance was left. And everybody knew what would happen if it's a wrong one.

After 2 wrong passwords, everybody needed a break. Mark had gone to smoke, while Eva wanted to have some food for herself and Sam.

It's not right. I am missing something. The Professor would not have made it so difficult. He didn't know that I would have friends, much less one of them to be a cryptologist. There must be some clue. He has kept a plan B in case an enemy finds this iPad and gives wrong passwords, the circuit will fry, and Hans' notebook would be lost forever. So, his plan A must have some clue.

But where can that be?

Sam looked around and searched for something.

Where is it? There must be something there.

There.

He found what he was looking for near the window and took it back with him in the table.

The notepad where he had written the letter from the Prof from memory.

'Eva.' He cried, at the top of his voice. 'Call Mark, I think I've found something.'

CHAPTER EIGHTY-ONE

10:45 AM

Ten minutes later, the trio sat together around the table.

The iPad and the letter sat in between them, on the table, near Sam. Beside him was Mark and opposite to them Eva, both of them bewildered by the sudden summon from the Indian.

Sam looked at them and enjoyed the look of bewilderment on the faces of both. A smile hung on his face.

'What's so exciting?' Asked Eva.

Without answering her, Sam extended his hand towards Mark.

'Can I have one of those cigarettes you were smoking?'

Without question, Mark passed a Camel to him and lit it.

Taking a deep drag, Sam looked at both with a smile and started talking.

'Don't be so surprised. I normally don't smoke. But needed to clear my head as well.'

'Yeah.' Said Eva. 'It's good that you are enjoying yourself, but can you tell us why you called us suddenly?'

'Certainly. You see, the professor has always provided clues for me. The *Mlechhita-vikalpa* in his tissue paper which pointed us to my home in India. Then the mirror image letter which then told me about Hans' diary.'

'Yes but…' Mark started but was stopped by Sam who was too much excited to get distracted.

'So, if he has set up a password in the iPad which I am supposed to open in order to get the details in the diary……'

'Then he must have left you with a clue.' Eva said, now understanding his point.

'Exactly.' Sam said. 'Now, except the letter and the iPad, there was nothing in the satchel I got from my home in Delhi. So, it came to my mind, that if there's some clue, it's got to be in the letter itself.'

'Oh…. kay.' Mark said now, looking at the letter.

'So, I started looking at the letter.' Sam continued. 'Is there anything that seems a bit off in the letter for you two?'

Mark stared at the letter for a few seconds, reading again from top to end, but once completed, just shook his head.

'Nope. It seems he was pretty straightforward about his letter, telling you about your parent's works and the details of Hans' diary and your parent's deaths.'

Sam looked at Eva.

'And for you?'

'Well.' Eva said, thinking a bit. Her eyes suddenly glittered, as if she had discovered something. 'This section here…...'

She pointed out at the end of the letter.

'Yes exactly.' Sam said, now grinning ear to ear. 'This section of P.S. At first I thought it's a prayer he had written in the PostScript.' He pointed out the whole line.

P.S.: *So sudden is the Advent of Mother and father.*

'But, it doesn't seem to match any idiom or phrase I have ever heard of. So, if there's any clue, then it must be here.'

'Hmm.' Eva said. 'But how does it contain a clue to the..........'

She stopped suddenly, noticing an oddity. Earlier she had also thought this line to be some prayer for good fortune from the parents, but there seemed to be something more in this.

'Why are these like this?'

She quickly took out a pen from Sam and circled a few things.

P.S. : So sudden is the Advent of Mother and father.

Both Sam and Mark also now noticed. The circled letters by Eva were the only ones which were in Capital letters.

'Why are these letters marked in capital?' She asked again, now looking at the surprised faces of her two male partners.

Sam had thought that he had discovered the way for the clue but was not ready for this. He had entirely overlooked the fact that only 3 letters were marked in capital whereas all others were small. So, it was easy to miss this. But now that he could see the marked letters, everything became clear to him.

'I know why these are marked in the capital.' He said after a minute.

Did the professor mean what I think he meant?

'Why?' Asked Mark from his side.

Eva just gave him a questioning look.

'Because it spells a particular name.' He said and took the paper and pen from Eva.

He wrote something and then showed them.

Both Eva and Mark were shocked to see what the Indian had written.

'My God.' Eva said, really surprised. 'You are right. He was a genius.'

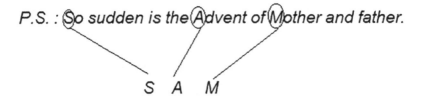

P.S. : So sudden is the Advent of Mother and father.

S A M

Mark was just too surprised to say anything.

It was Sam who spoke after a minute, breaking the silence in the room.

'The password is my name. He had given the clue all along.'

CHAPTER EIGHTY-TWO

'But that's 3 letters only.'

Mark was still getting his head to grasp on the scenario in hand. He had always thought himself of a smart man, been able to take decisions and device the enemy plans very quickly, but the codes and clues of the Professor for last few days have made him look like a kid in his own eyes.

'Correct Mark. But you forgot one thing.' Sam said with a smile. A look at Eva told him that she had already understood the clue.

'And what's that?' Mark narrowed his eyes. He got irritated with himself for missing yet another twist in the Cambridge Professor's clues.

'My full name is Sameer. As in S-A-M-E-E-R.'

Mark's eyes widened in understanding.

Of course. It all makes sense now. Everything has always been connected to Sam on this quest. His parents found the first clue for the Library of Alexandria, the Prof passed on all the clues to him only. So, it's quite natural that the password would be somehow related to Sam.

The other two burst out laughing seeing the embarrassed look on Mark's face.

'It's all right Mark.' Sam said once he was able to control his laugh.
'The Professor had all of us fooled with his clues.'

'Yes.' Eva supported him, though still laughing. 'We all had a hard time to figure out his clues.'

'Well then. What are we waiting for?' Mark said after both enjoyed making a fool out of him.

'Yes, let's see if we are correct.'

A minute later, Sam had entered the password in the iPad.

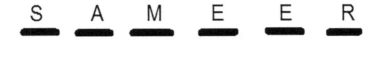

ENTER THE PASSWORD.

Before clicking enter, his finger hovered an inch above the screen.

'What happened?' Both Eva and Mark said from both of his sides.

'I might be wrong, and if that's true, then as soon as I click enter, the circuit will fry instantly. And…..And all will be lost. The diary of Hans, the Library of Alexandria, the Callimachus Scrolls, everything will be gone forever.' Sam's eyes seemed afraid, afraid of losing the last clue to a great archeological discovery of the century.

Eva touched his shoulder and pressed on, giving him the support. Sam looked at her, and their eyes met. Unexpectedly, a very different emotion crossed both their eyes and minds in turn.

The kiss. We will speak about that later, once everything is over.

'You are not.' Mark said from the other side. The emotion that crossed his friend's eyes have not lost on him, but he decided not to let that show. *They should be ready to speak about it.*

Eva supported him the same. 'Everything that led us here has been somehow related to you. The Professor, his clues, your parent's discoveries, their death – everything was always related to you, and you only. So, if there's anyone who could open it, and if there's any password to open it, that's you.'

That seemed to steady Sam. He looked back to the screen and with a shaking hand, clicked ENTER.

Nothing happened at first. Then……

'Oh God.' Sam said, looking at the screen.

CHAPTER EIGHTY-THREE

KATHMANDU, NEPAL
November 18,
18:05 PM

'Half an hour before we land.' Mark announced, coming out of the cockpit.

It took them nearly two days to ready themselves with all the gears and everything they needed for the travel. Mark had to report to his employer, and Eva had to take more approval for the leave. It would be time-consuming for them to traverse the mountains and reach their destination through the treacherous path.

It was 6 AM when they have started their travel, and it took nearly a bit more than eight hours for them to reach near Kathmandu. Mark had taken a nap in the jet, and just sometime back went to the cockpit to get an aerial view of Nepal from up here. The place really looked cool. At this time of the year, a few patches of white could be seen up north from here.

However, the best scene was seen around half an hour ago, the aerial view of Mount Everest itself. Though some parts were covered in cloud and it was still dark at that time, yet it felt like heaven for them. For the last one and half hours, it had been a visual treat for the eyes of the trio. All the most known peaks like – Kangchenjunga, Mount Everest, Mount Kailash could be seen from the top, though not as clearly as they would have liked. But that didn't deter them from pressing their noses on the windows of the jet and looking for the beauty of nature.

But their destination could not be seen from here, as was mentioned in Hans' diary.

Sam recollected precisely what happened that day with his name as the password.

The screen had kept frozen for a few seconds.

Sam was not sure if the touchscreen has worked, or if the password was wrong and, in the background, the circuit was being fried.

After a painful few seconds, the screen glowed with a message.

WELCOME
Password accepted
Enter here to go to the Ibook

Everybody exhaled visibly, and smiles were etched in their faces. Sam had held his breath most of all, in anticipation of what was going to happen. If he were wrong, everything would have been lost. But now, it seemed he had been correct, and the Professor indeed had kept his name as the password. A pang of sadness crossed his mind.

The Professor truly wanted to tell me about this, he wanted me to find out.

'Let's see what the old professor has for us in store.' Said Mark excitedly from behind.

Sam appreciated the excitement and clicked to open the iBooks.

A PDF document opened in the iPad on the click. It seemed that it's the only item present in the iPad itself. Once the PDF file opened, all three of them started reading it.

November 15, 1939

I have made a life-altering discovery, but have kept secret from the Ahnenerbe, not because I want the thing for myself, but I know what Ahnenerbe is. Their only goal is to get historical data which can help Germany and the führer – Herr Adolf Hitler to win the war, a war that has taken the life of perhaps a thousand Jews already and many more in coming days for sure. They are already calling it the Second World War.

Anyhow, let me get back to the point. When I went in early October to Greece for the archeological expedition of Olympia, on my way back, I had gone to Alexandria. It's a city mixed with ancient and modern ways. I have enjoyed staying there for two days. However, my curiosity drove me towards the old site of the Library of Alexandria, a place which has been repeatedly attacked and destroyed over and over in history. My curiosity was based on the question that what drove people to attack this library, a mere collection of books, scrolls, and texts again and again?

Alas! I did not get the answer, but during my visit, I found a secret tunnel built much further below under the Mouseion, as called in Egyptian for the Ancient Library of Alexandria. I believe that the destruction of the Library is a myth, a ruse taken by the people of Ancient Alexandria. The structure of the tunnel and its gate is contemporary of Ptolemy I, the creator of the Library. So, my theory is that Ptolemy had suspected that the Library may get under attack sometime in future, and as a result had created a secret pathway for the people in the Library to smuggle out the book, scrolls and texts to a predetermined location if needed.

The first entry had ended here. However, on the second page was a more interesting narration.

August 25, 1942

A few days ago, my book Erechtheion got launched, and it made me so happy. However, this is a ruse I had to take in order to get the approval from the Ahnenerbe to let me visit Greece from time to time, mainly to search for the details of the hidden location of the Library.

I normally don't write diaries, but you are the only one whom I can trust right now with the truth. And the fact is that I have made some more progress with my research. With the help of some Egyptian labors, I had entered the tunnel below the Library of Alexandria breaking the thin wall that was created long back to keep the tunnel hidden, which led to the further north from Alexandria itself, below the Mediterranean Sea, and then took a sudden detour. As far as my research goes, it seems the people in the Library had used this getaway to smuggle everything from the Library to a predetermined post in the Mediterranean Sea, and from there to the intended hideout. From my travels, the only thing I had been able to find out as of now is that the tunnel opened somewhere in an island in the Mediterranean, and from there, the route had been treacherous for the people. The Island seemed to be near to Syria, and that would be the most likely place for the people of the Library to Port. However, I am going again next year once to visit the site and to discover more details on it.

They scrolled to the next page for the next entry.

July 8, 1943

My suspicion seems to be correct. The people of the Library had taken refuge in Syria, and from there they had started their auspicious journey to the Northeastern side. Judging by the path they had taken, it seems to be somewhere around Iran or Afghanistan that they had traveled.
Evidence suggests that they have traveled through Syria and then Iran, without crossing the Caspian Sea. However, I have been asked by Heinrich Himmler himself once about my so many frequent journeys to Greece. I think they are suspicious on my travels now. I have to be more careful in the future.

This page ended here. With anticipation, they had opened the next page.

June 29, 1944

I came back last night from my travel from Afghanistan. Even my wife Lora seems to be suspicious of my trips now. This time I haven't informed anybody about my journey. Only Lora knew, but I haven't told her why I am going to that part of the world, and it made her suspicious. I can't believe that she thinks that I still have something for Anna from my college days. How can she ever feel that I would leave her and my twin sons with her here in between the war, and would go to Anna and stay with her in her home in Austria? She seems to have totally lost it.

Anyhow, need to be more focused. So, in my last entry, I had told that the people of the Library might have smuggled their stuff from Alexandria to somewhere in Afghanistan, but it seems I am wrong. The trail doesn't end there. It appears from Afghanistan; the people have traveled further east. My suspicion is somewhere in India. But it feels good thinking that all those incredible and valuable scrolls and texts and books are all safe somewhere. Julius Caesar, Caliph Omar- nobody had been able to destroy those precious items.

But you might ask me why I am not telling my own party about the discovery. Well, my auspicious diary, let me tell you frankly, I don't enjoy being in the Nazi party itself. But I have a family, a wife and two children I have to take care of now, and the Ahnenerbe provides me with the means to survive. And I love my country. Germany and

Adolf Hitler are not the same. Germany is much more than the wretched Hitler. And if I tell the Nazis about my discovery, then they will do nothing different than what Caliph Omar tried to do with the Library. So right now, silence is the best gift I can give to the Librarians.

The next page in the PDF was the last entry from Hans. And that described everything.

April 27, 1945

What I am about to write, might chill you to the core. I have decided to kill my wife Lora and my two sons, my two beautiful sons - Alexander and Konstantin, one of whose name I have given due to my obsession with the Library of Alexandria.
I have to do it. I can't let Himmler know about the Library's existence, or they will use my family as a weapon against me to let them know about all my voyages and its details. The war seems to be nearly over, as it seems that the American scientist named Oppenheimer may be on the verge of inventing the Atom Bomb. However, that does not concern me, as I will not be there to witness it, though I would very much like to see the destruction of the Nazi party and that wretched dictator Hitler.
But, that's not important. Time is running out. Himmler will be here in some time. Before that, I have to post this diary to you, Matthias.

I have found the Library of Alexandria. The location of this place is in one of the remotest places on earth. A place where nobody has ever gone before.

27°57'09.6"N 88°08'30.9"E

The latitude and longitude of the Library I have given above. I have never been able to go, but I believe that someday someone will find it, and all the books and scrolls in the Library will be again in front of the whole world to see. This is the result of my last 6 years of research on the Library of Alexandria.
Anyhow, I have to go now and send it through my servant to keep it hidden for you, Matthias. If you get this, know that I am not there anymore, but I love you always.

Hans.

'Will the helicopter be available?' Eva asked Mark, in the process jolting Sam back to the present.

'It will be, but in these conditions in the hills, the helicopter won't be able to travel much.'

'But I can't wait to see the Library.' Sam said, looking at both. 'It's a wonder of the ancient world.'

'I understand Sam.' Mark said, looking at Sam, and sitting on the seat opposite to him. 'But you must know that we can only travel near Kanchenjunga, and from there we have to go on foot. So, it will take time.'

'What if Alexander reaches by the time we go?' Sam countered, getting a nod from Eva, who also apparently was thinking the same.

'We have to go to Lhonak Peak, and from there we can travel.'

'Hmm, let me see what can be done.' Mark said, at last, contemplating the facts.

'Anyhow, here we are in Kathmandu.' He said looking outside. The jet had just landed and started taxying.

'Let's take rest for tonight.' Said Sam, grinning like a child.

'Tomorrow finally we will visit the Library of Alexandria.'

CHAPTER EIGHTY-FOUR

THE HIMALAYAS
November 19,
9:07 AM

'Whose Idea was it exactly to hike on foot?'
Eva's cry could be barely heard over the howling winds. For last two
and half hours, the group had been hiking the area, and right now
they seemed to be hopelessly lost. The latitude and longitude
provided in the diary of Hans put the area somewhere around this
border.

Instead of going the whole way on foot, Mark had arranged for a
HAL Cheetah transport helicopter with the help of his employer,
from the Indian Army base near the Himalayas. The Helicopter had
taken them from the Kathmandu air base and crossing the
Kangchenjunga, they had come near the Lhonak Peak around 3
hours ago at 6 AM in the morning. There the trio had jumped from
the Helicopter using the lightweight parachutes brought in by Mark
earlier. How his employer managed to get help from the Indian
Army was still a mystery to both Sam and Eva.

They both had asked many times about Mark's employer, but he had
always been able to dodge the question.

'Once the mission is done, you will know about him in time.' Was the answer they have always got. Exasperated, both of them have stopped asking now to the MARSOC soldier about his mysterious employer. For now, the Library of Alexandria mattered the most, the employer could wait.

The Lhonak Peak itself was a tourist spot and was visited by many tourists over the year, but this area remained closed from October to March every year, due to the ferocious winds, too much cold, the deadly snow and crevices, and the moving glaciers. And the place they were standing right now had never been explored yet by humans, at least nothing in recorded history.

'Who gave the Librarians idea to open their Library in the middle of nowhere?' Mark complained in his earphone.

The weather had worsened over the last hour. Winds were blowing with a power of nearly 140 kmh. Along with that the bone-jarring coldness and the mist around them. The visibility was near zero for all of them.

Though everybody was covered from head to toe with winter gears, still the wind was actually making them shiver, chilling them to the core. The place where the Library was supposed to be was arbitrarily near the Indo-China-Nepal border. In the map, the latitude and longitude given in the diary showed the spot to be around 40 kilometers from the Lhonak Peak towards the north, placing it exactly on the Indo-China border. Not much people except the military gets the permissions to get anywhere near that, but Mark's employer seemed to know magic, providing him with the necessary documents to traverse the area without any disturbance.

Right now, it seemed nobody cared to disturb them, as this was really one of the remotest areas on earth. Nothing could be seen anywhere except the three of them, tied together through hiking ropes and snow axes in their hands, and surrounded by pure whiteness in all sides.

Sam looked behind and thought he saw the peak of Kangchenjunga, a view that people wanted to see once in the lifetime at least, making them feel closest to heaven on earth before the winds and mist covered his view once again. The peak seemed to be tiny from here, and most of it was already shrouded from view by the nearest peak of Lhonak Peak.

'How much have we already traveled?' Sam asked, rather cried on his earphone. His own voice was drowned due to the winds.

He saw Mark stopping and getting his laser rangefinder out from his backpack. Eva and Sam were too much tired to get an answer and sat on the snow itself. Everywhere they could see, it was all white out there. Not a sign of any inhabitants anywhere nearby.

How can someone live out here? The place seems to be frozen all over the year. Nobody comes up here. Why would they set up the Library of Alexandria here?

'We have covered nearly 35 kilometers from the peak.' Mark said, looking into his rangefinder's screen. 'And we have to go that way.' He said, showing towards the left.

Sam looked that way and was greeted by another white mist, blocking his visuals.

He got up quickly. *So near to see an ancient history come alive. To see one of the most significant historical collection ever recorded.*

301

The promise of seeing the Library kept him standing and full of energy.

'Ok People.' He said into his earphone. 'Let's move.'

CHAPTER EIGHTY-FIVE

9:47 AM

It took them 40 more minutes to travel those last 5 kilometers.
By then both Eva and Sam had drained up their energy. Hiking through these mountains were treacherous enough, but in between the crevices were much more dangerous. Sam himself had fallen into one of those crevices. It was the quick thinking and reaction of Mark and the commonly tied rope that saved him from certain death. The only unfazed person was Mark, having traveled to different places like these all his life.

'Where is the Library?' Sam said, a little disappointed.

In front of them, a wall of pure white stood, instead of any library or any kind of inhabitation.

Mark and Eva also felt perplexed. The American soldier rechecked his rangefinder and compass.

'This is supposed to be the correct place as per the coordinates.' He said, still baffled by the wall in front of them.

'Can Hans had made any mistake?' Eva asked, looking on all sides. Everywhere the white snow reigned the area, and though it was mid-morning, still the sun had not been in its full power, causing the white mist to stay everywhere and block their visuals.

'I don't think so, Eva.' Sam said. 'He had risked everything, he killed his family, committed suicide. Unless he was sure that he was right, he wouldn't have done that.'

Eva nodded. Sam was correct. Unless Hans was entirely sure, he wouldn't have let his family and himself die in vain due to a mere assumption.

'Then, let's climb the wall.' Said Mark, showing the snow ax to them. 'Let's see what's on the other side of the wall.'

****

Ballav Sang was standing outside the door.

He has already reached and met the Grandmaster yesterday.

According to the old man, the Indian and his friends have found the location and were supposed to be arriving the Library today.

'Prepare to welcome them, my friend.' The Grandmaster had told.

'From what I know, Sam is a brilliant and kind man. He should be treated as such.'

'Yes, Grandmaster.' Ballav had replied.

The morning looked good. Cloud had covered most of the area, and though there were greeneries in this place, still, most of the part was covered in snow right now.

He was lost in his thought when Grandmaster came and stood beside him. The touch on his shoulder made Ballav aware of the presence of the Grandmaster, making him look towards him.

'They are here.' The Grandmaster said with a smile and gestured towards the front.

****

'It's really amazing.' Said Sam.

They have crossed the wall of snow in front of them, which took them around 20 more minutes. Once they were on the top of that wall, the other side presented itself.

'He was right.' Sam said, excited and smiling. 'He was bloody right. Hans had really found the place.'

'Yes Sam.' Eva said, touching his arm. 'The Professor, your parents, Hans, everybody was correct.'

'Yes, yes.' He said, still smiling like a child getting his first Christmas present.

'Look out.' Mark said, unspooling his Heckler and Koch rifle. 'Someone's coming.'

Alarmed, Sam and Eva looked forward. The place looked like heaven on earth. There was another wall on the far opposite to where they were standing right now, around 2 kilometers away. In between these two walls, was a small valley. And in this valley, there seemed to be some houses created. *No, not only houses. It's a village of a few people living here.*

The houses were made of red bricks. Only a few, Sam counted six on each side, houses were present, making a total of 12 houses. Behind the houses was an open field for farming. The whole place was really a small valley, a two by five kilometers long.

But it was the building on his exact opposite side, just on the foot of the other wall, that held Sam's attention. It was high, very high, nearly a ten-story building height. The top of the structure was conical, like that of a mosque or any Hindu Temple. But it was the material that had seized the attention of the trio. The tapered top was glinting in the daylight. *Gold. The top is made of gold.* The whole building itself screamed an Egyptian heritage. The structure was entirely cylindrical in shape, except the conical head. The door of the building was covered with Egyptian architectural statues of small sizes in different boxes. From here, Sam could not see all the structures, but he caught a glimpse of the figure of Ra, sitting on his throne in the middle box of the door. It seemed that the handles of the two doors to the building converged together to form this figure. The door was made of brass, whereas the building itself seemed to be made of the same bricks as the rest of the houses in the valley. But the decoration, ornamentation, and color of this building made it stand out. The building's all the walls contained decoration in the form of books, not actual ones, but paintings of different kinds of books, scrolls, text, in different languages. From his vantage point, Sam was not able to make out everything, but he was sure of one thing.

The Library of Alexandria. I've found it, at last.

The path to the Library from the summit of the wall where the trio was standing, was made of concrete, suggesting that the people here got their supplies from either Nepal, India or China. The whole valley itself was covered in a shroud of mist, a cloud. *That's why it's not in any of the satellite images.*

'Hold it there.' Mark cried, pointing it towards a person coming through the concrete road towards them.

'Stop, don't.' Eva said to Mark, stopping him to threaten the person coming and pushing his gun down.

By then, Sam also noticed something. In the gate to the Library stood a monk of some kind. From here, he couldn't be sure, but the Indian felt the monk was old, very old, and he was looking straight at Sam.

'Come in.' The man coming through the concrete road called out. 'We are here to welcome you.'

CHAPTER EIGHTY-SIX

11:01 AM

After an hour, being rejuvenated with some rest and lots of foods, including tofu, spinach, and fruits, the trio were all ready to go inside the Library.

'You sure you guys don't need more rest?' Asked the Nepali person who had escorted them to the temple.

The temple of the Muses, the nine goddesses of art, sat at the summit of the wall on the southern side of the valley, just below where Sam and his entail had first made their entrance to the valley. With the excitement of finding the Library of Alexandria, all three had missed the temple standing just below them. Half the size of the Library, the temple was also made of the gold top, brass doors and red bricks, the same as the Library.

The Nepali person, his name now known to all as Ballav, had escorted them to the Temple when they had come down to the valley. To Sam's surprise, the old person who was standing in front of the main door of the Library didn't come to them, to help or to aide them. According to Ballav, he was waiting for Sam and his entail in the Library.

And Sam couldn't wait to go to the Library.

'Yes, we are ready.' Sam said, completing the fruits given to him.

Mark was going to bite the last apple on his plate when he heard the exchange and saw Sam looking at him pointedly. Eva also had finished her food and was ready to go. With extreme unhappiness, the American soldier put down the apple and stood.

'Yeah, we are ready.'

'Good, now please if you would follow me.' With that Ballav turned and started, followed by the trio. Keeping the idol of the goddesses behind them, the entail followed Ballav, coming out of the temple, into the open air.

By then, the mist has dispersed a little bit, though still the sky couldn't be seen. But some rays of the sun were able to penetrate the clouds, causing the area to lit up a bit. They could now see many people working on their own in the farming land on the right, and children studying in the open-air school at one side of the library. Some women could be seen weaving or cleaning in front of the houses. All in all, it seemed that there were not more than a total of fifty people living here. And the lifestyle of them appeared to be simple and peaceful.

'The people here start their work at 6 AM in the morning, just after the prayer.' Ballav said, seeing them looking at the people.

Some of the people stopped their work in the middle, to check on the newcomers. An old lady, nearly of an age of around sixty, was walking close by when she turned and saw the newcomers. She stopped and after a good look at Sam asked the most surprising question to him.

'Are you Sameer Rawath?'

At first, Sam was dumbfounded. How could she know my name? I have only told my name to Ballav.

He looked at Ballav, who just shrugged in return.

'Yes mam, I am.' He said gently to the lady.

In return, the lady smiled in a heartwarming manner, and put her hand on top of Sam's head, gesturing a blessing.

'That was spooky.' Mark said after they were out of the earshot of the lady.

'Yes definitely.' Eva supported him. 'How did she know your name?' Sam just kept quiet, thinking the same thing. But he focused on what he was seeing. The questions in his mind would be answered shortly from what Ballav had told them. He checked the architecture of the buildings, the temple and the Library itself from the outside.

Everything was definitely of ancient Egyptian architecture, but there was a hint of different other cultures also.

'You have incorporated the other cultures too.' Said Sam, a little too loudly, which was heard by the Nepali.

'Yes indeed.' Ballav said. 'But all of these will be better answered here.'

He gestured for them to enter the Library, opening the big door with his hands.

And that was the first time in nearly 2000 years, that an outsider has set his foot inside the Library of Alexandria.

CHAPTER EIGHTY-SEVEN

'Wow.'

That was all Sam could manage to say out loud. The grandeur of this hidden Library of Alexandria was nothing he had ever seen or imagined. All three of them were staring in awe at what they were seeing.

'Its….' Eva searched for words. 'It's nothing I've ever seen.'

'Yeah. Me too.' Sam replied slowly.

It was all too much for him to take in. Mark being a soldier, had never been into books much, but he had seen the Library of Congress, the National Library, and the likes. But he was also never prepared for this. As a result, all three of them were mesmerized by the beauty and the way everything was immaculately arranged. Sam had seen a fair share of Libraries in his life. As a person growing up with academics, he had to go to Libraries with his parents and also with the Professor. He remembered one time, when his father went to Kolkata in India, along with his mother and him for a lecture on Archeology, in the Archeological Survey of India, and they had visited the National Library of India. Though not much of the memory stayed with him from that time, the one thing he remembered was the collection of books in the big Library. He had also gone to the Cambridge Library, one of the biggest in the UK, along with the Oxford Library. Both were big, but nothing like this. Sure, the Library of Congress was the World's Biggest Library and compared to this one much larger. Still, the collections and the grandeur of this one was awe inspiring.

The whole building was cylindrical, as was seen from the outside. From inside too, it was the same, rising to a height of 10 stories high. However, the whole building from inside was made of gold walls in stark contrast to the outside. None of the red bricks seen from outside could be seen here. The railings were all made of brass, along with the sections holding the books and scrolls. There seemed to be doors on every floor, and all of them were open. It seemed the people liked to pray there. The other thing that he noticed was that the whole library was lit with torches, not a single electric bulb anywhere, giving the entire library an ethereal appearance.

It's like a temple to them. They sit in solitude to read and pray here in the Library. They all have been carrying the Legacy of protecting and saving the library for generations.

The books and scrolls were covering the most part of the Library. From his point, Sam could see many scrolls and books being held in containers, under glass covers on different floors.

So that's how they are preserving the scrolls.

So entranced they were with the Library, that they didn't notice the old man whom Sam had seen earlier, coming in front of them in the corridor. It was not until he spoke that they came to know about his presence.

'Welcome Sam.' The man said, waving his hands. 'Welcome to the Library of Alexandria.'

All three of them looked at the person, while Ballav moved forward and introduced the old man to the outsiders.

'Sam, Mark and Eva, meet the Grandmaster of the Library.' He said, keeping his hands in a position suggesting *namaste* in respect to the old man.

The trio also bent their head in respect to the old man while he just stood there with his hands gesturing blessings to each of them.

'Now.' He said, turning around. 'I believe you have a lot of questions for me.'

'Yes, Grandmaster.' Sam replied, still fathoming the things he was seeing in the Library.

'Good.' He said turning around while addressing Ballav this time.

'Ballav, you can wait outside, while I speak with Sam and his friends.'

'Sure.'

With that, Ballav turned around and left the building slowly.

'Well, now that there's no distraction, lets come to the main hall and speak among ourselves. I believe I will be able to answer all your questions.'

CHAPTER EIGHTY-EIGHT

11:20 AM

The Boeing AH-64 Apache crossed the Kangchenjunga peak and took a right turn.

'They are not much far away.' Sabir said in his mike from the passenger's seat, behind the pilot.

A tablet was held in his hand showing the satellite imagery of the Himalayas, and in between that a red and blue dot blinking. The blue dot represented the helicopter, while the red dot was their quarry. According to the screen, it was still nearly 250 miles away from the place where the red dot was blipping.

'We have to take the turn from here 12 degrees to the right.' He said to the pilot, showing him the route, the helicopter must take.

'How much more time to reach?' The voice came in his earphone. But Sabir knew the person who was speaking.

Alexander Penbrose sat in the copilot's seat with a Desert Eagle in his hand. Though he couldn't see Dane's face from his position behind the pilot, Sabir knew what was going on in his mind. The billionaire could not wait for taking the revenge for what had happened in Copenhagen. The American soldier and the NSA bitch, along with one of their friends, had dared to come in his home turf and create mayhem there to get Sam out.

'It should take an hour for us to reach.' He said. 'The mist is dispersing with the day growing, so hopefully, we will not be delayed anymore.'

'Good.' Alexander's voice came into his earphone. 'Tell your men to be ready. And tell the other chopper to follow us closely.'

Sabir looked at the men beside and in front of him. Six people each side made a total of twelve in this helicopter. The other chopper, a Eurocopter Tiger, held ten more mercenaries. And there were loads of missiles and guns for them to take over an army. So being outgunned was not a worry. Also, in the second helicopter, Berthold was sitting with all the mercenaries. Alexander needed the German historian to authenticate the scrolls after taking revenge from Sam and his friends.

He looked at the screen in his hand. It looked like Sam, and his little entail have run out of time.

CHAPTER EIGHTY-NINE

'There's an underground vault as well?'

Eva's question boomed in the main hall of the Library. The Grandmaster had taken them to the table at the far end of the main hall and asked them to seat there with him. Beside the table, just a few yards away, a door was left ajar, stairs descending downstairs.

'No.' Said the Grandmaster in reply. 'The most prestigious collection of the Library is situated there.'

He looked at Sam, daring him to understand what the prestigious collection could be.

Sam thought for a moment, and the answer clicked in his mind almost instantly.

'It's the scrolls of *Callimachus*.'

'Bravo.' The old man said in joy. 'You are every bit the brilliant person I thought you would be.'

'But how do you know me?' Sam asked, now first time getting time actually to ask the questions running through his mind. 'There was a lady outside I met, and she called me by my name. How did she know me? What's going on? And how is the Library being set up here?'

Eva and Mark also seemed equally curious about everything. The Grandmaster looked at all of them and sighed.

It's time to tell them.

'Patience my boy.' He started. 'I will tell you everything. But first, let me sit down. At my age, it's not possible for me to stand for much time.'

The trio waited for him to sit and start explaining things.

'Before telling you about the Library being set up here, let me tell you the history behind it.' He started while sitting down.

'When Pompey first came to Egypt, a Civil War was happening in Alexandria. Pharaoh Ptolemy and his sister Cleopatra VII were having a dispute at that time. However, at the arrival of Pompey, both the parties were astonished. In the history books, it is now told that Ptolemy ordered the soldiers Achillas and Lucius Septimius through the eunuch Pothinus to kill Pompey, which is wrong. Though Pothinus is known for being the one who turned Ptolemy against his sister, later he felt remorse for his actions, causing him to side with Cleopatra secretly. He had somehow learned of the true reason for Pompey to visit Egypt, that of stealing and obtaining a particular scroll which provides the location of infinite power, making him unstoppable.'

The Grandmaster noticed the uncomfortable gazes of the trio in front of him on the mention of an unending power but chose to ignore it, continuing his story.

'So, Pothinus went straight to Cleopatra and told her all the details. In response, she asked him to turn Ptolemy against the newcomer Pompey, telling him that Caesar would be happy to see his enemy dead, which will help the Pharaoh to secure an ally in the form of the great Julius Caesar. So, the eunuch did as he was told. The other thing that Cleopatra did was to ask the then scholars of Alexandria –

Sechilius, and Archelius, to secretly smuggle the most important scrolls to *a place so secluded, that even the Gods won't be able to find.* The scholar brothers did as they were told, and by the time Caesar visited Egypt, they were out of the country with most of the important papyrus and other scrolls with them, along with a few more men. It took them nearly 3 years when in 45 BC they reached the foothill of the highest mountain in the world they had ever seen – The Mount Everest. But they soon understood that human curiosity would soon draw them to this mountain, so they searched for some other place nearby where they can set up the new Library.'

The Grandmaster stopped to catch his breath. The trio was entranced with the history of the Library and was listening intently.

'So, after one more year, at the start of 44 BC, in January, they reached here, at the gorge here and saw a place secluded from anywhere else on earth. The valley being hidden by the snow walls on three sides and covered by mists and clouds for the most part of the day, was perfect for them to set up a secret village. Adding to it, the frequent snowstorms ensured that no man would dare to come here. And that was how this Library was created here. It was after 3 years that the scholar brothers returned to Egypt, only to find Cleopatra returning from Rome after the murder of Julius Caesar, with her son Caesarion. When they met her, she told them to take more scrolls, books, texts, and papyrus with them back to here which were hidden during Caesar's visit, leaving only some skeleton scrolls there as a ruse, which they followed by the letter. At that time, due to different wars and tormenting of the ordinary people, not much people came to the Library, so it was not difficult to continue the ruse.

However, as and when new books came, messengers were sent here, in the new Library to inform about the new scrolls and books, which were later brought back here. So you see, the attacks on 391 AD by Emperor Theodosius I and on 642 AD by Caliph Omar didn't destruct much of the Library, since most of the things were already here.

We have been living in peace here since then, with all the scrolls, books, and texts intact here.'

'Wow.' Mark said at last. 'That's a hell lot of burden to carry for nearly 2000 years.'

'You are right.' The Grandmaster said, looking at them, at Sam mainly. It seemed he was expecting some more queries from the Indian.

As if on cue, Sam asked the question the guardian of the Library was expecting.

'But that doesn't explain how you all know my name.'

'Yes.' The Grandmaster replied, a little sadly. 'It was perhaps because of me that you are in danger right now. Hans Schleif had tried to find this Library his whole life. And he very well followed the same path that our forefathers had taken, following the breadcrumbs of the trail through the history. But it was his bad luck that he had to die before he could reach us. All he ever wanted was to find the Library, not anything else. No hunger for power, no fame. And we welcome such individuals among us.

But, it was not his fate. He had to commit suicide when the Nazi party was breathing on his neck, and his death saved us. We knew that he had found our hideout but couldn't help him without exposing us. And if we had exposed ourselves, then the Nazis would have easily got hold of the Callimachus scrolls, giving them what they wanted. The ultimate power. We couldn't allow that. I was a teenager at that time, but I saw my father take the tough call of not helping him.

However, we had found his diary later in a hidden hideout of his, where he asked his servant to keep it until his brother can come. But by then a letter was already posted to his brother. And that's how that German family came to know about the Library's existence. But, I am not sure for what reasons, they never came after us, or the Library. Until now.'

He said the last words looking directly at the trio. The meaning was not lost on them. Alexander, being a family of Hans was after the library now.

'Anyhow,' he continued. 'We had recovered his diary and kept with us. But it was in the year 2000 when one of my protégé told me about an Indian couple, who were noble and had hunger only for knowledge. My protégé met them quite accidentally in Germany when he was attacked by some bandits, and Rita and Hemanth had fought to save him, and ultimately were successful. It was then that I decided that these archeologists are good souls, and they must be rewarded with the knowledge of the Library. Though your parents were searching for the Nazi trail, it was us, who had provided them with the diary of Hans. During one of their excavations in an Ahnenerbe site, we had hidden the diary for them to find.

I had thought that once they find it, they will come straight to us, here in the Library, dedicating their lives to knowledge. But alas! That was not the case. Alexander had tried to buy them off once he learned that Hans' diary has resurfaced, but they refused. We were sure then that we have provided the trail to the correct persons. But we received news after a fortnight that some other historian had killed your parents and drowned them in *Markkleeberger See*.'

By then hearing about his parents, Sam's eyes have become moist. It was the Grandmaster who stood up and put a hand on his shoulder to console him, along with Eva of course.

'A historian?' Mark asked curiously.

'As far as we know, yes.' Said the Grandmaster. 'So, I sent some of my men to carry out a mission of mine. They found and secured Rita and Hemanth's body and brought them here.'

That made all three of them surprised.

'My parent's bodies are here?' Sam asked, a little too loudly.

'Yes, my boy.' The old man said, with a sad smile. 'We never wanted anyone to die. But see, because of us Hans has died, your parents and the good Professor too sadly. And I think some of the security people in Copenhagen too.' He said with his eyes narrowed.

'Anyways.' He continued. 'We had always kept an eye on you. When you were nearly ready to complete your Ph.D., and the Professor went to Frankfurt, my man had met him as a labor from your parent's archeological entail and told him everything about the diary. The Professor was skeptical and didn't believe it at first. But when the same person sent the diary and he read it, it was clear to him that what he heard was true. But before he could tell you, it seems he was also murdered.'

'Where are my parent's bodies?' Sam could ask the only question coming in his mind, barely hearing anything else.

'Right here.' The Grandmaster said, waving his hand downstairs.

'The underground vault contains the Callimachus scrolls and your parent's bodies, preserved perfectly. As I said, our greatest possessions are there.'

'Who was the historian that killed them?' Eva asked, ultimately breaking her silence.

'His name w ----'

Boom. Boom.

Before the Grandmaster could say anything more, serial blasts rocked the place.

CHAPTER NINETY

12:55 PM

The helicopters dangled in the air like angry birds out of the Arabian nights stories.

Alexander sat in the copilot seat and watched as the destruction unfold. Seconds ago, he had deployed a couple of the AGM-114 Hellfire missiles from the pods of the chopper. The first one had detonated on contact with the snow wall, just behind the Library building. The missiles were capable of destroying tanks, so it was not much difficult to obliterate the top part of the wall, resulting in a shower of snow, dust, and fire on the top of the building. The whole golden top of the Library was now covered with the snow and dirt. The second missile was targeted at the farm field on the right side of the Library, causing a billowing fireball to start there, and burning of most of the crops. With the sound of the twin explosions, all the residents of the small valley came out of their houses. Mothers tried to keep their children safe while the men tried to keep their families away from the fire and danger.

An evil grin crossed the face of the Dane billionaire.

'That's right.' He cried, spits coming out of his mouth. 'You motherfuckers. See the wrath of Alexander.'

He has gone insane. Sabir saw the Dane watching with crazy amazement all the destruction but didn't say anything.

Alexander looked back towards him.

'What are you waiting for? Let's get on with our business.'

With that, ropes were drawn out, and the mercenaries started zipping down from the two helicopters.

****

Mark saw everything from the gate of the Library.

As soon as he had heard the explosion, he knew it could be none other than Alexander himself. So, he asked the Grandmaster to stay in the building where he would be safe, while the trio ran for the main door. By the time they reached the gate, soldiers with black overalls and guns, have started climbing down from the helicopters. The 30mm minigun from the Apache started blazing violently, spatting a tongue of fire three feet long. The bullets came in hundreds, pinning the trio behind the door. Mark and Eva took cover in the two sides of the door, behind the strong walls. Sam remained pinned behind Mark, on the right side of the door.

'Eva.' Mark cried, in the onslaught of the firing. 'Take this.'

He threw a Kalashnikov towards her from his own backpack, while collecting an M4A1

Assault rifle for himself and looked outside. The bullets stopped from the minigun for a moment, probably for reloading, when Mark came out of cover and started firing blindly. From this distance, shooting at the helicopter was a hopelessly lost cause. So, the only thing he could fire at were into the climbers from the choppers. Most of his bullets went off course, but two of them found their mark. The first one hit the leg of a climber from the Apache, just scratching his calf, causing him to panic and lose his grip on the rope. The person fell quickly and swiftly, crying all the way down for thirty feet, where he landed on his back in the middle of the road with a sickening *splat*, painting the whole place in his blood and brain matters.

Mark's second bullet caught another man directly through the eye, who was climbing from the Eurocopter Tiger and caused him to lurch for a moment and then release the rope and fall all the way down. The bullet already had lodged itself in the hapless man's brain, making him dead long before he hit the ground.

Eva got out of her cover and tried to shoot as well, when suddenly the Eurocopter Tiger fired a missile of its own, straight at the door of the building, where the trio had been in hiding.

'Abandon post.' Cried Mark and started running, while at the same time dragging Sam with him by his arm.

Eva was frozen for a moment after seeing the missile on its way, but the cry from Mark brought her back to present. She started running back with all her might, following Sam and Mark into the building.

Booom.

A moment later, the missile connected to the gate and detonated. A billowing fireball started which obliterated the door to the Library almost instantly, taking with it half of the wall on the right side.

'Oh god.' Sam said, seeing behind him.

The fireball followed the trio like an angry monster from hell.

'This is not happening.' Eva said to herself, all the while running behind the men.

It was about to touch her when she dived forward as a last-ditch effort to outrun the fire and collided with Sam and Mark. Fortunately for them, the fire stopped some five feet behind them, while dust and rubble showered everywhere.

****

As soon as the mercenaries reached the ground, a total of twenty people now, after the loss of two of their comrades, they formed a perimeter around the houses. The people in the small village were all already inside their homes, to stay away from the firing. For the moment, the whole place seemed deserted and silent, with only the sentries from the choppers standing.

Once the perimeter was set up, the two helicopters - the Apache and the Tiger, both landed side by side, on the far corner of the valley. Alexander and Sabir came out of the lead helicopter, while Berthold came out from the second one, a little timidly. All the violence and killings for the last few days were not of his liking.

The Danish tyrant strode purposefully and full of confidence through the road and stopped near the dead body of the first person from his detail to die. He barely noticed the body of the dead man in the pool of his own blood and asked Sabir for the speaker that was brought in from the chopper.

One he was provided with the speaker, he stepped forward one step and started shouting.

'WE HAVE THIS PLACE COVERED. SAM AND MARK, COME OUT OF HIDING OR THE PEOPLE HERE WILL DIE.'

His voice boomed through the entire place.

CHAPTER NINETY-ONE

'What should we do?'

Eva asked the question which was on everybody's minds now. The four of them – Sam, Mark, Eva and now joined by the Grandmaster, were all inside the library in the main hall. The whole corridor seemed to be covered with dust and grits, along with some snow and ashes. The dust could still be seen in the air.

Thankfully, the fire had not reached here, which meant none of the scrolls were endangered. But in order to keep it that way, they needed to take a decision now.

'We should go out there.' Sam said, standing up. 'I have seen this madman up close in Denmark. He will kill all those helpless people outside if we don't go.'

'Sam is right.' The Grandmaster supported the Indian. 'We should save my people.'

'Yes, I got that, thank you.' Was the reply from Mark. He was still thinking on how to manage the situation best when suddenly something came into his mind.

'They never asked you to come out.' He said, now turning to Eva.

'That means, they don't consider you are a threat yet. Good.'

A smile formed in his lips.

'I am not going to like it, am I?' Eva said, seeing the hint of smile on the American soldier's face.

****

Two minutes later, the three people came out of the Library. Slowly, raising their hands.

Sam was in the middle while Mark and the Grandmaster were flanking his both sides.

'So Sam, we meet again.' Alexander said, smiling while stepping closer to Sam. 'You are one resilient son of a bitch.'

Sam said nothing in reply, just stared straight into the eyes of the Dane.

'And you.' The billionaire now moved a little right, to stand face to face with Mark. 'You have caused me more trouble than you can imagine.'

'I am happy to oblige.' Mark said, grinning.

Bam.

The punch connected his nose with great force, causing Mark to see stars in front of his eyes. Blood started oozing out of his nose slowly, and searing pain filled his face. It took a few seconds for Mark to focus his eyes on the person who had punched him in the face.

The Middle Eastern stood in front of him with his fists closed and ready for another punch.

'Oh no no Sabir.' Alexander said playfully to the man. 'Don't hit him so hard. He has to see what we are going to do.'

Though it looked like Sabir would have enjoyed punching some more, but he obeyed the Dane and stood down.

'And now.' The billionaire said, moving in front of the Grandmaster. 'Who might you be?'

'I am the Grandmaster of the Library of Alexandria, sworn protector of the Library and the knowledge it holds.'

'Oh! Is it?' Alexander laughed out loud. 'It sure doesn't look like you are doing an excellent job with that.'

The old man didn't bother to reply to the tyrant, instead stared ahead. It was then that Sabir noticed something.

'Where is the American woman?' He said out loud, looking at the trio standing in front of them.

'She is hurt.' Sam said, a little too defensibly.

'Then we shall fetch her out.' The Dane said. He then looked behind him, addressing two mercenaries.

'Bring the girl to me. If she tries something funny, put a bullet in her brain.'

CHAPTER NINETY-TWO

1:22 PM

Every single problem has a solution.

Eva had learned this lesson long ago while starting her career in NSA Cryptology department. There were times when everything seemed lost, and there was no way out. But a cool head could always find a solution in such dire times. Her boss, General Thomas had always taught this to his colleagues and subordinates, along with telling them how to keep control of the mind.

'Always take deep breaths to keep your mind calm.' He would say. 'Oxygen provides the brain with calmness.'

Now, pinned at the Library, with all the lights out in the floor, she had finally calmed her mind. And have put use to Mark's plan.

Let's just hope it works.

The two mercenaries entered the building and found themselves covered in darkness, among the rubble caused by the last missile detonation. But they recovered themselves quickly and put on their night vision goggles, turning the floor into a shade of dark green in front of them. Once that was done, they opened their rifles, a couple of Kalashnikovs and putting those in front of them, they started step by step, towards the inner sanctum of the Library.

The problem came after a couple of steps. In between the rubble, the first soldier while entering tripped onto something and fell on his face. The second person looked below and immediately saw the danger. A wire got disconnected from something, and a small black round object fell from somewhere in the wall on his right. The end of the wire carried a small silver colored pin.

Both the goons tried to cry out at the same time, somehow to warn each other and the others outside and to magically try and outrun the impending danger, but before any of them could say anything, a blast rocked the place, blasting both apart.

Eva came out to see her handiwork. The tripwire and the hand grenade have worked out perfectly. The idea of setting the booby trap from Mark had worked out.

Now she just hoped that both Mark and Sam were fine outside.

****

Alexander was looking at the Library, the architecture of it when he heard the sound of the blast inside.

Sam and Mark both smiled at that.

'There's something wrong in there.' He said, looking back at Sabir.

Sabir and Berthold were looking straight at Mark and Sam when the blast had taken place. Both looked towards the billionaire.

'Sabir, go inside with some of your men and see what that bitch is up to.' His face was contorted in anger.

Sabir just started to step towards the Library, when suddenly, unexpectedly, someone else called him up.

'No. Sabir you don't need to go there.' The sound came from behind Sabir and Alexander. 'We are here, and the Library is in our hands now. We will get the girl.'

Sabir just stopped in his tracks obediently, while the reaction of the Dane to this command was very different.

'Berthold. Who the hell are you to tell what I should do or not? You just shut the fuck up and stand where you……….'

Blam. Blam.

Before he finished his words, Alexander's body was hit by two bullets, bullets that came out of a Desert Eagle that had somehow magically appeared in Dr. Berthold's hands. Both the shots hit the Dane in his gut, causing the billionaire to lurch and fall. Alexander was so astonished and shocked by this, that at first he didn't realize what happened. It was after the blood started oozing out from his gut, that he got the full implications of the historian's actions.

'Why……why?' He asked very slowly, clearly being in pain.

'What the hell?' Both Sam and Mark shouted out in astonishment. The answer came from the most unexpected source. The grandmaster standing beside them, being captive in front of all the mercenaries, spoke out.

'I was about to tell you Sam, the name of the person who killed your parents. From what my sources had found out was that,' he gestured with his eyes towards the historian, 'Dr. Berthold Weber was the killer of your parents.'

CHAPTER NINETY-THREE

'You killed my parents?'

The shock in Sam's voice was unmistakable.

From childhood, after losing his parents, he had thought that they had accidentally drowned. Now only three days ago, from the letter of Professor Richard Hedley, he had come to know that they were in fact, killed. And now, when they had come to the Library, the Grandmaster had told them that a historian had killed them. But he had never thought that it could be Dr. Berthold, the fellow historian their parents had trusted so much that they had gone to the field with him. He was the person who had called up Rita and Hemanth to come to Germany for some research on the Nazis.

'Yes Sam.' Berthold said, a sinister smile forming in his lips. 'I needed your parents' help on some research on the Nazis, and that was the reason I had asked them to join me in Germany. But once they were there, your parents were contacted by someone who called himself 'one of the protectors of knowledge,' and that person entrusted them with a diary that would lead them to the Library of Alexandria. I was nearby at that time when they were speaking. The person told them not to speak about this to anybody. But I had thought your parents would at least tell me. How could they not? It was me who had called them, it was me who had given them a lead on Ahnenerbe, it was because of me that they came to Germany and

got in touch with the protector of the Library. BUT THEY DIDN'T.'
The German shouted out, at the top of his voice.

Sam watched in horror as the historian's eyes turned red slowly, indicating a hidden craziness now coming out. Mark, however, was watching something else. He had noticed that neither Sabir nor any of the mercenaries even flinched for once after the historian fired on Alexander.

He has them covered. They are all working for him.

'When I asked them about the diary of Hans, they denied having it. Can you believe? They simply denied while I had seen them taking the diary. So, my anger got better of me, and I just drowned them in the aquarium below my house. And Sabir here helped me out.' Berthold said with a smile.

'He was the one who was working with me during the excavation in Germany. But he was also hire for muscle who was used by Alexander many times. Therefore, he was the one who suggested the way out of this.' The German continued. 'He told me that Alexander had also known about the diary and had tried to get it from the Indian couple and that I should get in touch with him. It was then that I started working with Alexander to find out the Library. Because I need that power, a power that can grant me whatever I wish for.'

He looked at the sorry form of Alexander, struggling for his life and trying to staunch his blood oozing out of his stomach.

'I needed Alexander's resources and money to find the Library. And now that I am here, in front of the Library of Alexandria itself, just a step away from the legendary Callimachus scrolls, I don't need this person anymore.'

And with that, in that shocking instant, he raised the Desert Eagle in his hands and fired point blank at Alexander's head. The Danish billionaire's head exploded from the back, oozing blood and brain matters, and the tyrant dropped dead.

'Noooooo.' Cried out the Grandmaster. All the killings and bloodbath here at the heaven of knowledge had made him nauseous and filled him with sadness. 'No more killings. Please, take whatever you want.'

Sam personally didn't feel anything much about the death of Alexander though. After all, this person was responsible for the death of Professor Hedley. But that didn't cross out his hatred for Berthold.

He is responsible for my parents' deaths. He must pay.

But before he could think or do anything, Berthold pressed the Desert Eagle in his temple.

'Now, back to business.' He said. 'Where were we? Oh yeah! The lady needs to come out.'

He then shouted out towards the Library.

'COME OUT MISS EVA BROWN, OR SAM DIES.'

CHAPTER NINETY-FOUR

1:25 PM

'Don't hurt anyone.' Eva's voice came out of the darkness, from the inside of the Library. 'I am coming. I am coming.'

She had seen what happened in the last few minutes from the Library after her trap blew out the two goons. She had seen Berthold firing at Alexander, she had heard what the historian said about the death of the parents of Sam, and she had seen him kill Alexander Penbrose in cold blood. Though the Dane was not the best person on her list, still, nobody deserves to die like this, unable to defend himself.

She had also noticed the same thing Mark had. All the men of Alexander seemed to be working for the German historian now. And now that person was threatening Sam.

'Leave him.' Mark cried out, still his hands in the air. 'You don't need to hurt Sam.'

'Indeed.' The historian said, smirking. 'If the lady doesn't come out now....'

Blam.

Without saying anything more, he just shot, from point blank. The bullet just scratched the left ear of Sam, drawing blood. Sam, due to the sudden pain, reacted to that, contorting his face in anger and pain, holding his ear, which didn't do any good to slow down the pain, and blood still came through in between the fingers.

Mark tried to attack him, but Sabir just pointed his Heckler and Koch towards him, deterring the American to do anything stupid.

'I am coming, dammit.' Eva said from inside the darkness, still inside the Library. 'Just give me a min......yes, now coming.'

Both Sabir and Berthold looked ahead, towards the library and to their horror, saw very different things coming out of the broken door, instead of Eva. Before they understood anything, two red-colored things came out at breakneck speed. One of them hit Berthold square on his nose, knocking him down on his butt and drawing blood, while the second one hit the gun hand of Sabir, knocking his gun out.

'Attack Mark.' The cry and Eva, both came out of hiding at the same time.

Before any of the other people standing there could comprehend what exactly happened, Mark sprang into action. He hit the stunned Sabir on his face, breaking his nose in the process and taking the revenge of the punch earlier, and following his action by dropping low and somersaulting, just over the fallen gun.

Eva, on the other hand, had already come out with a gun of her own. The M4A1 Assault rifle blazed in her hand on full auto as soon as she came out of the hiding. The mercenaries were not at all ready for this kind of attack with everybody under observation and being covered by gun. So, they all scattered for cover as soon as she opened fire.

Sam and Grandmaster took a minute to understand precisely what was happening, when one of the mercenaries came straight towards them, brandishing his Kalashnikov to finish them off. It was at that moment, the exact same moment, that both Eva and Mark looked towards Sam and saw the impending danger. By then, Mark has already secured the gun that was earlier with Sabir, whereas both Sabir and Berthold have taken cover behind the nearest building. Both the Americans without any delay pointed their guns at the goon and fired on full auto. The result was devastating. The man had bullets continuously entering his body both from his front and back, resulting in a shower of blood and internal organs from both front and back, causing him to dance long after his death.

'Come on.' Eva said, commanding both the Indian and the old man to follow her. 'Let's get some cover.'

She had stopped firing and started reloading, while Mark kept firing a few rounds to keep them covered.

'That…. was unexpected.' The Grandmaster said, breathless, once they were all inside the Library, safe for now.

'Thanks.' Sam could only say, still trying to digest what all happened in the last few minutes.

'Yeah.' Mark said, still looking outside for any danger. 'Save that for now. We are still in danger.'

CHAPTER NINETY-FIVE

Sam looked away, still thinking about the betrayal of Dr. Berthold Weber.

'He is a good historian. I have not seen much people with such caliber and such detailed knowledge on different fronts of history and archeology.'

Sam remembered what his father had told once to his mother, around eighteen years ago, on a sunny morning, a few days before leaving for Germany. He was playing with his things in Hemanth's study when his parents were discussing their coming trip to Germany.

Never thought I would see him this way.

All four of them including the Grandmaster were huddled together just near the rubble, inside the entrance of the Library. After the small battle outside, Mark calculated, around seventeen more mercenaries would be there, considering he finished off two people at first, and later Eva set a trap and killed two more. Just before they came for cover, both he and Eva had shot the fifth one.

'I am out.' Eva said, throwing off her gun away behind her. 'Checking for another one.'

'We are still outnumbered and outgunned.' Mark said, thinking out loud. 'We need to even the odds.'

'And how do you propose we do that?' The Grandmaster said, gasping a bit due to the last few minutes tension and running for cover.

'I......let me think.' Replied Mark, while Sam went to help Eva.

****

'Sir, we need to do something.' Sabir said in a hushed tone, sitting just beside Berthold.

'I know, I know.' The historian replied, irritated. 'That bitch attacked me with a brick, can you imagine? A brick.' He said, while still nursing his nose.

The blood kept oozing out of the nose, though the pain had dulled a bit. But it was his ego that was hurt more than his nose itself. He had never thought that American bitch would attack them so suddenly and fiercely.

'I have a plan, sir.' Sabir said to him from his side.

They both were hiding behind the first building on the left, near the Library. From here, Sam and his friends could not be seen, but they both knew that the four people were still inside. More than the pain, what fumed Berthold more was the fact that he had the upper hand, the element of surprise, and now he had lost it.

'What's the plan?' He asked, still irritated, both with himself and with Sam, for having such resourceful friends on his side. Not only this time, but they had also outsmarted them earlier in Copenhagen as well.

He had planned for this moment for the last eighteen years. He had killed his colleagues Rita and Hemanth Rawath, he had done a deal with the devil by siding himself with that Danish billionaire Alexander. Now he couldn't lose the Library again, just because of Sam and his friends.

But he trusted Sabir. This person had helped him in the past as well and still was on his side. So he listened carefully what the Syrian had to say.

After a minute, once he heard the plan, he was quite impressed and nodded his approval.

Sabir is resourceful too.

****

'In case we die here today.' Sam said, in the darkness inside the Library, to Eva. 'Can we talk about what happened in Copenhagen, in the *Kastellet*?'

'You mean the kiss?' Eva turned towards him. Though it was darkness inside, still from somewhere a single ray of light was coming, probably a crack somewhere at the top, due to the missile blow earlier at the snow wall just behind the building. In that little light, both were able to see each other.

'We will talk about it once we are out……….'. She stopped suddenly, remembering something.

'What happened?' Sam asked, seeing her stopping in mid-sentence and clearly thinking something. 'What is it?'

'We didn't know about the location of the Library until we saw the scanned pages of Hans' diary from the locked iPad from the Professor, right?'

'Yes.' Sam replied, a little dumbfounded by the sudden change of topic, not sure where this conversation was going.

'Well, Alexander didn't know about the location either.' She said, still thinking.

Correct.

Sam now understood what she was implying. He didn't get the time to think about it either.

'Then how the hell they came here?' Both said in unison.

But before they could talk or think more about it, a volley of firing started from outside.

'Shit.' Sam said. 'They have regrouped and attacked.'

'Let's go.' Eva said while picking up a Wildey and thrusting it into Sam's hand. She herself took another Heckler and Koch from the abandoned bag pack of Mark. 'Mark needs our help. You think you can manage?'

She looked at him with her left eyebrow raised.

Sam looked at the Wildey in his hand and nodded with determination.

And they both started running to the front of the building to join the fight, where Mark and the Grandmaster were holed up.

CHAPTER NINETY-SIX

'Shit.'

The bullet just missed his head by a mere centimeter. He was just thinking how to get the advantage of numbers against Berthold when suddenly all the mercenaries attacked as one.

Not all, Mark thought.

With experience, he had learned one thing, how to calculate the number of people by hearing some subtle signs. The number of guns roaring, the sound of footsteps, the leapfrogging process. That experience had come in handy in many field operations for him over the years. And now also it came into his mind.

From the roaring of guns and by judging the number of bullets, it felt to him, that it was around twelve people firing at them.

That's odd. As per his calculation, except Berthold and that middle eastern man, Sabir, there should be seventeen more mercenaries. *So where have these men gone?*

He looked out for a second from his cover and before a bullet found its mark, he moved his head back behind the broken hinge of the door of the Library. He had seen what he needed to see. The men were coming straight towards them, in a classic leapfrog formation. When two people fired, the third man skipped those two and moved forward, and then he would shoot and give a chance to the other two to move forward. And that way the cycle continues until the enemy was overwhelmed.

There's decidedly less time.

'What's the situation?' Eva and Sam reached behind him and crouched.

'Well, short version. It seems they are setting a trap for us.' Mark said, looking back at them. 'The enemy is about to overwhelm us and......'

He stopped for a second. He suddenly had an idea what the other missing five might be doing.

He looked back towards his friends. An Indian archeological student holding the Wildey like his mama's kitchen spoon, an old man cowering behind the rubble, more a liability than an asset, and an NSA cryptologist who had proven herself more competent in the field than he would have thought her before, but she still needed some more work, some more training.

Not good. But if I need to save everyone and everything, I have to do what's unthinkable.

All three were looking at him, trying to understand the predicament.

'Grandmaster.' He said, looking at the protector of the Library. 'You and me. We are going to the Callimachus scrolls. Now.'

He looked at the stunned faces of Eva and Sam.

'You two.' He said, with an authority that the others had not seen these few days. The cold precision of the soldier was back. 'You have to hold the enemy here. They are trying to set a trap. Around twelve people are firing. The others must be going for the scrolls. I trust you guys. And Sam....', he said looking at the Indian. 'For God's sake hold the Wildey towards the enemy, not me.'

Sam looked at his hand. Indeed, he was holding the gun pointed somehow towards the American. Mark held his hand and positioned the weapon correctly.

'Now, just point and shoot.' He smiled.

With that, he left with the old man towards the rear of the building, to the main hall. From there, they must travel down into the basement, to the most prized room that the Grandmaster had told them about.

****

Blam.

The sound of the gun going off nearly stunned Sam. *And the jolt.* It felt like his shoulder would be wretched out due to the recoil of the firing.

'You need to straighten your hand more, and put a little more pressure on the arm, instead of putting all pressure on your palm.' Eva said, from the other side.

She had seen how awkward the gun looked in the Indian's hand, suggesting this man had never even in his dreams used any firearm.

'Thanks for the suggestion.' Sam smiled. But the nervousness made his smile look like a horse chewing.

'No time like the present.' She smiled back, and, in a flash, moved out and fired straight, in a short three-burst firing mode.

The nearest mercenary fell on his back, never to get up. One bullet has put a hole in his leg, while another one burst opened his brains out.

That would give us a few seconds.

Blam. Blam.

The 9mm bullets from Sam's gun accidentally hit one of the goons in his chest and face, who was leapfrogging his mates on the left side, near one of the buildings. The man flew back a few feet, with all his hands and legs dangling high, and fell on one of his mates, who was about to fire on Sam. The result was somewhat unexpected. The second man's finger was already on the trigger, and the dead body of the first man caused him to fall on his back as well, causing him to pull the trigger accidentally.

The man's Kalashnikov was on full auto when he fell. As a result, his bullets started firing on the opposite side and hit two people on stomach and legs, who were parallel to the hapless man.

'That.... was.... unexpected.' Sam said, shouting.

'Good work soldier.' Eva said and looked at Sam, who was smiling awkwardly. 'Wait, you didn't hit him on purpose, did you?'

The Indian's smile gave her all the answer she needed.

'Accidental or not, we have three people less to worry about now.' She said while firing at the same time.

'That should hold them off for some time.'

CHAPTER NINETY-SEVEN

The room was nothing Mark had ever expected.

Only two torches were there in the room, illuminating it in a dull yellow light. Minutes ago, they entered through the hidden door and the bare steps there, which consisted of the wall on one side and a thirty feet void on the other, from the main hall of the Library. The door to the basement was at the end of the main hall on the right. It took them a minute to reach the end. The steps stopped at a big circular hall which was lit with torches, and a door at the eastern end of it.

Once entered through that door, Mark's eyes fell immediately upon the only three things present in the room. The first one was in the middle of the room, inside a glass case. It contained a papyrus scroll, faded to yellow due to age, but otherwise well preserved. The scroll was majestically sitting on a pedestal, around 4 feet above the floor of the room. It was open in full, like that of a big book kept open in libraries and museums all over the world.

So, this is the scroll. The Callimachus scrolls, for which all the fuss is about.

And then he saw the other two things. Both the things looked entirely out of place in the room, albeit the Library itself. Both looked like glass boxes, some six feet long and two and a half feet in breadth. The ornate covering was nothing he had ever seen on any glass. It was only after he took a few steps to take a good look, that he came to see what was inside them. And it shocked him.

Bodies. Two of them, in two sarcophaguses.

One of a man, a man with fair skin, middle-aged, around forty of age, black hair and closed eyes. The second one was that of a woman, a beautiful woman, also with fair skin, age somewhere around mid-thirties, with black hair and closed eyes, same as the man. Both people looked serene. Both the bodies were covered with salt and the sarcophaguses were sealed, keeping them preserved fully.

He suddenly remembered what the Grandmaster had told them earlier in the main hall.

They found and secured Rita and Hemanth's body and brought them here.

So, this is what happened to them.

'We have shown our utmost respect to them and preserved their bodies for Sam to come and do the final rites.' The Grandmaster said from behind him.

'Yeah.' Mark replied, a little too slowly, with respect to the couple's dead bodies. 'I got that.'

****

Thud.

Sabir landed softly on the floor of the main hall. The four other people with him were still dangling from the rope above, making their way in. They all had made it through a crack on the top of the building, which got created when the first missile had detonated, and the snow wall dropped on the top of the Library.

It was the plan of Sabir that he had discussed with Berthold ten minutes ago. While they were hiding behind the last building, it was then that he noticed the crack from his vantage point and the plan formed in his mind. Quickly, he decided to keep Sam and his friends busy by sending all his men to attack them, giving himself and a skeleton crew of just four people the opportunity to go from the top. 'Come quick.' He said in a hushed tone to the others. 'We should be in and out before they know.'

While waiting for his men to come down, he looked onwards. Something important like the Callimachus scrolls would be hidden, and not in plain sight. While coming down, he had seen all the floors above and not seen anywhere where a scroll or a book could be hidden.

It has to be somewhere here.

He looked everywhere, and that's when he saw the door. A door on the right side, just where all the bookcases have ended.

What's a door in that place doing?

The door couldn't have been seen if not there was a crack, where the door was left open a bit, albeit a little one. Anyone would miss it, but since Sabir was looking for exactly something like this, he was able to notice this quickly. The color of the wall, the bookcases, and this door were all the same, making it nearly impossible for anyone to notice it.

If there's anywhere a scroll would be hidden in this Library, this would be it.

He waited for the last of his men to descend into the hall and then started towards the door.

But why was it open?

Two of his men followed him, while the other two went forward. Once the door was opened ajar by the lead person, some stairs could be seen descending to the basement. Sabir was not able to see anything after the third step, and that made him uncomfortable. There was not a single source of light, and the whole place was plunged into darkness. But while the door was open, they would not be able to use the night vision goggles due to the little light coming from the main hall.

As a result, the first two people started descending slowly, giving Sabir and the rest two room to climb down the stairs.

'Be careful.' Sabir instructed his men while drawing his ARX160 A3 Assault Rifle at the ready, all others following suit. He then closed the door behind him and started the descent.

The first two people had already reached the fourth and fifth stairs respectively when the door was closed. They just started to get their night vision goggles out....

Blam.

Suddenly, shockingly, without any warning, a gun fired somewhere nearby and a there was a sound of someone falling. Before Sabir could get a grip on what happened, there was another sound, a sound of two people fighting.

CHAPTER NINETY-EIGHT

Still, nine people left.

That was the main thought in Sam's mind right now. But before he could think more, a curious site greeted him and Eva, when they tried to look outside.

It seemed Ballav had somehow managed to get some more people with him from the village buildings when the mercenaries started attacking the duo. Now, at least thirty people gathered outside and started throwing whatever was available for them as weapons, towards the mercenaries. Some of them used the knives, while others used stones and snowballs as weapons.

'You are not welcome here.' The cries started coming. 'Leave us in peace.'

The sudden attack from behind made the last nine people baffled, making them rooted to their spots for a minute. A minute that cost them their advantages. Both Sam and Eva came out of hiding and started firing on the mercenaries, while they were distracted by the attack from the villagers. Eva was able to cut off the last three people of the group standing closest to the Library, while Sam fired four shots. Luckily one of those hit a goon on his back, incapacitating him.

Some of the mercenaries were able to get off a few shots before the villagers overwhelmed the rest five people, causing two of the villagers to take bullets and die. But that did nothing to discourage the villagers. In fact, that made them more enraged, and within a few minutes, everything was over.

Five minutes later, the remaining three goons were all tied up and circled by the villagers. Two more have died while fighting with the protectors of Library, while the villagers have also lost two more. The whole place now held dead bodies of nine mercenaries and four villagers. Some of the other villagers also seemed to have suffered injuries.

But that was the least of concerns for Sam.

Where's Berthold?

'Berthold is not here. As is Sabir.' Sam said to the cryptologist.

'Yeah. It seems they have gone with others to collect the scroll.' Eva replied while doing a round of the village and coming back near the Library door, where Sam was still standing.

'Ok.' Sam replied. 'We have to go inside and help Mark. He is outgunned and outnumbered too.'

'Yes.' Ballav came up beside them. 'You should go and help your friend there. We have here covered.'

His eyes looked sad, due to the loss of four friends in the battle. But there were no tears.

'Thank you for helping us here. Now go.'

With that, the duo started running inside the Library.

****

Mark was fighting his own battle.

He had plunged the hidden place in darkness before Sabir and his four goons came and was waiting for them to step into the stairs in darkness and close the door behind them. With the whole place in total darkness, Mark had assumed correctly that the attackers would not be able to afford to keep the door open and use their night vision goggles at the same time, as that would enhance the light coming from the crack outside, causing them losing their eyesight, either temporary or permanent.

And there was very little time after Sabir closing the door and his people donning their goggles, which he used perfectly.

With the thermal imaging goggles already donned over his eyes, the first thing that Mark did was to put a bullet in the head of the lead person at point blank range from the seventh step where he was waiting in an alcove on the right-side wall, the wall that was connected to the stairs, causing the man to double over and fall from the bare stairs to thirty feet down with a heavy *thud*, dead before he hit the ground. Next, he threw a punch straight at the second person coming through the steps, causing his nose to break straightaway, exploding with blood. While the man was not able to do anything, and falling on his back, a strong kick on his stomach made him fall on his mates who were following behind.

The limp body of the man fell on the next two people behind him in the constricted space of the stairs, causing the first one to lose his balance and fall off the stairs, following his dead comrade, the first one to die.

He cried all the way before a *crack* sounded, suggesting the breaking of his skull on contact with the concrete floor below. The last person to follow Sabir was on the other side of the stairs, and even though he lost his footing, he was in no immediate danger, except banging his head hard on the wall adjacent to the stairs. But Mark was not about to give him any respite. Before the man recovered, he fired two quick shots, causing the bullets to enter the body of the man in his chest and face. The whole fight took less than ten seconds.

Blam.

Just as he was about to turn around entirely and attack Sabir, suddenly a bullet hit his arm, causing him to lose his gun, and the next instant a strong kick connected his stomach, blowing the air out of his lungs. Before he recovered from that, for an instant, a ray of light came from the door behind Sabir, making him think Eva and Sam have arrived on his aide. But he couldn't contemplate much on that as another punch from Sabir connected his shoulders, and he lost his balance and started painfully rolling over the stairs.

It was after a few seconds that he fell to the end of the stairs, covered in his own blood and devoid of all energy, where the Grandmaster was hiding in a nearby alcove.

'Well, well, well. It seems Mr. Mark here tried to put up quite a fight.' A voice boomed inside the subterranean place, followed by a strong flashlight.

The voice of Berthold Weber.

CHAPTER NINETY-NINE

1:45 PM

The door seemed to be closed from inside when they reached. Both Sam and Eva have heard muffled gunshots while coming here. Fearing the worst, they arrived at the door, only to find it bolted shut from inside. The last shot they have heard was a few seconds ago and after that nothing. Shouting Mark's name from outside didn't help either as there was no answer from him. They were not even sure if Mark was able to hear them through the closed door.

'Seems like they are in trouble.' Eva said, sharing worried glances with Sam. 'Both Berthold and Sabir are not outside.'

'Yeah.' The Indian replied. 'They must have gone inside for the scrolls.'

It was at that moment that Ballav entered along with two of the residents of the village. All were fuming in fury due to the damage to the Library. The only respite was that there was no damage to the inside of the Library of Alexandria, in turn keeping all the thousands of books and scrolls unharmed.

'Let us help you.' Ballav offered, seeing their predicament.

After another minute of trying, the door finally cracked under the combined weight of all five people. A couple of tries more, and the whole wooden door fell from its hinges. Sam and Eva sprinted through the stairs, without waiting for anything else. From their vantage point, a sliver of light could be seen coming out of a door on the eastern side of the hall nearly thirty feet below. No other illumination in the hall or the stairs, causing them difficulty to see in the darkness.

But without thinking about that, the duo started running towards the end of the stairs. In between they crossed two bodies, bodies wearing black coveralls, suggesting them to be the men of Alexander, or of Berthold, considering what happened earlier.

Mark seems to have given a hard time to them.

Both of them crossed the bodies, and sprinted down the stairs in the near darkness, only illuminated by a sliver of light from the open door below. The light source coming from below didn't seem enough to illuminate the hall below, but Eva and Sam didn't bother. They jumped off the stairs once they reached near the end and ran with all their might. Both carried guns with them, Sam holding the Wildey and Eva with her Heckler and Koch.

Again, a couple of bodies, both bloody, both already dead. *An example of Mark's handiwork.*

They jumped above them, crossing on the fly and reached the door ....

.... And stopped dead on their tracks.

'Welcome my friends.' Berthold said, looking at them, pointing his Desert Eagle straight at Sam.

CHAPTER HUNDRED

'Welcome my friends.'

Berthold was pointing the pistol straight at Sam's head, from near the door and was smiling with pleasure.

The whole room couldn't be seen from where they were standing. But from what Sam could see, it didn't look good, not good at all.

'Oh, no.' Eva cried out from beside Sam, looking inside the room. Mark was down completely on the floor, his face bloody, one eye seemed to be swollen and while blood dripped from the other. He appeared to have sustained a substantial injury and was currently out. He was fallen on the floor on his chest, and his left hand could be seen from where Sam was standing. A deep gash on his left hand suggested a terrible injury, even a fracture may be, and blood kept oozing out in trickles from the wound.

Other than Mark, there were some other things to be noticed by them as well. Firstly, Sabir was standing near a glass case, which stood on a pedestal in the middle of the room. The case seemed to contain a yellowed scroll of some kind. *The Callimachus Scroll,* Sam guessed. Next, beside the pedestal, the Grandmaster was sitting in a kneeling position with his hands behind his head, and the Syrian was pointing his gun straight at his temple. The old man seemed to be sorrowed too much and kept looking at Mark's fallen body while praying silently, with tears in his eyes.

Lastly, the things that most intrigued Sam were two glass boxes at the far end of the room. From his position, Sam was not able to see what those boxes contained inside them.

'Good for you two to join us.' The German said, in cold humor. 'You three have caused me quite a lot of trouble.'

'What have you done to Mark?' Eva asked, looking straight at the historian.

'It was not me, really.' He said, mocking sadness but still pointing the gun at Sam. 'It was my trusted friend Sabir, who got the better of Mr. Mark.'

'You fucking---' Sam started to step forward towards the historian---
-

'No Sam.' Berthold said while moving the gun between Eva and Sam. 'Both of you, throw away your weapons. I have seen you playing with those for a long time. No more.'

Both Sam and Eva looked at each other.

'DO IT.' Shouted out Berthold, prompting them to throw away their weapons. 'Or else the old man here, dies.'

Sabir's finger tightened around the trigger of his gun. Out of options, the duo was forced to throw away their own weapons.

In the meantime, Ballav and two others reached the bottom of the stairs and were quickly able to assess the situation from their position. The Nepali gestured his two people to move back and slowly all three of them quietly returned into the shadows, all the while keeping themselves away from Berthold or Sabir's eyes.

'So, at last, it seems I am successful.' Said Berthold. 'After all my troubles, after so much deception, at last, today, I am standing in the fabled Library of Alexandria.' He laughed, like a crazy person. 'The Callimachus scrolls are here, as are the bodies of my friends Hemanth and Rita.'

The last words were explicitly said for Sam, which had its intended effect.

So that's what the glass boxes contained. My parents' bodies.

Tears welled up in his eyes while looking at the glass sarcophaguses. 'Sam.' Eva said from his side, trying to get hold of him. 'Don't listen to him. He is just trying to make you weak. Don't let him win.'

'There's nothing to win here Miss Eva Brown.' The German said to her, all the while pointing his gun at her while looking at Sam. The Indian suddenly seemed to be in a trance, looking straight at the life-sized glass boxes, which held the bodies of Rita and Hemanth Rawath.

'We have won already.' The historian continued. 'Because of Rita and Hemanth, I came to know about the existence of the diary of Hans. With the help of Alexander, I was able to arrange resources to aide my search of the scrolls. After that, I was the one who asked that fool to put a transmitter in Sam's shoulder while he was patching up the injury so that if he ever finds the Library, we can also find it simply by following him. And we have already communicated outside for a pickup, which will be arriving in some time. Now, you see Miss NSA, I had the contingencies always prepared. It took me eighteen years, but in the end, I have won.'

With that, keeping his eyes on Eva and the fully tranced and crying Sam, Berthold moved towards the pedestal.

'It's not for you to hold.' The Grandmaster shouted out seeing the German advancing towards the pedestal, still kneeling on his knees.

'That I will decide old man.' He spat out in anger while advancing towards the glass case holding the scrolls. 'Sabir, keep an eye on them. If they even blink, kill them.'

In response, Sabir just nodded and kept his eyes on all of them.

Berthold reached the glass case, and without so much of remorse, he lifted the glass and let it fall all way to the floor, breaking into thousand pieces. But he never looked at it.

Instead, he grabbed the yellowed Callimachus scrolls very carefully, with a huge smile on his face.

'Finally. The secret to the infinite power is mine.'

CHAPTER HUNDRED-ONE

Thwack.

'Ahwwwwww…. aah.'

A sudden sound and a painful shout came up behind the German historian, causing him to whirl around.

'It seems that you have an unending stupidity too.'

The voice came from below him, and before he knew what happened, two mighty kicks connected his both kneecaps at the same, bending both his legs at an awkward angle.

Crack.

The sound of both his knees breaking simultaneously resounded in the whole room.

'Oh, you fuck.' He shouted out, looking at his attackers while falling on the floor slowly.

Sam stood in front of him, with a smile of triumph on his face.

Beside him, Mark was just getting up from the floor.

It was a few minutes ago, when Berthold was talking about the bodies of Hemanth and Rita that Mark had regained consciousness.

It took him a second to get the idea of what's happening in the room, but it was Sam and the persons he had seen creeping up behind Eva, that gave him the idea. He had seen Ballav and two more people advancing the room through the shadows brandishing knives. He then saw Sam looking at Sabir from the corner of his eyes, trying to judge the distance, all the while keeping the deception of being an emotional person with tears flowing from his eyes alive.

Sam is not an emotional fool. But he made Berthold believe that he was, trying to get an advantage out of this.

The Syrian was keeping his eyes on Eva, oblivious of the danger looming for him just behind her. He was ignoring Mark because of his broken state, and Sam, primarily because he was in an entranced state and was advancing towards the sarcophaguses of his parents. The same people whom he had helped Berthold to murder in cold blood all those years ago.

Sam has fooled everybody.

It was then that Mark's eyes met Sam and Mark gestured him to attack Berthold on his signal, and at the same time gesturing Eva to duck once their eyes met, while Ballav and others threw their knives towards the Syrian. And then all hell broke loose.

Two of the knives were out of the target, while the third one had entered directly in the thigh muscle of Sabir, tearing his jeans and the flesh, drawing blood and a painful cry from him in the process. At that moment, Mark made his comment, making the German turn towards them. And then as if on cue, both men threw powerful kicks simultaneously, breaking both kneecaps of the historian at the same time.

A well-deserved punishment.

Eva, on the other hand, didn't want to give Sabir any room to fight. While the Syrian was trying to get the knife out of his leg, she ran and collided with him at full speed. Both fell on the ground at the same time, but Sabir was quicker to react. He got the knife out of his leg and was about to plunge it into the extended leg of Eva----

'No, you don't.'

A powerful kick connected his wrist, causing him to lose the knife. This time the kick came from Mark.

He had already got up, and came to Eva's aide, while Sam, Ballav and other two were taking care of Berthold.

Sam kicked hard on the face of the German, drawing blood and one of his teeth to the ground.

'You will pay for this.' The historian shouted out on the top of his voice. 'You cannot win this fight.'

Blam.

While broken and bloodied, Berthold still had the gun in his hand, which he fired suddenly towards Sam. Strangely, the Indian felt nothing this time. No sharp kick of the bullet, no blood, nothing. It was then that he noticed what just happened. In a kind of slow motion, the Grandmaster started kneeling on his knees, with his back towards Sam.

'Noooo.'

Sam dashed towards the old man, while Ballav plunged a knife directly into the palm of the German historian, in the process getting rid of the gun in his hand and throwing it away from the room, through the door.

'They will find the power.' Berthold cried out shouting.

A kick on his face, this time by Ballav, and Berthold was out cold.

'No Grandmaster, what have you done?' Sam said, reaching the old man, and supporting him with his hand.

A trickle of blood flowed from the chest of the Grandmaster, result of coming in between Sam and Berthold at the last moment and trying to save the Indian from the bullet.

'It's ok……Sam.' The Grandmaster said, with quite a difficulty. 'I…. I have done what I was supposed to….do.'

He said, in between ragged breaths. It took all his effort to speak up.

He is dying.

The bullet had actually hit him in the chest, making it impossible to save him now.

'Nononono.' Sam cried. 'You will be fine.' He said while trying to make the old man comfortable in his lap. He suddenly remembered a week ago, in a similar situation, in a café in Cambridge, holding the Professor in his lap in the same way.

So much death. For what?

The Grandmaster smiled. A smile of a man who knew he was dying. 'You can't save me….my boy.' He replied. 'You are a good man……a man what your parents……wanted you to be.' He stopped to take a breath. 'Give them your respect…... and keep their blessings with you.'

'Ballav…,' he said, looking at the Nepali standing behind Sam with two others, tears flowing from his eyes. 'You…... have…. served...us well. You…. will…be…the next Grandmaster.'

With that, the old man stopped talking, and his eyes rolled. A second later, his head lolled to the side.

Dead.

CHAPTER HUNDRED-TWO

While Sam was taking care of the dying Grandmaster, Mark and Eva had their own things to worry about.

Mark attacked Sabir with a classic open palm hit, which Sabir was able to deflect easily, by using his left hand, while with his other hand he punched hard in the American's gut, causing him to double over and keeping him winded. Mark was already weak and broken and bloodied, and was not able to see clearly, due to the fall earlier from the stairs, so it really made him weaker this time.

But, before the Syrian was able to celebrate, a hard kick connected his lower jaw, this time coming from Eva, that left his head ringing. He was about to recover when he saw two kicks coming from his two sides. Both the Americans started attacking him at the same time. He used both his hands to defend himself from the attack, while the other two did something curious.

Mark and Eva looked at each other for a moment and decided their attack plan. While Sabir defended himself from their kicks, they did something unexpected together. Both the Americans launched themselves in the air and used their feet together to strike Sabir. All four legs kicked out hard and connected the Syrian's chest together. The hit was so hard that Sabir thought he heard one of his ribs breaking, making him airborne for a moment.

He landed on the western side wall hard, hitting his back. Blood came out of his mouth in the form of a cough.

'That ought to keep you quite.' Mark commented.

Bam.

A punch on his face now from Sam, who came up after Ballav and the two others took the unconscious Berthold and the dead body of the Grandmaster out.

'This is for helping a killer.' He said out loud.

Sabir collapsed in a heap on the floor, out cold

'Well, that went fine.' Mark said. 'Now who's going to carry this guy to the top?'

CHAPTER HUNDRED-THREE

4:45 PM

Sam looked at the black smoke with moist eyes.

It flew from the ground and met the clouds above. Not that it had to travel too much high to do that. At this height, sometimes, the clouds were below, in the valley too. At this hour, everything was shrouded in twilight, even the clouds. The houses below in the valley, even the big Library itself, could not be seen now. The broken pieces of the helicopters, 3 of them including the backup one which Berthold had told earlier were also shrouded in the mist, to be taken care of later.

'They are in peace now.' Ballav said, from his side.

Sam looked behind him.

All the villagers stood behind him with fresh tears coming out of their eyes.

Every one of them has come to pay their respects to the Grandmaster.

The three flames burnt steadily, but with a hue of orange. The pyres were nearly done now. Sam could see his friends standing beside him too. Mark stood at the far right, looking somewhere in the sky, lost in his own thought. Eva however, stood beside him, holding his hand, giving him strength. And beside him on the other side, stood the new Grandmaster of the Library of Alexandria, Ballav Sang.

They all wanted good for the society. Now they all are gone.

He looked at the two pyres near him. It has taken all his mental strength to finally see his parents' bodies, preserved for the last eighteen years in the underground room with the Callimachus scrolls. The people here had kept them for him only, paying their utmost respect to them. Both his parents were looking the same as he remembered them. His father looked the same manly as before with his mustache, broad shoulders and the fair skin.

Rita, on the other hand, his mother, looked as beautiful as ever, even after her death. Her skin still seemed milky white as he remembered, with her tender face and the life-altering smile. Both of them looked in peace with their eyes closed, and the smiles on their lips.

Finally, I know what happened to them.

So, he felt it fitting to do the final rites of his parents here, on the top of the northern side wall of the valley which housed the Library of Alexandria.

The other pyre, on his left, was that of the Grandmaster. Since there was no heir of the old man, he had named Ballav as his successor for being the Grandmaster of the Library. A tribute for serving the old man for so many years without questioning. And the Nepali had paid his respect by performing the final rites of the Grandmaster himself.

'We all have paid prices for saving the Library from the tyrants over two centuries.' Said one of the villagers from behind Sam. He looked behind and found the same old lady he had encountered earlier coming towards him.

'Your parents were the most respected persons here. We had always paid respect to them and prayed for your arrival.' The lady said. 'I know it is hard for you but think about it. They have raised you, and you have become what they wanted. In fact, you are as good as them. You found them, and you found the Library.'

She offered her blessing to him, which Sam took hesitantly.

'What about Sabir?' Mark asked Ballav.

After the fight below, Berthold was taken out into the open, where he had been offered as a tribute to the Himalayan snow leopards and bears, who from time to time attacked nearby in search of foods and were respected by the inhabitants here as Gods. The villagers have taken their revenge by hacking his legs and arms from his body and feeding the same to the snow leopards while he watched. Sam and Eva had been inside the main hall, not able to see the violence with their own eyes, but in their minds wanting the same fate for the historian.

A fitting end to the madman.

It was afterward that they left his body for the snow leopards and the Himalayan bears to feast upon. His cries had dried down nearly an hour ago, suggesting that the animals have done their duty.

'He will be punished for his crimes as well.' Ballav replied, looking at the extinguishing fires in front.

Sabir was also tied and taken to one of the last houses and kept as a captive there, to be taken care of later.

****

THEY WILL SEEK OUT THE UNENDING POWER. YOU ARE NEVER SAFE.

The note was the only thing that was there in the room.

It was half an hour later that everybody reached the valley below and entered the house where Sabir was kept captive. But instead of Sabir, they were greeted by a simple note, left behind clearly by Sabir.

'How did he get away?' Eva asked, surprised.

'He might have his ways.' Mark answered, from her side, clearly depressed due to Sabir's disappearance. 'Military training involves evasive maneuvers as well.'

'What about the Callimachus scroll?' Eva asked, suddenly remembering.

'Its fine with us.' Ballav replied to her with a smile. 'It's been kept securely now, inside the Library.'

'But who are they?' Asked Sam this time.

'That….' Mark said, 'is something we would worry later.'

'Yeah.' Eva said, with a smile and holding Sam's hand. 'Right now, we should celebrate your discovery. After all, you are the first person who discovered the legendary Library of Alexandria and the scrolls with it.'

'Yes.' Sam said with a smile, looking at her. 'That we should. But it was not only me.'

He looked at Mark and Eva both.

'It was all three of us who discovered the Library of Alexandria.'

EPILOGUE

WASHINGTON D.C., USA
March 14,
7:45 PM

'Why are we going here?'

Sam looked at the building looming in front of him. Mark and Eva accompanied him on this trip. He was wearing a black suit today as per Mark's request, looking a little out of place. He was always more comfortable with t-shirts and jeans rather than these formal wears.

'You have to wear a nice suite for the trip Sam.'

Mark had told him repeatedly before his visit to the USA this time. After everything that happened with the three of them three months ago, Sam had never thought that he would be able to revisit the USA so soon. But here he was, back. Last time he was here, an RPG launcher blasted the living room of Eva in Maryland.

Hopefully, nothing like that would happen this time.

His research paper had scored the highest grade in Cambridge University Archeology department for this year. His article contained the details of the Library of Alexandria and its contents. As the discoverer of the Library of Alexandria, he has become one of the most famous persons in the World in the last couple of months. Blogs, Facebook, Twitter, and other social media networks have gone crazy over the news of the discovery of the fabled Library. The internet is still flooding with the news and the details of the discovery. And he was awarded the Ph.D. Certificate along with a prestigious position in the Cambridge itself.

But I am not sure I want to take the job in Cambridge.

A statue of Professor Richard Hedley has been erected on the main campus of the Cambridge University, in remembrance of the good Professor.

'I want to give you two a surprise.' Mark replied with a huge smile.

It was last week that Mark had called Sam after he got his Ph.D.

'You need to come to Washington on March 14th.' Mark said over the phone.

'Why suddenly Washington?' Sam asked.

'Someone has insisted on meeting you and Eva here.' Mark replied.

'You have to wear a nice suite for the trip Sam.'

That was odd.

'What's with the suite?'

'We will be going for dinner.' Mark replied cryptically. 'A dinner with someone significant.'

Even after asking a lot of times, Mark has refused to answer his question about who the dinner is with. Sam had asked Eva on the same thing too. She also got the same call from Mark and in the same way. Therefore, she was also in the dark for this trip. Though her dress was not as dark. She wore a stunning electric blue one-piece dress that made Sam thinking of a few more things in his mind, other than the impending dinner.

However, for Sam, it was a golden opportunity to meet Eva after a long time. Granted, they have met on the occasion of Sam revealing his discovery to the world on the Library of Alexandria, but that was also nearly two months ago. He still remembered their discussion on the Himalayan village three months ago.

'So, can we talk on what happened at the Kastellet?' Sam asked, at last, drawing all his courage.

Eva looked at him from the side. Sam couldn't see her face, plainly because she was covered wholly to be safe from the cold. To make matters worse, her eyes were also covered with goggles, the same as Sam's. As a result, the Indian was not able to see her eyes, or anything, as a matter of fact, to judge her reaction.

'It was what it was.' Eva replied, looking back towards the valley. Ballav and others in the village were working for the last couple of days to fix the broken Library and its surroundings. Mark was also helping them out, though he was covered with bandages everywhere mostly, while Sam and Eva came up here at the top of the southern wall, to speak, away from all the hustle.

'The emotion came out suddenly.' She said, after a pause, making Sam's heart skip. 'I had been attracted to you the moment I have seen you, outside the Delhi airport.'

Sam couldn't speak for a moment. It felt like a lump in his throat is causing him to choke.

'I....', he started speaking at last. 'I felt the same too.'

They both looked at each other. He felt an emotion, an attraction like a magnet, the same one he had felt the first time he had seen her.

It was after a long minute, that they kissed each other again, this time more passionately, without anyone disturbing, or trying to kill them.

'With whom are we having the dinner?'

Eva's voice brought Sam back to reality. It was after 3 months that he had met Eva yesterday.

The White House of America stood before them like a magnificent empire of a fairy. The fountain before them glowed a little yellow, while the building itself glowed in white with all its glory. The pictures on the internet or the video footages of the Hollywood movies don't do justice to the real beauty of the building. Sam remembered a movie he had seen recently, *Olympus has Fallen*, which had shown the White House being broken down due to terrorist attacks.

Well, that's certainly not the case here.

'You will know soon enough.'

****

Ten minutes later, all three of them were sitting inside the famous Oval Office inside the White House of America. From his position on the sofa, Sam can see on his right the Resolute Desk, famous now due to Nicolas Cage's movie *National Treasure-Book of Secrets*. The architecture and the intricate designs on the front of the desk really captivated him. Behind the desk, he could see the two flags. The dark blue flag on the left side, known as the *Flag of the President of the United States*, with the famous emblem of the Coat of Arms of the President with an Eagle holding an Olive Branch in one hand and a bundle of thirteen arrows in another, along with a white scroll inscribed "E PLURIBUS UNUM" in his beak. Behind and above the eagle is shown a radiating glory Or, on which appears an arc of thirteen cloud puffs proper, and a constellation of thirteen mullets argent. The flag for the United States of America stood on the right side, with all the fifty stars, representing all 50 States of USA, while the thirteen stripes represented the thirteen colonies which declared their Independence from the British.

All the doors in this room remained closed now. Except the three of them, Sam can't see anyone here. Eva was sitting beside him, while Mark sat opposite to him.

Click.

The door behind him opened with a soft sound, and a person's voice came to him.

'Welcome Mark.'

All three of them stood up in an instant hearing the voice.

The President of The United States of America strode confidently and purposefully into the room and came straight to Sam and shook his hands firmly.

'Welcome Sam.' Trevor Broad, the President of The United States of America, said. 'I have been waiting for this meeting for the last four months.'

'Four months?' Sam asked while the President shook his hands with equally surprised Eva.

'Yes.' Trevor Broad looked back towards him, purposefully. 'I am the one who employed Mark to help you.'

That explains Mark's secrecy and access to all those things which seemed impossible for any other person to have access to.

'But how? And why?' The questions came out of Sam's mouth involuntarily.

'Sam, let's start our dinner, and discuss.' The President said, gesturing them to start the dinner which was served just before he came into the room.

'Do you know that I was a fellow student of archeology in Harvard, along with your parents and Professor Richard Hedley?' Trevor asked.

Sam's shocked expression suggested he knew nothing about that. The same applied to the other two present in the room. Both Mark and Eva looked towards Sam, then to the President and at last at each other.

'That's true.' The President said, looking at all three. 'I am a friend of all three of them. We all had worked on the research papers in Harvard. From that time both your parents and Professor Richard Hedley were obsessed with the Nazis. The only difference was that Professor Hedley was a few years senior to your parents, and as a result, they have not met until one decade. It was later that they all met in Poland, during an excavation there. I, being their common friend, was able to get them closer to each other. While they were all interested and worked on the fields of history, I, being the son of a famous industrialist, was dragged into a totally different world. Years passed by, and I came to know about the death of your parents. However, that didn't strike me as odd, owing to the fact that it was all over the news saying that Rita and Hemanth Rawath had died due to an accident.'

All three of them listened intently to the President while having the lavish dinner.

'It was not until Hedley spoke to me and showed concern over the deaths of your parents, that I knew the details of your parents' deaths. That was nearly six months ago before everything happened. But when he went to Denmark to search for some more Nazi relics, that's when all hell broke loose. He came to know about Alexander, and somehow everything connected to your parents.

In the meantime, I was searching for someone capable enough to protect you, should you need help, or you get into any problem. The suggestion was from Hedley himself. Alexander was someone who could be a very dangerous person when he is agitated. Some of my special agents and a private investigator were tracking Mark, which he very evidently got wind of, and confronted one of them. I was not the President at that time. Fortunately, the Professor got the problems building up only after I became the President, and as a result, I had asked Mark to be ready to pounce if needed anytime.'

He looked at Mark, smiling. 'Evidently, that time came when Hedley died, just after a few days of receiving the package and speaking to me on it. And that's when I decided to get you help, help that you needed, in the form of Mark.'

He stopped for a second and then looked at Eva.

'You, Eva Brown, however, were the unknown factor in the whole equation. I had never expected you or anyone else to be a part of this fight, but you came out with flying colors. And congratulations on that. I would not have expected an NSA cryptologist to be such a good field agent.'

Eva beamed, accepting the praise heartily.

'Considering my position as the President of United States of America, forgive my secrecy.' He continued with a passive expression. 'I had to keep things secret, as nobody could know about the involvement of me in this. Things would have been very shaky if people knew about my involvement, as anything I am involved with can be termed as an involvement of the United States itself.'

'Then how are we meeting today?' Sam asked this time.

'You are forgetting one thing, Sam.' The President said, with a smile. 'I am meeting an archeologist now, who discovered the Library of Alexandria. You are a famous person now. And now, as you know, the United Nations Educational, Scientific and Cultural Organization, or UNESCO, is taking care of everything in the Library and anything related to it. They will keep the Callimachus Scrolls for now regarding restoration, and it will be given to you and Ballav to check on the so called ultimate power source. If it's a weapon, then that needs to be kept away from the common people, and if it can be used as an energy source, that needs to be checked too. And I am relying on you Sam, to check on that.

So, as The President of The United States of America, I am meeting you and holding a press conference in....', he looked at his watch, '5 minutes.'

'What's the press conference about?' All three of them asked simultaneously.

'I am offering the two of you jobs in the United Nations. Sam in UNESCO, Eva in the department of International Telecommunication Union or the ITU, while Mark continues to work in MARSOC.' He said, cryptically. 'Do you accept the offer?' The smiles around him gave the answer.

************************THE END************************